Charles Rathbone Low

The Autobiography of a Man-o'-War's Bell

A Tale of the South Sea

Charles Rathbone Low

The Autobiography of a Man-o'-War's Bell
A Tale of the South Sea

ISBN/EAN: 9783744709262

Printed in Europe, USA, Canada, Australia, Japan

Cover: Foto ©Andreas Hilbeck / pixelio.de

More available books at **www.hansebooks.com**

THE AUTOBIOGRAPHY

OF

A MAN-O'-WAR'S BELL.

" I stepped forward, eagerly seized a paper, when, oh, horror! there appeared before my eyes, as I hastily opened the slip, the single word—*Death!*"

THE

AUTOBIOGRAPHY

OF

A MAN-O'-WAR'S BELL

A Tale of the Sea

BY

LIEUT. C. R. LOW (LATE) I.N.

WITH ILLUSTRATIONS

LONDON AND NEW YORK
GEORGE ROUTLEDGE AND SONS
1875

THE

Autobiography of a Man-o'-War's Bell.

CHAPTER I.

THE autobiography of most bells, of those, indeed, with which the generality of the kind folk, who will favour me by perusing the following pages, are familiar, would deal with subjects far dissimilar from those of which I am about to treat. In this category of bells, I do not allude to such humble productions of human ingenuity as the household implements which lie in rows in the basement floors of all modern houses; though, doubtless, were the tongues of many such to give utterance to their feelings, they could tell some unpleasant truths of the opinions of " their betters," freely ventilated by the servant-kind, who "live and move and have their being " in the kitchen, and the regions that "thereunto adjacent lie." Dear me! what tales of cross-grained mistresses and dyspeptic masters, could not these bells,

1

well-nigh dinned to death by continuous and violent tintinnabulations, unfold to mortal ears. No, I pass by the domestic bell as unworthy my muse; I tune my lyre to a more pretentious lay than the retailing of the adventures of such very small fry. Neither am I about to sing of the experiences of the solemn and highly respectable class that are to be heard, but not seen, in contradistinction to the golden rule laid down for the guidance of all little boys and girls, and of which we have a lively remembrance from our earliest infancy, high up in the ivy-grown church tower. These bells speak of time and eternity, of births, marriages, and of deaths; and their voices recall to mind the saddest and most solemn, as well as the happiest moments of our life. But upon this theme I will not dwell. It is of the bell of a man-of-war, the great bell of a majestic ship of the line, that I now propose to write; and, after just premising the circumstances under which I heard the narrative I am about to relate, I will stand on one side, and allow the time-honoured tongue (I cannot degrade it by applying to it the homely title of clapper) to wag in its cavernous old jaws and speak for itself, as it has so often and so effectually done midst the battle and the breeze in days long, long gone by.

One hot summer day—it was just such another

grilling afternoon as Charles Dickens describes with marvellous graphic power in " Little Dorrit "—I was strolling about the museum of the Royal United Service Institution, and inspecting the interesting and curious collection of odds and ends in the naval department of the museum. I say inspecting, advisedly, for had it been the winter-time of year, or had the thermometer marked a range some twenty degrees lower, one would have been inclined to wonder at and admire the models, and particularly the Nelson and Franklin relics, but with the mercury at eighty and something or another degrees —I forget the odd number, it was too hot to count— how could any mortal be expected to do aught that militated against the adoption of the *nil admirari* principle of viewing things. No, the one thing a man *could* do with success, under conditions that would have melted the stoutest frame, was to, in short, take a nap; so I thought at the time, and as there was no one in that portion of the museum, and I felt overcome with sleep, I thought I would just indulge in forty winks ! Vast heaving ! paul,* there. When I said just now, there was no one, I should have excepted the worthy porter, an old petty officer

* The " pauls " are stops in the capstan, which prevent it from going back when heaving round.

of the navy, for whom I entertained a regard, having
had many a chat with him about matters and models,
nautical; but still he was of no account on this occasion, as I know from testimony, auricular as well as
optical, that he was sleeping the sleep of the weary,
for he was snoring in the most uncompromising
manner.   By the by, I hope this revelation, given in
strict confidence, may not fall under the observation
of any of the authorities at the Royal United Service
Institution, so that it may in any way prejudice the
interests of the old petty officer in question.

Feeling overcome with the heat, I looked about
for a seat, and, at length, "brought myself to an
anchor" near a great bell, an inscription over which
informed me that it was the bell of the French line-
of-battle ship, "Ville de Paris," the flag-ship of
Admiral Count de Grasse, in his memorable action
with Lord Rodney, on the 12th of April, in the year
1782.   I gazed long and curiously at this interesting
relic of that famous fight, and of the brave men who
immortalized themselves on that day, so long, indeed,
that I found myself musing over the stirring events
that were enacted beneath its shadow on the high
forecastle, and the tales it could tell were its iron
tongue gifted with language.   From first musing, I
found myself nodding—bad examples, we know, are

contagious ; and just then I was startled by a loud snort from my friend the porter, followed by a renewal of the gentle snoring, indicative of profound repose, so nothing loth, I resigned myself to the blandishments of the " sleepy god," and fell into a deep slumber.

"What, you would like to hear something of my early life," said a deep muffled voice at my side. Now, though this question proceeded from the bell that I had been so attentively regarding, the pheno-menon of an inanimate object, like a ship's bell, entering into conversation, did not strike me as in the least singular ; indeed, in our dreams, though we deal almost exclusively with phenomena, and discard common sense views of everything, nothing strikes us as extraordinary.

" Yes," I replied ; "I should like nothing better than to hear the story of your life."

" Listen, then," said the bell ; and straightway, without more ado, it unfolded in deep sepulchral tones, the following veracious narrative, being the Autobiography of a Man-of-War's Bell :—

I was cast in the year 1757 at a foundry in the south of England, and I remember debating with a lot of my brothers and sisters who first saw the

light, as you would say, at the same time as myself,
as to what might be the fate of each of us. I wonder
how many of them are in the land of the living now.
Though most of the number were destined for peaceful purposes, and not to ring forth war's alarms, and
calls to "fire quarters," yet, I doubt not, many came
to grief, and gave evidence of a flaw, or " cracked their
cheeks," diseases to which we are, from our composi-
tion, peculiarly susceptible, long years ere this.
However that may be, I must not be indulging in
sentiment, as if you have only patience to listen, I
have a great deal to tell you.

I was taken down with a wagon-load of others
to Portsmouth, and speedily found myself on board
one of the frigates of His late Majesty King George
the Second. The " Melpomene " was fitting out for
service in the year 1757, and I was proud enough, I
assure you, to be selected for duty on board such a
handsome ship, one of the crack frigates of the service. I saw some queer sights during the time she
was being fitted out. Those were the days of press-
gangs, and in seaport towns it was a dangerous
thing for a man who could not give a satisfactory
account of himself, to be seen wandering about.
Often such fellows were brought on board, quite
insensible with drink, the man-o'-war perhaps sailed

the following morning, and the deluded wretches did not regain their consciousness until the ship was far out on the blue waters, and all chance of return to their friends was at an end. Several such instances came under my personal cognizance, and on numerous occasions during the many years after this, my first induction to a seafaring life, I have been shipmates with gentlemen of good birth, who were thus entrapped into the navy; such cases occurred during the commission of the "Melpomene," and the romantic history attaching to these men, of which I propose now to speak, will, I trust, interest the readers of my autobiography, as much as they interested me during its development.

In 1757, there was a great want of foremast hands for the navy, and, in consequence, the press-gangs were particularly busy at their detestable trade, now happily abolished. No less than seventy-eight of the hands out of the frigate's crew of four hundred and seventy men, all told, had been impressed into the navy at different seaports, and sent down to Portsmouth to be drafted on board the ships of war in which there might be a paucity of seamen. Strong guards were required to escort pressed men, in consequence of the indignation the system excited in the minds of the populace, who frequently turned out in mobs, and released the unhappy fellows who had been seized or cajoled into " fighting the French," which was the seductive phraseology used by the " crimps," in seeking to induce landsmen to join His Majesty's fleet, though a portion of the navy was serving in distant climes, where the French and prize-money were not to be found. There was another method also of recruiting for the service besides pressing, and that was by the time-honoured mode of cajolery, which, indeed, is out of date now-a-days. Soldiers and sailors had to be procured, and they were procured in the same way as the Jew is said to have directed his son to get money—" honestly, Moses, if you can, but get it." The manner of recruiting, therefore, not being closely scrutinized, the results only being looked to, a school of harpies, or land-sharks, sprang into existence, who lived by inveigling "likely," but unwary, men into the hands of the recruiting parties, getting a portion of the bounty for each fresh hand they shipped.

No sooner had I joined the "Melpomene" than I commenced to adopt the habit I have since prac-tised all my life, and which is now in me a second nature—namely, that of studying the faces of those with whom I may be thrown into contact, and form-ing therefrom my own opinion of their characteristics.

I then watch with interest the gradual development of character, as shown by acts, which are the great, and, indeed, the only touchstone of what is in a man, and what a man is. From long observation I have become such an adept in the art, which like every other is perfected by practice, that I find I am now rarely at fault in the estimate I first form of those falling under the scope of my personal observation. I was scarcely settled in my place at the back of the top-gallant forecastle, a fine position for observing all that went on around, than I began to take notice of the men and boys whose duty it was to strike the hours upon me. This was done by means of a short line or lanyard that was fastened to the knob at the end of my tongue, and was the work of one of the quartermasters, a friend of mine, who took the greatest interest in keeping me clean and bright as a new pin. The lanyard was a perfect work of art, manufactured of the finest cords, which the quartermaster had bought with his own private money, and worked up at some expenditure of time and trouble, and then studded at intervals with fancy knots, that only an experienced seaman could have wrought. While making this elaborate ornament, and, after it was finished, when cleaning me every morning with bits of rag dipped into a small saucer filled with lamp

oil, cunningly concocted with other ingredients, he
would talk to me just as if I was one of his own
species and could answer him.   However, he used to
say I amply repaid him for all the time and trouble
expended on my adornment, for he was never tired of
reiterating that I was the sweetest-sounding bell he
had ever been shipmates with. To be candid, I think
he was not very wide of the mark, for " though I say
it as shouldn't," I was never tired of hearing the
mellifluous sounds ring out, as my tongue sounded
loud and clear the hours and the half hours, or " the
bells," as they call them on board ship.   During the
years I was on board the " Melpomene," they echoed
through the frigate, day and night without once
ceasing, except when in action.

Aha! I think I hear some one of my readers
exclaim, "Though your voice was strong and mellifluous, you had your weak points, and we have not
been long in finding out that personal vanity is one
of them."

To the sharp individual who has probed my
" weak point," as he calls my self-complacency, I can
only reply that "it is a fault I have in common with
a large majority of mankind, who love to hear themselves talk on all occasions and in all places ; and I
suppose, my kind censor, I contracted the bad habit

from having been thrown all my life among your fellow-creatures." As Lord Palmerston once said to Mr. Cobden, when they had a sharp and acrimonious encounter across the table of the House of Commons, " I always like to give as good as I get."

The " Melpomene " was a crack 48-gun frigate ; this was her first commission, and the captain was considered exceedingly fortunate in having been appointed to command the latest accession to the navy—a ship in all respects as handsome as any in the service. He was given almost *carte blanche* in his requirements while fitting her out for his pennant, and having good interest with my Lords —Parliamentary interest which was everything in those days, and by the same " token " (as the Irish say) is not a bad thing in the present year of grace— he found the dockyard and harbour authorities very amenable, and had no difficulty in securing all the stores he required for a long commission. Captain the Honourable Jasper Gaisford, was a fine, sailor-like officer, and worthy the confidence reposed in him, and the high responsibility of commanding in a time of war one of the representative ships, as it were, of the service, a heavily armed frigate, specially designed and manned beyond her proper complement, by more than a hundred hands, with the avowed object of engaging frigates of the enemy in single combat.

The times in which our tale is laid were stirring times. In the month of May of the previous year, war had been declared against France, and on the 14th March, 1757, was consummated one of the most disgraceful acts in the history of this country. On that day Admiral Byng was shot on the quarter-deck of the flagship of the Admiral Commanding-in-chief at Portsmouth. The brave but unfortunate officer met his doom with the calm courage of a sailor. Having taken leave of his friends, he came up on deck at noon under a guard of marines, and handing to a friend a paper exculpating himself from all blame in regard of the disgraceful charges laid to his door, sat down on an armchair, bandaged his own eyes, and giving the signal to the firing party, dropped dead pierced by five bullets, the whole transaction having occupied only three minutes. Thus was committed a foul judicial murder, for though Byng showed want of enterprise, if not pusillanimity, in not renewing the indecisive en-gagement off Minorca, yet it was owing to the neglect of the ministry of the day in sending to the Mediterranean a fleet notoriously ill-fitted for service and undermanned, and this notwithstanding the pro-

THE DEATH OF ADMIRAL BYNG.

MAN OF WAR'S BELL.

test of the Admiral himself, that success was rendered impossible. After some changes in the ministry, the elder Pitt, better known as Earl of Chatham, returned to office, nominally under the premiership of the Duke of Newcastle, but in reality he wielded all power. William Pitt found the country disgraced and dispirited, and by his splendid talents and wonderful energy raised it to the highest pinnacle of glory it has perhaps ever attained. It was at this juncture of affairs that Captain Gaisford commissioned the " Melpomene." The dockyards and arsenals of the kingdom resounded with the clang of preparation, and the Parliament voted money without stint to carry on the war against the ancient foe. The captain strove his utmost to fit his ship out before other commanding officers who had got the start of him, and he succeeded ; for one morning when the flagship " made daybreak " with one of her guns, the " blue Peter " was seen fluttering at our fore-royal mast-head, and before noon the gallant ship was under way down the Channel with her complement of hands filled up, and every man and boy on board anxious to have a brush with any Frenchman that might heave in sight, short of a first-rate.

Of course much had to be done after getting out into blue water, in the way of drilling at the guns those of the crew who had never served in the navy. As far as handiness aloft went, the men who had been bred in the merchant service required little teaching beyond learning those habits of smartness and cleanliness that mark at once the old man-o'-war's man; but in handling the great guns and the small arms (under which are enumerated cutlass, pike, and musket), the merchantmen were as much novices as the greenhorns who began to feel, for the first time, the direful effects of sea-sickness. However, healthy Englishmen quickly get over this temporary ailment, and my shipmates soon got all right. They formed as fine a body of men as ever I saw together; and I remember the first morning they mustered at divisions, toeing a line on the quarter-deck in double rows on the starboard and port sides, being struck with the gallant appearance they presented, all dressed in their spick-and-span new slops served out to them by the purser, who took care to cut their wages for the same to a pretty tune, for pursers in those days were not very particular as to pounds, shillings, and pence—that is, where Jack's balance was concerned, for I never heard complaints of punctuality and accuracy in paying No. 1. This was the first occasion on which I had an opportunity of observing the captain, who appeared to great advantage, as he marched down the lines of noble fellows, all bound to obey his every word and look.

Captain Gaisford was not what is called a fine man, but he was just of the stature and bulk that make the smartest seamen. Somewhat below the middle height, he was well knit and muscular, and looked every inch a sailor. There was an air of command about him that at once stamped him as one accustomed to be obeyed, and the self-confidence with which he gave his orders and carried on the duties of the ship, on such occasions as "general quarters,"— for the captain of a vessel of war always leaves the details of the management of the discipline and working of the ship to the first lieutenant—this self-confidence was inspiring to the officers and men, as nothing tends so much to a lax state of discipline and general inefficiency among the hands before the mast as the knowledge from personal observation, of the fact that "the skipper doesn't know what he is about." Captain Gaisford knew well what he was about, and all "malingerers" soon discovered that they had come to the wrong ship for shams, when the captain came down into the "sick bay" with the doctor, and closely questioned them, while his dark, piercing eyes looked through and through them, bringing the blush of shame to the cheeks of the detected " sham Abraham men." The first-lieutenant was a first-rate seaman, and one of the " old school," for even in those days it was becoming antiquated ; I refer to the school that habitually swore at men, and indulged in a quid of tobacco. This manner of naval officer is popularly known as the " Benbow " school, but it would ill become us were we to sneer 30 at a class that has produced redoubtable warriors like Cloudesley Shovel, and scores of others. Now-a-days one never meets with an officer who has made his way to the quarter-deck "through the hawse-pipes," and yet in holding up to admiration our present practice of excluding forecastle men, we ought not to forget that the proudest triumphs of our navy were gained in the days when such strict rules of exclusiveness were not enforced. Nelson, no mean authority in naval matters, as I suppose even the staunchest upholder of competition for naval cadetships will allow, had a saying " more honour abaft, more seamanship forward." The other officers scarcely call for any comment here, as they do not form prominent members of our *dramatis personæ*.

While the captain, accompanied by the first lieutenant, is inspecting the ranks of

> " The twice two hundred iron men
> Who all his will obey,"

we will take advantage of our privilege and jot down notes of any that may attract our attention. There is nothing in the appearance of the seamen proper—those I mean that have been in the navy, or merchant service—to call for especial notice; there is the usual liberal allowance of broad shoulders and muscular limbs, with bronzed cheeks and full whiskers, betokening the hardy tar who has fought his country's battles, or weathered the breeze in all climes, from the frozen north and the Baltic in midwinter to the tropics and the coast of India, where some of them have met the traditional foe of Britain in the struggle for the mastery of that fair empire, at that time in progress under the auspices of 'Clive on shore, and Watson at sea; indeed, this year, 1757, was signalized by the most memorable event in Indian history, the victory of Plassey, gained over the "subadar" of Bengal, by the soldiers and sailors under those two great commanders.

But when we come to the ranks of the landsmen, those who have been recruited by the pressgang, or voluntered for service, there are two or three faces that immediately arrest one's attention, as in fact they attracted the notice of the captain, who stayed his step in each instance, and asked his first lieutenant some questions as to the name and pre-

vious occupation of the persons alluded to.   As three
of these individuals will play important parts in the
incidents that passed under my observation, I will
not apologize for describing them to my readers, as
they appeared to me on this my initiation into naval
routine.

After passing, without a remark, some half a
dozen raw young men, who looked as if they had
taken to the sea simply because they did not know
what in the world else to do with themselves,
Captain Gaisford suddenly brought up opposite an
aristocratic and very handsome, though dissipated-
looking man, the last person you would ever have
expected to find voluntarily partaking of the exceed-
ing hard fare of "weevily" biscuits and "salt horse,"
and performing the uncongenial work of a seaman
on board one of His Majesty's ships.   So, evidently,
thought the captain, who, himself of aristocratic con-
nections, knew a born and bred gentleman when he
saw him, notwithstanding the attempt made by this
man to disguise himself in order to baffle the curiosity
that inspired his superior, and which appeared to be
anything but agreeable to him.

"What is your name?" asked Captain Gaisford.

"John Mullins, sir," was the reply, accompanied
by a graceful bow, which so greatly amused some

weather-beaten, genuine sons of Neptune on the opposite side of the deck, that they could not control themselves, but hiding their honest faces in their hands, grinned hugely and audibly behind those " horny " extremities. His attention being then called to the mistake he had made, John Mullins, quickly raised his hand, and, naval fashion, touched the rim of his hat, with the forefinger and thumb of his right hand, while, with the extreme sensibility of a gentleman unaccustomed to ridicule, his face flushed a bright crimson all over. The captain, and Mr. Higham, his first lieutenant, smiled, and the former asked him why he came to sea, and where he came from ? Answering the latter question only, he said somewhat curtly, " From London, sir."

A pause ensued, while Captain Gaisford waited for a response to his first interrogation. " Well, and why have you come to sea ? Have you no friends on shore who could have helped you to some employment ? "

This close questioning disconcerted John Mullins, as he called himself. He had clearly not prepared himself for more than the first two interrogatories, or if he had, the piercing glance of his superior confused him in his replies.

" Yes, sir," he stammered out, in an unequal

attempt to keep up the vulgar accent he had assumed.
" I have no friends."

The officers saw the man was for some object
concealing the truth, and as neither of them was in-
quisitive, they passed on, the commander merely
remarking to his first lieutenant, " Queer sort of
fellow; don't know what to make of him. Is a
gentleman though; keep your eye on him, Higham."

" Yes, sir," promptly replied that officer. " I'll
knock it out of him, or my name isn't Jacob," and
he turned on one side, and squirted some tobacco
juice through one of the open gunports. Had the
commander of the " Melpomene " seen the expression
that animated the face of the seaman he had just
been addressing, as he turned away and continued his
inspection, he would have pondered longer on the
lineaments of his countenance, and have taxed his
memory as to whether he had ever seen that face
before. Had he done so, he would have answered
the question in the affirmative, though the first
meeting took place under widely different auspices
from the second. But I must not anticipate.

The brave sailor thought nothing more of the
circumstance. I, however, from my vantage ground,
noted well the entire scene, and was astonished to
watch the demoniac expression that, like a dark

cloud, swept over the handsome but hitherto stolid features of the "landsman," while his eyes followed the retreating figure of his unsuspecting superior, with a gleam of malignity that betokened, I thought at the time, a condition of insanity.

The two officers passed several men who looked like mechanics, or shopmen; clearly, some at least of them were the fruits of the press-gang, and Captain Gaisford prudently forebore to ask any questions, but stilled the promptings of his conscience by a reference to the "exigencies of the service." Crossing over to the port side of the deck, where they were joined by the second lieutenant, who was in charge, the officers began the inspection of the port division, and beginning from forward, commenced with the boys and inexperienced seamen, or "landsmen," as they were rated on the ship's books There were boys of all sorts—country boys and town boys, strong, healthy youngsters who would do well under the hardships and privations of sea life, and a few puny, and delicate-looking lads, who it didn't require prophetic foresight to predict would languish and fade away, or at least do no good in the profession they had selected. Among the number was a tall, slim youth, with a fine, frank, engaging face that at once arrested the notice of the observant captain.

He was a boy of that description, judging from his outward appearance, who would do well anywhere where manliness and resolution were required for success in life. On Captain Gaisford questioning him as to his name and object in coming to sea, he replied with the most amusing frankness and in unexceptionable English, that his name was James Duckworth, and that he wanted to see the world, and was sick of the hum-drum routine of school; but on a second query being put to him as to the name of the school, he laughed, changed colour, and looked disconcerted. The captain, evidently pleased with his naïve manner and manly bearing, did not press for a reply, but directed the first lieutenant to station him at quarters with the signal quartermaster, as he appeared intelligent and smart. There was a third man who drew the attention of Mr. Higham, though this was on account of his commanding stature and muscular development, which description of endowment alone took the fancy of the first lieutenant, who regarded his new hands with approval, only in so far as they promised to be smart at the "lee-yardarm in a breeze of wind," or good at need when boarding a Frenchman in action. The thews and sinews of this man were all that could be desired for an athlete or champion of the prize ring, and the lieutenant, as he passed on, made a mark opposite his name in the roll of seamen he held in his hand.

The inspection finished, the men were told off to their respective stations at "general quarters," "aloft," "at the boats," and in the "fire bill;" in which latter I was to play a very prominent part, for any one was authorized, on the discovery of a fire, to depart from the decorum of man-o'-war routine, and arouse all hands with my alarum tones.

Some little time passed without anything occurring to vary the monotony of daily life in the navy. We had, of course, the usual amount of exciting reports of suspicious-looking craft in sight, that make a time of war at sea so exhilarating to those who play the hounds in the sport; and on several occasions we gave chase to ships of the mercantile marine of the enemy, whose feelings, like those of the hare, cannot be of quite so jubilant a character, but on every occasion we were rewarded with ill success. We always happened to sight the most promising looking craft so late in the evening that they managed to effect their escape during the darkness of night, by adopting one of the numerous stratagems in vogue at sea' among merchantmen seeking to escape an enemy. This was all very annoying, for the " Melpomene " was a new frigate, and considered the swiftest in the service ; however, the more philosophic among us made up our minds for better luck, and only bided our time, which was certain to come. On one occasion we chased a fine, full-rigged ship all day, and, thanks to a stiff breeze, having gradually overhauled her, were almost within cannon-shot, when the wind towards sunset died away, and at nightfall we found ourselves in the same relative positions. The vexatious part of the business was that the captain more than once had almost decided to man and arm the boats, and send them off to take possession of her, but the sky looked so full of wind, that he was afraid by doing so he might lose us altogether, for were the breeze to spring up during the absence of the boats, she would quickly show them a clean pair of heels. So he waited the advent of the wind, which, when it came, as it did during the early part of the middle watch, enabled the stranger to elude us altogether, for the heavens being overcast with heavy clouds, we lost sight of her, and when daybreak broke she was nowhere to be seen. These repeated disappointments made the captain, whose chief failing was hastiness of temper, not so amiable as could have been wished. He used to stride rapidly up and down the quarter-deck, or poop, with his glass under his arm ; on the slightest provocation he would sweep the horizon with it, and hail the look-out man with the oft-reiterated question, whether anything was in sight yet. Woe betide the seaman on the masthead if he, the captain, first sighted a sail from the deck !

On one occasion this happened, and he immediately called the unfortunate fellow down from aloft, and forthwith gave him two dozen lashes with the cat-o'-nine tails. He was in a particularly bad humour that day, for it was the morning succeeding the escape of the large French ship I have spoken of above; but I knew he regretted his hastiness, and indeed would have let the unhappy fellow off his flogging, but that he promised it to him on the first discovery of his negligence, and was too proud a man to withdraw from his word.

Notwithstanding this, Captain Gaisford was no tyrant, and was immensely popular with his officers and men, who would go anywhere or undertake anything at his bidding. The landsmen "being knocked into shape," had no easy time of it, and some lazy "ne'er-do-weels," who came on board ship to skulk, quickly discovered their mistake. Drill was the order of the day, both aloft in all the various nautical manœuvres, such as "bending," and "unbending" sails, sending masts and yards up and down, when the fine weather admitted of it, reefing, furling, etc., and on alternate days at quarters with the ship's guns, and in the use of the cutlass and musket.

I watched everything that went on with lively interest, and flatter myself I soon became well up in the details of drill. I was glad to see that the boy James Duckworth justified the good opinion formed of him by the captain and myself, and taking an interest in all his duties, quickly mastered the rudiments of his profession; but I was not so pleased to find that he had fallen into what I considered bad company, for John Mullins, who had given such an unsatisfactory account of his past life, had so ingratiated himself with the boy, that the pair were always to be seen together off duty. Though displeased at this, I was not surprised, for Mullins had the most winning way with him, and as he had repelled, with hauteur singularly out of place, and unusual before the mast, the friendly advances of some of the seamen, who in their rough way were prepared to fraternize with him, young Duckworth was flattered at this preference.

It was not long before the frank-hearted youth divulged to his newly-made friend his previous history, and as the recital took place one fine evening, when they were sitting together close beside me on the break of the forecastle, I was an attentive listener, but observed with suspicion that his associate always avoided any reference to his own life, though he let drop expressions which satisfied me that he was a man of good family, and that his conscience was ill at ease, either on account of some crime committed or meditated. The friends were sitting, as I have said, close beside me, when James Duckworth said in reply to a question, "Well, you have been kind to me, so I don't mind letting you into a secret, and indeed I am glad enough to do so, for I hate mystery, and all that sort of thing, as I hate a certain black gentleman. The truth is, I have run away from Eton, to which my guardians sent me, on the death of my parents. I hate school, though I like sports, and more particularly boating. I daresay you wondered at my proficiency at boat duty with the remainder of the boys the other day, when the first lieutenant said he wished to see which of us could pull the best oar, so that he might select the coxswain of the jolly boat. Well, I owe my promotion to the tiller of the 'jolly' over the heads of those other chaps,—who, because they had been pulling about Portsmouth Harbour when attached to the guard ship, considered themselves quite old sailors— I owe this good luck entirely to my Eton training, as I was stroke of one of the school boats for nearly a year before I left. Well, you see, I made up my mind to bolt from school, as I had had enough of it; so one night I lowered myself out of one of the windows by a piece of rope I had concealed during the day under my mattrass in the dormitory. Another fellow went with me, and we agreed to walk to Portsmouth and ship on board a man-o'- war, but just as we cleared the college gates by climbing—no joke it was, I assure you, for I cut one of my ankles and split my trousers—the lodge- keeper's son, who was coming home, gave the alarm at the lodge, and then chased us. The beggar had been poaching, I know, for he had his gun over his shoulder, and it was pretty well known that he was a loose screw, as far as the law of *meum* and *tuum* went. We took to our heels, and as it was a fine starry night, I rather liked the chase than other- wise, and thought it a good beginning for a life of adventure, though I hope when we see a Frenchman we will not show our stern quite so smartly as I did. The fellow who was running after us, finding we would not stop for all his shouting, got into a rage, and said he would fire at us. 'I say,' said Wilkins, who was running like a deer by my side, 'we must stop, and give ourselves up.'

"'Not I,' I replied, 'he dare not fire at us.'

"Hardly had I said so, than the gatekeeper's son bellowed out again at the top of his voice, and swore that he would bring us down, unless we surrendered. I did not say a word, for I was getting blown, having a small bundle of clothes under my arm. Crack went a fowling-piece, and a lot of shot passed whizzing over our heads, proving that, overcome with passion, he was as good as his word.

"'I say, I can't stand this,' said Wilkins, in a terrible funk, while the perspiration stood on his face with fright.

"'What,' said I, 'can't you stand fire? You'll never do for the navy.'

"Just then our friend in the rear (he had not given up the pursuit) hailed us again with a second volley of oaths, finishing up by an announcement that he would let fly the other barrel at us, and that he had got the 'elevation this time, by —— '

"'I say, Duckworth, I didn't bargain for this,' gasped out my companion; 'I am going to give myself up.'

" 'You fool,' I replied, 'he hasn't another barrel to his gun; come on, and don't be a coward.'

"But it was no use. The threat had its desired effect, and Wilkins surrendered at discretion. My pursuer returned with his prize, and finding I was not chased, I slackened my speed, and walking all night, crept into a barn soon after daylight. As it was Sunday, there was no likelihood, I thought, of my being discovered, so I turned in among the straw and slept for several hours. But I wasn't clear of danger of discovery yet. I had brought a little food with me, and had some few pounds in my pocket to purchase what I required while making my way to Portsmouth. About mid-day I made a frugal repast out of my little store, and feeling thirsty, determined to make my way to the neighbouring farm-house and get some milk. Climbing over the barrier that did duty for a door in the barn, I heard the wheels of a carriage of some sort driving rapidly along the road, and nearing the building. Lifting my head carelessly to see who was passing, I was horrified at observing it was no other than the gate-keeper's son, who was driving a little trap in which also was seated one of the under-masters. Luckily it was near a turn in the road, and they were looking ahead at the time, so they did not see me. Didn't I

let go my hold and drop backwards into the straw,
with the agility of a practised acrobat? That young
sneak, Wilkins, must have betrayed me, for how
could they have known that I had taken the road
that led in the direction of Portsmouth? My
amiable friend, the poacher, was not animated with
very Christian feelings towards me, for as the chaise
whirled past at a quick pace, I heard him exclaim, in
response to some remark of the under-master, "Yes,
sir, and I'll screw his neck"—the rest of the sentence, relating to his obliging intentions towards me
in the event of his laying hands on me, was lost in
the distance; but I chuckled inwardly as I recommended him, at a perfectly safe distance, to catch
his hare first. This incident, however, taught me
caution, and I took to the fields by the side of the
road, and eventually after some days' walking arrived
at Portsmouth. Now I was obliged to be more care-
ful than ever, for I had little doubt but that my pursuers were on the alert, and only awaiting my arrival
at the 'Hard,' or in the quarters most frequented
by seafaring men, to pounce upon me, and bear me
back to Eton, where I would become the laughing-
stock of my late schoolfellows. However, I was
soon relieved from all anxiety as to my recapture and
removal back to the irksome studies of school-life.

" The very evening of my arrival at Portsmouth, as I was taking some refreshment at the bar of a public house in the suburbs of the town, I was accosted by a rough-looking fellow, who asked me where I was bound to with a wallet over my back. Like a robber who thinks he sees in ' every bush an officer,' I replied, with assumed nonchalance, that I was going to see a relative on board a man-o'-war.

" ' What name, mate ? ' asked my pertinacious companion.

" ' Johnson,' I replied, promptly ; one name I thought would do as well as another, and Johnson wasn't a very uncommon patronymic.

" ' No, boy, the name of the ship,' persisted my interrogator.

" Here was a puzzler, and for a moment my courage failed me. I had not the remotest idea what ships were lying at Spithead or refitting in the harbour, so seeing that boldness was the only policy, I answered in as gruff a tone as I could assume, ' Come, now, what's that to you, mind your own business ;' so saying, I turned my face aside to hide the flush of alarm that overspread my features. Recovering myself instantly, I cast a guinea piece down on the counter, demanded my change of the fat old woman at the bar, and, taking up my bundle, prepared to leave the house. But I was not to get off so cheaply. I felt a heavy hand on my shoulder, while the same voice saluted me, with 'This won't do, young gentleman,' and he laid particular stress on the two latter words; 'I see through it all, as plain as a pike-staff. You have run away from school, you have; and you want to ship on board a man-o'-war, you do. That's just about it; make a clean breast of it, and we can come to terms; otherwise, you shall go before the mayor along with me.'

"I saw it was no use riding the high horse with a great powerful fellow who could pitch me over his shoulder and carry me, bag and baggage, before the magistrate aforesaid, so with a deep feeling of humiliation I asked what he wanted.

"'Well, boy,' he had dropped the young gentleman now—'I'll not be hard on you. How much of the rhino have you got?'

"I put my hand in my pocket, and pulled out my purse containing all my riches, and counted it out before him; six pounds four shillings and eightpence there was in all. At this juncture the fat old landlady interfered.

"'Don't rob the boy, Jerry,' she said. 'You remember you got into trouble about that business of the "Vanguard." It ought to have taught you

3

better nor that. If you hurt a hair of the head of that child, I'll inform against you, that I will.'

"'Who's going to hurt him?' growled out the individual who went by the name of Jerry; adding, with a sneer, 'I 'spose you are going to stick up for him because he is a pretty boy.'

"'Never you mind,' she answered; 'I'll not see him harmed, and if you don't account for him, you know who'll make you.'

"It was perhaps fortunate the good dame had thus befriended me; for these crimps, I hear, are a dangerous lot, and are not particular how they come by their money, and I saw by the avaricious gleam of Jerry's eyes that he was naturally not so inclined to let me off cheaply as he would have me believe. The mysterious allusion, however, to the person who could make him account for my safety had its effect, and telling the old woman she knew where to find him in case she wanted to see the pretty boy, he told me to follow him, and he would get me a berth in the ship of which he had spoken. I must own to having felt somewhat crestfallen at the ignominious treatment I had received, more particularly at being called a pretty boy, for I am fourteen years old. I followed him through some dirty lanes until he got into the nautical quarter of the town, and soon arrived at his house. Inviting me in, he told me not to mind what the old woman had said, but to keep quiet, and he would go out immediately and see some of the petty officers of the frigate, who were on shore every day about this hour looking out for hands, and particularly young boys like me. He soon returned, and said when the coast was clear a little later, he would take me on board the man-o'-war, and once shipped, he added, no man could remove me from her. I agreed to give him three pounds for his trouble, and he appeared quite satisfied, and I may say behaved very well in the matter. That night he pulled me on board the frigate in a light wherry, received a sovereign for shipping me from the captain, and asked me, before taking his leave, to give him a line to the old woman who had taken my part, as she would not leave him alone unless I satisfactorily accounted for my disappearance. He made his request in a jocular manner, and with a knowing wink ; but, nevertheless, I saw he feared the old woman, who knew more about him than he liked. I willingly did as he wished, and so bidding me good-bye, I saw the last of Jerry. This was the way in which I came to join the 'Melpomene,' and I have no cause to regret the step." The boy stopped, but cheerily added—

"Hallo, there is eight bells going. It is our

watch below ; I am going to turn in, as it is our middle watch to-night."

"Sail, ho !" just then sang out the look-out man, whose voice chimed in with the last notes rung out by my iron tongue.

"Where away ?" asked the officer of the watch.

"Half a point on the starboard bow, sir," was the reply.

"What do you make her out to be?"

There was a long pause, while the look-out man gazed at the tiny speck on the horizon long and carefully. On learning that a sail was sighted, a great number of the sailors came tumbling up the ladders in hot haste, and lined the rails, and stood in clusters on the topgallant forecastle as they strove to make her out from the deck, but all in vain. Again was heard the voice from the topgallant cross-trees, "Can't make her out, sir ; seems a largish, square-rigged craft."

Many of the men rubbed their hands with glee at the prospect of her proving a prize, or, better still, enemy. The officer of the watch having descended to the ward-room and reported the circumstance to the first lieutenant, left the deck in charge of a mate, and sprang up the rigging with a glass slung round his neck. Some little time elapsed before he had made out sufficient of the stranger to enable him to report to his superior; nearly half an hour passed away, and it was getting rather late to see clearly, though being midsummer we had some hours of daylight yet. One bell, half-past four, struck before the lieutenant of the watch returned to the deck, and when he did so, he communicated to Mr. Higham his suspicion that the stranger was a Frenchman, as she had altered her course, and was steering in the direction of the French coast. In the state of preparation for eventualities in which the "Melpomene" was kept, there was time enough for clearing for action; a few minutes sufficed for that. So the first lieutenant, who was not in the least excited at the prospect of fighting—why should he be, indeed, for he was confident his ship would come off victorious, and as to his own safety, that never entered into his calculations—leisurely made his way to the Hon. Captain Gaisford's cabin, and stated his belief that the strange sail was a Frenchman. The captain took the matter with equal nonchalance, and merely looking up, said, " All right, Higham, you know what to do ; let me know when she comes within reach of our bow-chasers, though perhaps I may come on deck before that." So saying he stretched out his legs in his swing-cot, with an air of satisfaction as a

man might do, who has had a good dinner and in-
tends to digest it at leisure, and resumed his perusal
of a pamphlet he held in his hand, Dr. Samuel Johnson's "Defence of Admiral Byng." Two, three, four
bells struck, and, as Mr. Higham had not yet reported that the strange craft was within range of his
foremost guns, the captain, glass in hand, made his
appearance on deck, and coming forward on the forecastle, surveyed the vessel attentively.

"Higham," at length he ejaculated to his second
in command, "she's a Frenchman. Clear the ship
for action. Beat to quarters;" and shutting up his
telescope with a sharp click, he turned on his heel,
and was preparing to leave the forecastle. Near him
with his eyes fixed upon his officer, and with a look of
fierce hate, stood John Mullins, and, beside the latter,
the boy James Duckworth. The captain for a
moment regarded the seaman, who dropped his eyes
under the searching scrutiny, while an expression of
surprise was distinctly observable on the captain's
face, and he muttered a few words, which I just
caught, as he brushed past me; "Like a face I have
seen somewhere," was all I heard. He turned and
was descending the ladder, when he noticed the fair,
frank face of the boy, lit up with a smile. "Well,
boy," he called out, stopping a moment, with one

hand leaning on his telescope, which rested on the deck, while the other held the man-rope, " aren't you frightened ? That's a Frenchman, and we are going to fight her."

" Frightened, sir," replied the youth, while he broke out into a ringing, boyish laugh it was pleasant to hear, "not a bit; I ran away from———," and he quickly checked himself, as he had found in his glee he had well nigh betrayed his secret, and confusedly added, " I came to sea, because I wanted to fight the French."

"Bravo, boy," said the captain with a hearty laugh, " you are made of the right stuff," adding, as he went below to the first lieutenant, " that youngster has run away from school."

" And quite right, too, sir," replied that officer, " if he wanted to come to sea."

Duckworth had risen amazingly in the estimation of the latter by this confession, and calling him down, he ordered his servant to give him a stiff glass of grog, and told the boy to come to his cabin after the action was over, and they had taken the rascally Frenchman, and inform him all about it.

The decks were now the scene of bustle of preparation for the stern ordeal of battle. The drums and fifes beat merrily, and the seamen repaired with

responsive cheeriness to their stations. Perfect
order and discipline was there. The manœuvre of
clearing for action had been gone through a hundred
times before, and now occupied no more time than
it daily did at general quarters. The hatches were
covered with gratings, the magazines, shell-rooms,
and shot-lockers thrown open, and their contents
passed up rapidly by the ship's-cook, his assistant,
and other non-combatants, under the directions of the
gunner and his mates ; the hammocks had not been
piped down yet, so were all stowed in neat rows as
usual in the nettings, where they are so serviceable
in screening the men from the musketry fire of an
enemy. The boatswain and his mates passed up
stoppers for the running and standing rigging that
might be shot away, with plenty of spare rope for
lanyards and other purposes ; the carpenter and his
crew had his shot-plugs all handy; the sailmaker,
his mates, and a party of men were told off under
the directions of the boatswain, to keep the sails
trimmed during the fight, as the successful issue
of the approaching engagement would depend as
much upon the prompt and seamanlike manœuvring
of the ship as upon the skilful gunnery of the brave
fellows at the guns ; the marines (or soldiers, who
in those days were embarked on board ships of war,

to do duty as marines, for the latter gallant corps did not then exist) were drawn up on the poop under their officers, a few of the crack marksmen being in the tops. The guns were " wormed," " sponged," loaded, and run out in a trice, the side tackles were coiled down in readiness for the recoil, the hand-spikeman stood by the " rear chocks," handspike in hand, the " rear tackleman," not to be behindhand, held the end of the tackle ready to gather in the slack, when the gun recoiled; last of all, the captain of the gun stood waiting for the order to prime. All was attention, and the most perfect, almost peaceful stillness reigned throughout the ship even to the cock-pit, where the surgeon with his assistant and dressers stood waiting for patients to commence his ghastly work, and knife in hand, spoke in whispers, and gave directions by signs, as if fearful to break the solemn quiet that brooded around on sea and air.

Thus we neared the Frenchman, who with his courses hauled up, was forging slowly a-head on our port bow, awaiting the action that it was seen was inevitable.

CHAPTER II.

THE "Melpomene" was, as I have said, built for a 48-gun frigate. Her armament was as follows :— 26 long twenty-four pounders on the main deck, 16 thirty-two pounder carronades on the quarter-deck and poop, 6 guns of the same class and calibre on the forecastle, 1 long eighteen pounder used as a bow-chaser, and a twelve-pounder boat carronade, which made a total of fifty guns. The enemy appeared to be a heavy frigate of at least equal size and weight of armament with ourselves, as well as we could gather.

At length we were near enough to commence the deadly duel. Two bells of the second dog-watch had been struck—in plain English, it was about a quarter past seven o'clock when the action commenced by the "Melpomene" firing a shot as a summons to the enemy that she must haul down her colours and surrender, or fight. The Frenchman preferred the latter course, to our very great relief.

But the fates were adverse still. Before the enemy fired a gun in return, as a notice that she had accepted our challenge, three or four sail were descried in the distance bearing down upon the scene of action. Whoever they might be, whether friend or foe, it was clear they were not wanted, but might be classed with that "third party," who obtrudes himself or herself at the critical moment when an anxious and timid lover is making his declarations to an equally coy mistress. Seeing what was up in the wind, the Frenchman trimmed her yards to the wind, and so we found ourselves baulked.

The "Melpomene" was quickly under all sail in chase, and so night closed in, and found all hands disappointed, and not in a very amiable mood, while we blessed the interlopers, whoever they were.

We chased all that night, and as it was clear and starlight, with a full moon, we never lost sight of the enemy. When morning dawned it discovered us under all sail, steering about east by north, with the wind now at north-east by north. To our great relief we found that our obsequious friends had disappeared, and we were once more alone with the stranger, so that we might settle our little account amicably together. But to our disgust, our friend, the enemy, declined to accept our invitation to adjust our differences by the exchange of powder and shot, no doubt fearing a repetition of the untoward interference of yesterday.   Hence, though we fired a gun or two at about half-past six, as a delicate notice that we were prepared to give her a warm reception, she treated · the attention with a silence more painful to be borne than the noisiest responses.   Towards noon the wind decreased, and the " Melpomene," in consequence, began to draw up to the Frenchman, which made every effort to escape.   At about one, the latter commenced lightening herself, by starting the water out of her tanks, cutting away the anchors, throwing overboard provisions, spare spars, boats, and every article of the sort that could be got at ; to make her sails draw better, she also adopted the plan of keeping them constantly wet, from the royals downwards.   This change in her tactics would have been extraordinary were it not that it was attributable to her fear that were she engaged with us, and lost any of her masts, our consorts, guided by the thunder of the cannon, might come up during the action, and then, even were she victorious, she would fall a prey into their hands owing to her crippled state.   That portion of the coast of France, in the neighbourhood of Bordeaux, was not very far distant, and she doubtless also counted upon running in under the protection of land batteries, from the superior force which she feared would overhaul her did she engage us.

At two o'clock the Frenchman opened fire from her stern guns at the " Melpomene," which half-an-hour later we returned with our bow-chaser. The enemy's fire was at first ineffectual, but in a few minutes a shot came through the port lower-studding sail, the foot of the mainsail, and the stem of the barge, which was stowed on the booms, and sweeping the quarter-deck, without doing any damage to life or limb, passed out to sea. So matters progressed till five o'clock ; at that hour, owing to our advance on her starboard quarter, the stranger luffed up occasionally, so as to bring her stern guns to bear, and was evidently much galled by the fire of our bow-chaser, while the greater part of her shot passed over the " Melpomene." At half-past five, we having for the last twenty-minutes maintained a position within half point-blank range on the quarter of the Frenchman she " brailed " up her spanker, and bore away to the southward, in order to bring her antagonist upon her beam, and so enable herself to escape to leeward. But Captain Gaisford was not to be done out of his prize by the display of any amount of seamanship ; so putting his helm " hard a-weather," the "Melpomene " met the manœuvre, and the two frigates thus came to close action in a parallel line of sailing. At four minutes past six, the Frenchman commenced with musketry fire from her tops, to which our marines replied with alacrity. Captain Gaisford manœuvred to close his adversary by occasionally hauling up, though without losing the bearing of his broadside upon the enemy. The two ships were now not more than half musket-shot apart; the "Melpomene" with her rigging and sails considerably cut, and the Frenchman with the principal part of her damage in the hull, as betrayed by the slackened state of her fire.

Captain Gaisford now looked forward for a favourable opportunity to board, as he was afraid of the enemy, from the comparatively uninjured state of her rigging, might escape. For some little time the opportunity sought for did not offer, but at forty minutes past six, the Frenchman hauled up, apparently to avoid her opponent's fire. The captain of the "Melpomene," profiting by this, poured in two raking broadsides, and, hauling up, also placed his ship on the starboard quarter of the enemy. Soon after this some good practice on their part,—and I will do them the justice to say that they carried on the action against the splendid gunnery of the "Melpomene" with the greatest spirit,—shot away a cutter from our port quarter, as also our lower and main top-gallant studding sails. Satisfied with this, or bent on repairing damages, the Frenchman kept up a feeble fire for some little time, while our brave fellows on their mettle, blazed away with the utmost vigour, and plumped the round shot into her in fine style. Recommencing again at about half-past seven, the enemy shot away our maintopmast, studding sail, and main brace, which was, however, quickly rove afresh by the practised riggers, under the direction of the boatswain. Having effected all this damage to our rigging, the Frenchman suddenly hauled to the wind, as if to try the strength of our masts. We had no fear for them, however, as they were not seriously wounded; so we also trimmed sails and hauled up, giving her at the same time a raking broadside, to which our adversary, who was evidently much shattered, only replied with a discharge from a stern gun. Just then her maintopsail halliards were shot, and the yard came down on the cap by the run, carrying away the topgallant sheets.

At this moment Captain Gaisford thought it high time to lay the enemy on board, so at about a quarter to eight he bore down upon her, and ran his bow-sprit between the Frenchman's main and mizen rigging on the starboard side. The heavy swell lifting the " Melpomene " ahead, her bowsprit, after carrying away the former's mizen shrouds, stern davits, and spanker boom, broke in two, and our foremast went at the same moment, falling inboard right upon the foremast and waist guns on the port or engaging side. These guns became in consequence completely disabled, but we still kept up a hot fire from the main-deck guns, whose muzzles were almost locked in those of the enemy. Our gallant tars did not care one jot, but, leaving their guns, prepared to follow their officers to board the Frenchman. The first lieutenant, Jacob Higham, calling away the first division of boarders, swang himself over the ship's rail, close to me in the fore part of the ship, with about seventy fine fellows at his back, while the captain leaving his ship in charge of the second lieu-tenant, was about to board from the quarter-deck as soon as the two ships came alongside, when a musket ball broke his right arm, and his sword fell out of his grasp. With the utmost calmness he picked his weapon up with his left hand, and refused to go below, or to allow the surgeon, who, with his assistants, was busily engaged in the cock-pit, to attend to him. Declining to have him summoned up, the captain got one of his seamen to bind up his shattered arm, and, once more waving his sword, and encouraging the gallant fellows round him by voice and example, led them to the forecastle to follow the first lieutenant's party, as the enemy's ship appeared as though about to fall off, and there seemed to be no immediate probability of his being able to board from abaft.

In a short time Captain Gaisford joined his first lieutenant in the deadly struggle progressing on the Frenchman's deck; all the great guns were hushed, and the cutlass and bayonet did their more silent, but no less deadly work. Not only were the decks the scene of a sanguinary and determined struggle, but the topmen were engaged in the exciting contest in which the lives and honour of all were at stake. The marksmen who crowded the main and mizen tops kept up a hot fire, while the foretopmen of the " Melpomene," taking advantage of the foreyard of their ship becoming locked in that of the enemy, ran along the yards like cats, and carrying their cutlasses in one hand, balanced themselves by the lifts with the other, as they boarded the Frenchman's foreyard.

Only one man of the latter waited to receive them, the remaining number preferring to seek safety, if such a thing could be had anywhere just then, on the deck, where at least they would have standing ground, and, if they had to fight, would not

4

be exposed to the additional peril of being hurled from a great height, with the certainty of being either drowned or mangled by the fall. The gallant fellow who remained behind and prepared singly to contest the possession of the top it was his duty to defend, made ready to receive the midshipman and half a dozen seamen of the "Melpomene" who now approached him. Stepping nimbly, almost running, along the yards, they made their way in Indian file until they reached the slings of the Frenchman's foreyard; to encounter them Johnny Crapeaud knelt down on the top, and grasping the rim with one hand, leant over to deal a blow with his cutlass on the head of the first man he could reach. The English party was headed by a brawny fellow who looked rather puzzled when he approached near enough to engage his adversary.

"Go ahead, Sawyer," laughingly said the young midshipman, a gallant youth, who treated as a monstrous good joke what many people would have considered a serious business; "go ahead, and drag the rascally Frenchman down. You are big enough, and ugly enough too."

At the same time he drew his pistol, which he had taken care to load before leaving the top of the " Melpomene," and steadying himself with one hand on the lift, covered the unlucky Gaul, and was about to fire, when the latter seeing certain death before him, threw his sword overboard, and putting his hands together in an attitude of supplication, prayed the young officer to spare him, as he would surrender himself a prisoner. Thus the enemy's foretop was gained, and soon the others were cleared. But a desperate fight was meantime progressing on the decks below.

The enemy's ship—as was the case in the French navy in the old days of the monarchy, when the Bourbons reigned on the throne of France—was commanded and officered by the scions of the old aristocracy; the maxim of *noblesse oblige* held good in war, if not in court morals, and the young nobles of France were taught to meet death fearlessly, even if it was in a losing cause. A baron of ancient lineage commanded the French frigate, and he, surrounded by his officers, as gallant a band of gentlemen as ever drew a sword, met the British boarders as they sought to set foot on their decks, and did all brave men could do to drive them back.

It was useless; the French sailors were no match, individually or collectively, for the British tars, and were borne back inch by inch, and foot by foot, until any furthur resistance appeared to be wanton obsti-

nacy, and a useless effusion of blood. Still the
French captain would not yield, though at length he
found the death he seemed, by the exhibition of the
most desperate valour, to be frantically determined to
win. He fell overpowered by a dozen seamen, in a
last effort to lead on men who would not follow, and
then the senior officer who succeeded to the command
by his death, flung down his sword, and calling to a
subordinate to haul the colours down, surrendered
his ship, the " Maréchal Turenne," to the victors.

The decks, on the conclusion of the hard fought
action, presented a spectacle that could never have
been forgotten by those who witnessed it, while the
cries and groans of the wounded and dying were
harrowing in the last degree to me, who had now,
for the first time, seen the dire effects of a naval
action, in which a large proportion of the wounds,
being occasioned by splinters and grape shot, are of
an unusually ghastly character.

A prize crew was put on board the " Maréchal
Turenne," and then both ships commenced to repair
damages. The principal injuries received by the
" Melpomene " have been detailed in the description
of the action. Her foremast was badly hit, but none
of her other masts to any serious degree. Our sails
were, however, cut to ribands by the bar and chain

shot used by the enemy, one of which had torn away twelve or fourteen cloths of the foresail—stripping it almost from the yard. In the short space of fifty-four minutes, our seamen, besides repairing the running rigging, bent new courses, main topsail, jib, fore topmast staysail, and spanker, and having trimmed them to the wind, hove the ship to, looking as fresh as when she began the action, and as ready to encounter a second Frenchman, should another be good enough to heave in sight. Out of our complement of four hundred and seventy men and boys, we had lost one officer, (a master's mate,) twelve seamen, and one corporal of marines killed, and three officers, twenty-four seamen, and three privates wounded.

On the other hand it may be said regarding the Frenchman, that if high firing displayed its effects in the disordered state of the rigging and sails of the "Melpomene," the low firing of the latter was equally conspicuous in the shattered condition of the hull and lower masts of the "Maréchal Turenne." The starboard side of the ship was riddled from end to end. Almost every port sill and port timber, both on the main and quarter-decks, exhibited marks of round shot. These shot had entered the lower deck, and had knocked away the bulkheads of the after powder magazine. Several had struck between wind and water, and some under water, which had cut the knees and timbers. A great many had also passed through the ship, between the main and quarter-decks, and in the waist. With so many shot holes in her hull, it will not be surprising that the ship, when she surrendered, had six feet of water in the hold, and that it required all the exertions of the carpenter and his crew to plug up the holes in time to prevent her from sinking under their feet.

We found that her complement before the action consisted of five hundred and sixty-five men and boys, and out of this she had her captain, two lieutenants, four midshipmen, and other officers, with forty-two petty officers, seamen, and marines killed, and her first lieutenant, and six junior officers, with seventy-six seamen and marines wounded. She was of slightly greater tonnage than the " Melpomene," and carried two more guns, but the difference of force between the two ships was so small that it may be said they were equally matched, and our victory was in every way a most creditable one to ourselves, while it must be owned that the enemy did all brave men were capable of, though fortune did not crown their efforts with success.

I had plenty of opportunity of observing the demeanour of the individuals whom I have introduced to the notice of the reader. They all conducted themselves as brave men should, and this eulogium applied equally to the boy James Duckworth, who followed close on the first lieutenant's footsteps when he boarded the French frigate. If he was not the first man to plant his foot on her decks, at least he was the first boy, and that in spite of the injunction of the good Lieutenant Higham, who spying him out by his side as he sprang up the top-gallant forecastle ladder, bade him peremptorily to remain where he was.

Young Duckworth had pluck enough to disobey his superior, and when the action was over, Captain Gaisford, at his first lieutenant's request, rewarded the boy by conferring on him the rating of a first-class volunteer, which in those days was a similar rank to that of naval cadet in the present year of grace. Being now an officer, he was removed from his quarters among the ship's crew to the midship-man's berth, and quickly rose to popularity among his new messmates. Of course, he had to fight his way into the good opinions of these youngsters, and being good-natured and manly, and, above all things, fearless, as I think is shown in the incidents of his career we have already related, he was able to take as well as give a fair share of the hard blows that are always going on in a well-constituted middy's berth. Fortunately for himself too, he was a gentleman by birth and breeding, and so the oldsters let him off cheaply in his initiation into the mysteries of a frigate's gun-room.

I was surprised to see that his partiality for the companionship of John Mullins did not end with his removal from his mess. Of course, he had not the same facilities for associating with him—this the regulations of the service forbid—but still whenever he had an opportunity for a minute's conversation, he never failed to avail himself of it.

This partiality on the part of Duckworth was not astonishing, for from closely observing his friend, I found that the seaman was not only a man of refined tastes, but also a most accomplished scholar, and possessing a mind stored with the information of a well-read and travelled man. Now Duckworth, though a runaway from school, and fond of adventure, had the desire for intellectual improvement, which is generally found in boys trained in our great public schools ; as scholarship was a thing scoffed at in the navy, more particularly in the midshipman's berth, as a sign of effeminacy and want of manliness, he would seek to improve his mind by conversation with his friend who, having similar tastes, was delighted with the companionship of the young Etonian. This was the link that bound together in friendship souls in other respects utterly dissimilar, for there could not well be a stronger marked contrast than that existing between the boy, frank and high-spirited, and the man, handsome but somewhat effeminate-looking, and with a strange restless manner, and a sinister expression of eye and mouth that would have repulsed any person of more mature years, or greater experience of mankind.

William Morris, the third character of whom I have spoken, was a brave, jovial fellow, who made the best of his position, though he clearly felt it very irksome. I could not make him out, or the reasons that had induced him at his time of life (he must have been thirty-five years of age) to ship on board a man-of-war, and encounter all the hardships and dangers of the sea. He was, I felt convinced, a gentleman, and the more I observed him, and I did so closely, the better I liked him.

One day an incident occurred that nearly cost Morris his life. He was stationed in the mizen top and prepared to go aloft one evening, with the rest of the topmen, to reef topsails at sunset, as men-of-war usually do when not chasing an enemy or sailing against time.

" Man the rigging," called out the first lieutenant, after the boatswain and his mates had piped the hands to reef topsails, and the master-at-arms had cleared the main and lower decks.

Up sprang all the topmen, some crowding on the rails, others on the lower ratlines of the rigging.

" Away aloft," sang out Mr. Higham in his stentorian tones, and up streamed the cluster of Jacks vieing with each other, and the hands of the other tops, in a generous rivalry as to who was the smartest.   Round the broad rims of the great tops, which in those days were made much larger than in the present year of grace, scrambled helter-skelter the rough fellows, tumbling over one another in a way that would have made a landsman's hair stand on end, for it seemed morally certain that some of them, as they clustered and climbed like bees, would inevitably be pitched headlong from their giddy elevation, unless like those interesting little creatures, they were also gifted with wings which would bear them in safety away, or back again to the busy swarm.   But matters .aloft were safer than they looked, and the seamen accustomed to this rough and tumble sort of game, reached the tops without accident, and springing up the topmast rigging were soon assembled in dense masses round the " parrals " * and quarters of the yards ready to lay out along the foot ropes at the word of command. All the details of manœuvring are worked in this method of uniformity in the navy, in this, so greatly differing from the merchant service, in order that the duties aloft may be carried out with precision and steadiness, besides giving a more ship-shape look to eyes nautical.

" Stand by your booms," was now the order of the officers from the deck, followed after a moment's pause by "Trice up ; lay out, and take in the first reef."

And the jolly tars did carry out the nautical opera-tion of " laying out," with most commendable celerity. Before they had well settled themselves in their respective stations they commenced picking up the topsails, the first reef bands of which their ship-mates on deck had previously hauled out " taut " along the yards by means of reef tackles. While all this was going on, the wind had quickly increased in strength, and was blowing in strong gusty squalls that felt chilly as if they had come from the farther confines of the North Pole.

* A parral is a sort of collar, by which the yards are fastened at the slings to the masts, so that they may be hoisted and lowered with facility.

The look out to windward altogether seemed gloomy and unpromising. In a minute the reefers aloft had hurled out the weather reef earrings, and the captains of the tops had given the word to their fellow topmen on the lee-yardarms to "haul out to leeward," when the accident to which I have referred took place. As the sailor next to the captain of the maintop of the starboard watch, who as the ship was on the port tack was on the lee-yardarm, was helping the petty officer to haul out the lee reef earring, the ship gave a sudden weather lurch, and then as suddenly righting herself, rolled with a sharp jerk over to leeward. The sailor of whom I have spoken, was intent on the duty of finishing with smartness the reefing of the maintopsail, and like all seamen worth their salt, thought chiefly of his top being first in concluding the evolution, for the maintop men were generally the smartest in the ship, a rather unusual thing in the navy, where the foretop generally carries off the palm. The sudden sway over to leeward caused him to lose his footing. Unfortunately he was employing both hands in assisting the captain of the top, and was resting on the yard somewhat sideways on his chest, so before he could recover himself with his hands, having already lost his foothold, he reeled for a moment in the unstable foot-rope, clutched wildly at the air, and then tumbled headlong down into the waters that seethed and hisséd alongside the ship.

There was an instantaneous cry of " man over-board;" and almost before his form disappeared beneath the waves, one man at least prepared to save his comrade, William Morris—it was none other than he—from a watery grave. The instant Morris's chum, the captain of the maintop of the starboard watch, saw what had occurred, he seized the starboard topmast backstay, which he was able to do, the yard being braced in as the ship was close hauled on the port tack, and sliding down it stood in the hammock nettings below; but only for a moment, for raising his hands over his head, he sprang overboard, and in coming to the surface struck out astern after his friend.

It was a bold deed, and right promptly done. From the deck we could see Morris struggling wildly with the waves; nothing but a miracle could save him, for he could not swim, still those who knew the gallant fellow who had plunged in after him, hoped for the best, for he was the most powerful swimmer in the ship, and had before now saved a fellow creature from a similar death. But it must not be thought that all this time the officers and ship's com-

pany were idly looking on at this exciting scene ; on
the contrary, no sooner were the words " man overboard" sung out and taken up by the people below,
than the first-lieutenant piped the topmen in from the
yardarms, and down to the deck, and putting the
helm " hard up," and squaring in the after yards,
" wore ship." The jib sheets were flattened in, and
the gallant frigate's head fiew off from the wind.
Now the head yards were squared away, she was
soon before the wind when, bracing up, first the
"after" and then the " head " yards on the starboard
tack, the " Melpomene " stood back in her former
track.

One of the quarter-masters had run up the mizen
rigging in order that he might not lose sight of the
unfortunate men, and now when the first lieutenant
asked him if he could see them, he was enabled to
reply in the affirmative, and point out the spot where
their heads could be descried above the wild and
boisterous sea, as occasionally they rose on the crest
of a huge wave, and until they once more descended
its precipitous sides. All hands breathed again
when they learned that the petty officer had succeeded in reaching Morris before the latter was
exhausted with his efforts to keep himself afloat, and
great hopes were expressed that both would be

saved. The second cutter, which was hoisted on the port, or lee-side of the ship, was quickly got ready so as to be lowered, when the frigate approached near enough to enable the crew to pick the two men up.

Swiftly the "Melpomene" approached them, and she seemed as if eagerly desirous of carrying out the errand of mercy as she sped before the favouring gale. Now we neared the drowning men, and expectation rose to fever height, as all eyes watched the small specks that appeared one moment only to disappear the next, as the gigantic ocean rollers rose like a wall between the two struggling seamen and their anxious shipmates. Soon the "Melpomene" was close enough to essay the task of rescuing the brave fellows ; she was hove to, and almost instantly, before indeed she had lost her way, the cutter was lowered away with her crew on board.

Both Morris and his preserver were such great favourites with all hands, that when the crew were called out the boat might have been manned three times over, so many volunteers stepped forward anxious to take part in the rescue. Hundreds of heads anxiously peered over the rail, or scanned the scene from the rigging, for it was felt, even now, at the eleventh hour, every effort might be in vain, and the boat arrive too late ; indeed, it denoted the pos-

session of a wonderful degree of strength and
dexterity in the art of swimming on the part of the
captain of the maintop, that he should thus be able
not only to keep himself afloat in such a sea, and for
so long a time, but that he could support his shipmate as well, under circumstances as trying as can
be conceived. But he was destined to receive his
reward for this noble act of unselfish devotion.
Every one on board the "Melpomene" drew a long
breath of relief as the boat ran up alongside the two
sailors, and it was seen that they were drawn in by
many willing and stout arms.

But sighs of relief could not altogether dispel the
overwrought feelings of honest Jack, and cheer broke
forth upon cheer, as he greeted this happy consum-
mation of what was nearly proving a tragedy. The
men were both speechless with exhaustion, and it
took a considerable time to bring them round. However, this was brought about by rubbing, and by the
administration of copious libations of grog, which
taken "neat," helped to qualify the nauseous doses
of salt water previously imbibed. The British sailor
must indeed be far gone in his journey towards the
confines of "Davy Jones's locker," if Jamaica rum
taken hot and often does not neutralize the effect of
any amount of exhaustion.

When they were able to speak—and many questioners asked the captain of the maintop how he ever managed to keep Morris who could not swim a stroke above water—he replied that the credit was due entirely to Morris himself, who had showed the greatest self-possession, and after the first minute or two succeeded in keeping himself afloat, by adopting the method pointed out by his preserver. The former, on the other hand, attributed his preservation to his friend's assistance; but there can be little doubt that had Morris been at all flurried, and seized his preserver by the throat or the limbs, the struggle would have been very soon over, and old ocean would have added two more victims to the countless thousands immolated on his altar owing to the want, on their part, of a little self-possession. Perhaps it is easier to preach the desirability of exercising this virtue from the comfortable depth of an arm-chair than to practise it in the terrific gorges of a mountainous sea; and this, the writer of these lines, as having had some little experience in that line, will not gainsay. However that may be, Morris always declared that he learnt to swim on this occasion, and it is certain that he was enabled to practise this manly accomplishment ever after.

Let us hope that none among my readers may

have so terrible a lesson, but that, should such be their fate, they may equally well profit by it. After this, as may be imagined, William Morris and Johnson, as the captain of the maintop was called, became the fastest and firmest of friends, and the former took his preserver into his confidence. It had been a long time evident to me, as I watched these men, that—in spite of a roughness which, though not exactly assumed, was, even when most exaggerated, not the roughness of ill-bred men— Morris had not always been in the position of life in which he now found himself, but I could not for the life of me account for my idea, except that his speech was that of a man of education and a gentleman, even though he occasionally swore, which in those days was no uncommon thing for any one " to the manner born."

As the two friends took their pipes together in the fine evenings, or the rough nights on the fore-castle, Morris often spoke of what he hoped to do for his chum, and sometimes half hinted at his not being what he seemed; but Johnson, honest old fellow as he was, did not apprehend the drift of his friend's remarks, and being well satisfied in his con-science, and as he considered, amply repaid by the approval and admiration of his officers and shipmates for what he had done, did not seek for any other reward, but listened to his companion's disjointed proposals with the good-natured indifference of a man who attributed them to the gratitude of one who would do much if he could.

However, my curiosity was soon destined to be satisfied, and from my eyrie on the break of the forecastle, I became the interested, but unsuspected confidant of the history of Morris's life. As some events of great importance, and of a stirring nature, preceded the date of this disclosure, I will keep to my plan of narrating this history in its strict chronological sequence.

CHAPTER III.

The "Melpomene" continued her cruise off the French coast in the waters of Bordeaux, and one morning descried a frigate which ran down towards us, and, on learning our nationality, signalled us to close. This we did, and were then informed that a fleet was mustering at Halifax, in Nova Scotia, under the chief command of Admiral Boscawen, for the conquest of the French possessions in Canada, and that he, the captain of the frigate, had received orders from the Admiral at Gibraltar to whip in all single ships he might encounter, and make the best of his way to the rendezvous. All hands on board the "Melpomene" were delighted at the prospect of a change, for we were getting disgusted of the monotony of cruising off a coast where neither prize-money nor glory seemed very plentiful, and where scurvy appeared to be the chief memento of their cruise our fellows were doomed to carry off.

We sailed in company with the "Jason," 44-gun

frigate, and arrived at Halifax without the occurrence of any event worth chronicling. On dropping anchor in the port, we found an enormous armament assembled, perhaps the most powerful England had ever gathered together for any conquest. It consisted of 157 ships, including transports. The naval part of the expedition was, as I have said, under the command of Boscawen, one of the most redoubtable of British admirals, while the land forces were led by Major-General Amherst, and numbered 12,000 men. This estimate does not include the troops under Generals Abercrombie and Forbes, consisting respectively of 16,000 and 8,000 men, with which, however, we have nothing to do here, as their points of attack were Crown Point, a fort situated on Lake Champlain, and Fort du Quesne, which stood a long way to the southward, near the river Ohio. The object the joint naval and military expedition had in view was the reduction of Louisburg, and the entire island of Cape Breton.

The armament sailed from the harbour of Halifax on the 28th of May, 1758, and on the 2nd of June, part of the transports anchored in the Bay of Gabarus, about seven miles to the westward of Louisburg, while the ships of war, the " Melpomene " among the number, proceeded towards the

town. The commanders learned that the garrison of
Louisburg, led by Chevalier Drucour, consisted of
2500 regular troops and 300 militia; towards the
end of the siege, they were further reinforced by 350
Canadians and Indians. The harbour was secured
by six French ships of the line and five frigates,
three of which the enemy sunk across the harbour's
mouth, in order to render it inaccessible to the English ships. The governor had taken all the pre-
cautions in his power to prevent a landing of our
troops, by establishing a chain of posts that extended
two leagues and a half along the beach; intrenchments were also thrown up, and batteries erected.
But the French commander, though a brave officer
and skilful commander, had to deal with sailors led
by a Boscawen—a man remarkable, even among the
many brilliant officers the navy numbered in those
days, for it was the age of Rodney, and Hood, and
Hawke, for his splendid dash—and by such soldiers
as Amherst, and his lieutenant, the immortal
Wolfe.

The dispositions being made for landing, a detachment in several sloops under convoy passed by
the mouth of the harbour towards Lorembec, in
order to draw the enemy's attention that way, while
the landing, it was intended, should be effected on

the other side of the town, in one of the intermediate spaces on the beach between the intrenchments and batteries that the enemy had thrown up.

All the night of the 7th of June, the fleet was busy in making preparations for the disembarkation, and when day broke on the 8th, the troops were all assembled in the boats in three divisions, while several sloops and frigates that were stationed along shore in the Bay of Gabarus, began to sweep the beach with their shot. After the fire had lasted about a quarter of an hour, the boats containing the left division of troops, commanded by Major-General Wolfe, among which were those of the "Melpomene," pulled towards the shore, while the two other divisions, on the right and centre, commanded by Brigadiers Whitmore and Lawrence, made a show of landing, in order to distract the attention of the enemy, and so take off a portion of their fire. Nothing daunted by the very severe discharge of cannon and musketry from the enemy's batteries, which did considerable execution both among the seamen and soldiers, and the heavy surf by which many boats were upset and numbers of lives lost, the gallant Wolfe pursued his course towards the shore with unflinching determination, and was well backed up by both services, who vied with each other in courage and enthusiasm. As soon as the water was knee-deep, the soldiers leaped out of the boats with the utmost alacrity, and, gaining the shore, attacked the enemy so fiercely, that in a few minutes they abandoned their works and guns, and fled in the utmost confusion. The other divisions landed also, but not without an obstinate resistance, and the stores, with the artillery, being brought on shore, the town of Louisburg was regularly invested.

The sailors of the fleet had a most arduous task before them, in landing stores and equipment, with all the heavy material of war necessary to carry on siege operations. The weather set in very boisterous, and the nature of the ground being marshy, was unfit for the conveyance of cannon.

The Governor of Louisburg, perceiving that he would have to stand a siege that would tax all his energies and military resources, destroyed the grand battery that was detached from the body of the place, recalled his outposts, and prepared for making a vigorous defence. The French troops maintained a severe and well-directed fire against the besiegers from their works in the town, the island battery, and the ships in the harbour, while numerous sallies were made though without much effect. In the meantime our people were not idle. General Amherst made his approaches with great judgment and success; while Bragadier-General Wolfe marched round the north-east part of the harbour with a strong detachment, and took possession of the Lighthouse Point, upon which he erected several batteries against the ships in the harbour and the island fortifications, which last he soon silenced. On the 19th of June, one of the French frigates escaped from the harbour, and attempted to elude the vigilance of the fleet, but she was intercepted by two line-of-battle ships, and taken possession of. She was discovered to be the " Echo," and from her officers the admiral learned that another frigate had sailed on the day of the disembarkation of the troops, and that a third had since successfully followed her example. Admiral Boscawen was anxious that his sailors should earn distinction by taking a prominent part in the operations for the reduction of the place, and was soon fortunate enough to have the coveted opportunity. On the 21st of July, three of the French line-of-battle ships were set on fire by a bomb-shell projected by one of the batteries raised by General Wolfe's division, and all three ships were speedily reduced to ashes. None remained now in the harbour but the " Prudent," of 74, and the "Bienfaisant," of 64 guns, and old Boscawen undertook to destroy these, though moored in the middle of the harbour and surrounded by the enemy's batteries.

Accordingly, on the night of the 25th of July, the boats of the squadron were mustered in two divisions, and placed under the command of two young and enterprising post-captains of the names of Balfour and Laforey. The night of the 25th of July was dark, and the boats' crews of the " Melpo-mene " as they mustered on her quarter-deck were inspected by Captain Gaisford, who examined their arms and accoutrements by the aid of lanterns. It was a desperate service, that on which the seamen of the fleet were about to embark, but it was not ex-pected that it would be attended with more risk than most cutting-out expeditions, which in those days were a common description of enterprise, and, perhaps, more than any others, have added a dis-tinctive feature to the glory of our naval annals.

My young friend, James Duckworth, was most anxious to be sent, but both the captain and first-lieutenant were obdurate, and refused to accede to his request, for the boat in which he was midship-man in charge was not ordered on service, and, moreover, both these officers discouraged the sending on such a hazardous duty a boy of his age.

" He lowered himself rapidly down."

However, the youngster was not to be thwarted, and when the men had "laid into" the boats, and just before they were starting, he managed in the darkness to elude the observation of any one, and swinging himself over the ship's side by the life-line that hung from the davit-head near the foremost boat's fall,* lowered himself rapidly down and whispered to his friend, John Mullins, who pulled bow, and who was in the secret, to receive him. The latter caught the young officer as his feet touched the boat, and stowed him away in the bottom under his thwart. The boat's crew saw the transaction, but only grinned and expressed their admiration of the pluck of the middy in the terse and forcible ejaculations usually employed by Jack to vent his satisfaction.

The fourth lieutenant, the officer who took charge of the boat, having received his final instructions from the captain, now stepped into the boat, and the word being passed that all was ready, the cutter shoved off, and joining two other boats from the "Melpomene," under the chief command of the second lieutenant, took up their stations in Captain Balfour's division.

All the boats were divided into subdivisions and

* See Illustration.

sections, according to a plan drawn up by the admiral, and then rowed off with muffled oars in the direction of the harbour. The divisions, pulling a good, ordinary stroke, so as to avoid fatiguing the men, were not long in finding themselves at the mouth of the harbour, but no sooner had they entered than they became the object of the lively attention of the enemy. Their approach had been discovered notwithstanding the darkness and the noiselessness of their advance, and the French batteries, as well as the line-of-battle ships, opened a terrific fire of cannon and musketry. There was no thought, however, of backing out of the enterprise. The boats' crews cheered with one accord, and the loud British hurrahs could be heard, clear as a clarion, above the din of the tempest of shot that rained upon them. The fire of the ships which formed the object of this cutting-out affair, directed the boats to their position, and they made for them, the crews giving way with frantic energy and enthusiasm. Captain Balfour's division, with which were the boats of the "Melpomene," being the smaller in point of numbers, made for the 64-gun ship, the "Bienfaisant," but they had nevertheless the more arduous task to perform.

The "Prudent," of 74 guns being aground, was

set on fire and destroyed, the crew escaping ashore as best they could; but the "Bienfaisant" was afloat, and received the advancing boats with a deadly fire from her guns, while every port-hole and her top-sides were illuminated with the volleys of her small-arm men.   Notwithstanding every species of opposition, the boats closed, and the British tars, drawing their cutlasses and clutching them between their teeth, clambered up the lofty sides of the line-of-battle ship, and jumping, or forcing their way through the ports, carried the great vessel by storm.

It was like magic, the celerity with which was worked the transformation scene, to borrow a theatrical simile, of the conversion of a French ship-of-war into an English prize.   The trick was done in a few minutes, and the enemy either killed, driven overboard, or compelled to surrender with the swords of the British seamen at their throats.

The "Bienfaisant" was now cut adrift from her moorings, and then a number of the boats proceeded to tow her out from under the batteries. This was done successfully in spite of the works on shore, the guns from which kept up an indignant roar at the disgrace that had befallen the Gallic arms.   Thus was this affair brought to a triumphant conclusion, though not without a heavy loss to the victors.

Among the killed at the very commencement of the action, was the fourth lieutenant of the "Mel-pomene," who commanded the cutter in which Duckworth had secreted himself. This young officer was shot through the breast, as, sword in hand, he was in the act of leading his men on board the "Bienfaisant." The musket was fired by a Frenchman who leant out of a gun-port and took deliberate aim, and so close was the muzzle of the gun to his victim's body, that the clothes of the latter were set on fire by the discharge. Young Duckworth saw his officer fall, and, springing forward, extinguished the fire, but, finding that he was already past human aid, he laid his body gently down on the boat's thwarts, and releasing the sword from out of the grasp of the fingers of the dead man, followed the gallant band who were making their way on board the line-of-battle ship.

The command of the boat's crew now devolved upon him, and he assumed it in sober earnest, boy as he was, and was fortunate enough to get through the fighting without receiving a scratch, which was a marvel, for, notwithstanding his courage, one would have thought the physical weakness of so young an antagonist, must have brought him to grief in so desperate an affair.

On his return on board his ship, he sprang up the rope ladder on the port side with all the assurance of his nature, and reported his return in command of the cutter, to the first lieutenant and captain, who were both waiting at the gangway to learn particulars of the affair. The latter feigned displeasure at the disobedience of orders, but Lieutenant Higham could not contain his admiration of the hardihood and pluck of the "younker," as he called him, and asked Captain Gaisford to forgive the breach of discipline in consideration of the gallantry he had displayed ; to which the coxswain of the boat, anxious to screen the young officer from the consequences of his fault, bore witness.

"I axes your parding, sir," said this worthy, addressing the first lieutenant, and touching his hat, while he pointed to the youth, who stood by, having in one hand the sword, so disproportionate to his size, of the lieutenant he had succeeded, his face flushed with excitement, "I axes your parding, sir, but this 'ere young gentleming was among the first on us as boarded the ' Ben Pheasant,' as them French chaps call the line-o'-battle ship as we cut out, arter Mr. Harness was knocked over. He led us on to wictory, and no mistake, he did your honours, arter that distressing ewent."

This burst of eloquence concluded, the honest fellow appeared so overcome at his apparently un-wonted flow of words, that he stood as if rooted to the spot, while his face bore the expression of a schoolboy who has been caught in the very act of committing some offence.

However, Holroyd was speedily re-assured by the captain, who replied, " All right, you can go forrard ; Mr. Duckworth shan't suffer for what he has done."

Turning to the abashed midshipman, Captain Gaisford invited him and the first lieutenant to accompany him to his state cabin, as he wished to learn particulars of the action and also of the death of Mr. Harness, for, being a kind-hearted man and taking a deep interest in his officers, he always made a point of personally communicating the intelligence of the death of any of them to their relatives. The captain also invited the officers who commanded the other two boats to join them, and then the party adjourned to the comfortable and roomy quarters of the commander of the " Melpomene," where our young hero, over a good stiff glass of grog, " fought his battle o'er again," and related what he saw of the affair that had ended so propitiously. The captain, though the strictest of officers on duty, indeed he was regarded as somewhat of a martinet, could relax on such occasions, and play the part of a host with all the grace and *bonhomie* of a polished gentleman.

Young Duckworth's adventurous conduct came to the ears of Admiral Boscawen, and that gallant officer, who could sympathize with the eagerness of the youngster to acquire fame (his own career from his childhood having been passed amidst scenes of bloodshed) sent a note to Captain Gaisford, asking him to dine on board his flag-ship, and bring the boy with him.

The honour of having attracted the attention of the commander-in-chief of His Majesty's ships and vessels, was enough to turn the brain of most young middies, but Duckworth fortunately was gifted with common sense, that rarest of all good qualities, and though pleased, he refrained from giving himself any petty airs of superiority, but "bore his honours meekly," and so avoided giving offence to his messmates, who though perhaps individually jealous, were still unanimous in speaking of him as "a right good fellow."

The admiral not only praised the boy and drank

6

his health at dinner, but offered to take him on board his own flag-ship and keep an eye upon him. This flattering offer, however, James Duckworth declined with many thanks, saying that he liked his ship and all the officers so much, that he would rather remain where he was. This refusal, though unexpected, tended to raise our hero still further in the estimation of the commander-in-chief, as it did, you may be sure, in the good opinion of Captain Gaisford and all the officers of the frigate.

The siege of Louisburg still continued with unabated resolution, on the part of the general and admiral respectively commanding the sea and land forces, between whom also the utmost harmony existed. The admiral cheerfully assisted General Amherst with cannon and other implements for conducting the siege operations, and sent on shore detachments of marines to maintain posts on shore, and otherwise assist the soldiers who were greatly harassed, owing to the extent of ground over which the necessary works were spread. Not content with thus aiding his colleague, Admiral Boscawen formed a strong naval brigade to act on shore as pioneers, but chiefly to assist in working the heavy guns and mortars. On their part the besieged displayed great pertinacity and resolution of purpose as well as skill.

The fire of their guns was kept up with ceaseless activity, and great perseverance, but at length it became evident to the Chevalier Drucour, that he could not hold out much longer with any prospect of success. The French shipping had been all taken or destroyed, the two principal bastions were in ruins, while two or three practicable breaches had already been effected; to render matters desperate, forty out of fifty-two pieces of cannon had been either dismounted or rendered unserviceable by the British fire. The commandant, therefore, in a letter to General Amherst, proposed a capitulation by which he and his garrison should be allowed to march out with all the honours of war; that is, with their arms, and flags flying. These were the terms that had been accorded to the English troops at Port Mahon in the Balearic Isles in the previous year, after Byng's unsuccessful attempt to relieve them. To this proposal, however, General Amherst declined to accede, but informed the Chevalier that he, together with his garrison, must surrender themselves unconditionally as prisoners of war, otherwise he must prepare to expect, on the following morning, a general attack by the fleet under Admiral Boscawen. The French commander, a high-spirited man, piqued at the severity of these terms, replied that rather than comply with them, he would stand an assault, and be buried in the ruins of the fortress it was his duty to defend. Such was his fixed determination, when the commissary-general and intendant of the colony presented a petition from the merchants and inhabitants of the place, requesting him to accede to the terms of the English commander, and pointing out the futility of further resistance. Sorely against his grain, the Chevalier yielded to this prayer, and agreed to capitulate on the original terms.

On the 27th of July, three companies of grenadiers, commanded by Major Farquhar, took possession of the western gate, while Brigadier Whitmore was detached into the town, to see the garrison lay down their arms and deliver up their colours on the esplanade, and to post the necessary guards on the stores, magazines, and ramparts. Thus the English obtained possession of the important town of Louisburg, together with the whole island of Cape Breton, and to this day it has never changed masters. The victors became possessed of two hundred and twenty-one pieces of cannon with eighteen mortars, and a considerable quantity of military stores and ammunition, while the total loss incurred in achieving these great results did not exceed four hundred men killed and wounded. The merchants and those of the inhabitants who were non-combatants, were shipped off to France in English vessels, but the garrison, together with all the naval officers, seamen, and marines, to the number of 5637 men, were transported to England as prisoners of war.

The loss of Louisburg and of the ships in the harbour, was keenly felt by the French people and by their King (Louis), while in England the nation was carried away with feelings of exultation proportionate to the depression of their neighbours. The despatches, giving particulars of the event, were immediately sent to England in a vessel detached for that purpose, and Captain Amherst, brother to the successful general, was also entrusted with eleven pairs of colours. These were, by order of his Majesty, old King George II., then in the declining years of his life, carried, with every circumstance of pomp, escorted by detachments of horse and foot-guards, with kettle-drums and trumpets, from his residence, the palace at Kensington, to St. Paul's Cathedral, where they were deposited as trophies under a salute of cannon and amid other noisy expressions of national triumph. But these rejoicings were not confined to the capital; the joy was universal throughout the British dominions, and addresses of congratulation on the conquest of Louisburg and reduction of Cape

Breton, were presented to the King by a great number of considerable towns and corporations.

After the occupation of Louisburg, some ships, among which was the "Melpomene," together with a body of troops, were despatched to take possession of the Island of St. John, which also lies in the Gulf of St. Lawrence, and, by its fertility in corn and cattle, had, since the beginning of the war, supplied Quebec with considerable quantities of provisions. This island was likewise the asylum to which the French neutrals of Annapolis fled for shelter from our Government, and the retreat from whence they, and the Indians, made their sudden incursions into Nova Scotia, where the latter perpetrated the most inhuman barbarities on the subjects of Great Britain. What these barbarities were, may be gathered from the fact, that several scalps of our countrymen were actually found in the governor's quarters, proving the truth of the allegations of the English settlers, that the savages received not only encouragement to perpetrate these outrages, but even a premium for every scalp they produced. The inhabitants of St. John showed themselves as cowardly as they were cruel, and did not attempt any resistance against the English force. They submitted to the number of 4100, and brought in their arms. The island was stocked with 10,000 head of black cattle, with vast quantities of corn. This concluded for that year the naval part of the operations against the French possessions in North America.

The "Melpomene" returned to England with Admirals Boscawen and Hardy, and a small squadron, the greater part of the fleet being left at Halifax. We arrived in England in the beginning of November, after having given chase to six large French ships which were descried to the westward of the Scilly Isles, but were unable either to overhaul them, or bring them to action. The gallant Boscawen was received with applause by his King and country, as were also the captains and crews of the ships of his squadron. Not many months elapsed before both he and they were engaged in fresh enterprises, but I must leave my readers to learn details of Admiral Boscawen's later achievements from the naval histories that treat of that period, and will confine myself to the autobiography of so uninteresting an object as a man-o'-war's bell.

CHAPTER IV.

At this time the whole English people were nearly beside themselves with a war fever, chiefly directed against the country's old traditional foe, France. The nation was filled with pride and triumph at the recent successes, not only as we have seen in America, under Amherst and Boscawen, but with the news of the great victories achieved by Clive and Admirals Watson and Pocock in the East Indies. Parliament voted large subsidies, and increased the taxes to raise the sinews of war, and the people, so far from being restive under the additional burdens, acquiesced in the imposition of these new and burdensome imposts. The arsenals resounded with the clang of preparation; the ships of the Navy were repaired, and their number augmented; and, in order to man the different squadrons with which our dockyards were crowded, the administration resorted with greater rigour and success than ever to the practice of pressing—a proclamation was issued offering a

considerable bounty for every seaman and every landsman that should by a certain day enter voluntarily into
the King's service. As an additional encouragement
to this class of his subjects, George II. promised his
pardon to all seamen who had deserted from their
ships, provided they returned before the 3rd of July;
while those deserters who neglected to surrender
themselves would be tried by court-martial on apprehension, and suffer the penalties of military law
without any hope of mercy.

William Morris and his friend Johnson, the captain of the maintop, had together concocted a plan
for deserting from the ship at Plymouth, where she
was refitting for foreign service on some distant
station, as was manifest by the large amount of
stores and war material she was embarking; but so
strict was the supervision kept over the men, even
when they went on shore on leave, that their chance
of escape appeared a very slender one. The Government issued a mandate to all justices of the peace,
mayors, and magistrates of corporations throughout
Great Britain, commanding them to make particular
search for straggling seamen fit for service, and to
forward all that should be found to the nearest port,
that they might be sent on board whatever ship lying
there that might be in want of hands.

As there was almost a certainty of being captured should they attempt to escape, the friends came to the determination to give up the scheme, but not without great reluctance on the part of Morris.   However, he had become accustomed to the discomfort of a nautical life, and on learning that the "Melpomene" had been ordered to proceed to the East Indies to reinforce the fleet of Admiral Pocock in those waters, reconciled himself to the prospect of a further lengthened period of service.   The frigate was to go out for a period of two years, the remainder of his commission, as Captain Gaisford informed his officers and men one morning when they were all assembled on the quarter-deck for grand divisions.   The gallant captain promised his men lots of prize-money, as well as a "bellyful of fighting."   The announcement was received with a grin of delight from one end of the double line of seamen to the other; the rules of the service did not allow Jack a more demonstrative method of testifying his approval of the object and prospects of the forthcoming cruise, or else he would have cheered; as it was, he simply grinned, and touched his hat in respectful acquiescence.

So the "Melpomene," having filled up with stores and secured her proper complement of men by a moderate application of the press-gang system, sailed from Plymouth in the latter part of April, leaving, doubtless, many sorrowing hearts behind in old England, and carrying away on board her some that were heavy also at the thought of the long parting, with all the chances and dangers of war time, and the ordinary perils of the sea; yet I should say that the major part of the gallant fellows, both officers and crew, were unspeakably relieved when, as the nautical saying has it, the " fore-topsail paid their debts," a rather unpromising method of liquidating one's liabilities as far as the unhappy creditor was concerned.

Nothing of moment occurred during the first days of the passage to the southward. No French ships were sighted, but one morning a large fleet was seen standing to the nor'-westward. This was soon made out to be the squadron commanded by Admiral Sir Edward Hawke, who had been dispatched to blockade the harbour of Brest, in which was shut up a powerful fleet, which the French Government proposed to send to sea under M. de Conflans, with the object of effecting a descent on the Irish coast. After exchanging signals, the "Melpomene" proceeded on her course, and ran down with a fair wind nearly to the line. Here she was detained some two weeks with variable and light airs, known as the " doldrums ;" but at length edging away to the southward, she caught a fine south-east trade-wind, and stood away a couple of points to the westward of south, with her yards braced sharp up on the port tack, and every stitch of plain sail drawing. For many days not a rope-yarn was touched in the way of trimming sail. During these pleasant long days, many and tough were the yarns I heard recounted under my shadow. Some, I assure you, were beyond my capacity to swallow. There was only one, however, that would greatly interest my readers, and as it relates to William Morris, who has played so prominent a part in these pages, and whose history I had long entertained a curiosity to learn, I will give it to my friends as nearly as possible in the language employed by the narrator himself :—

"You must know then, in the first place, that my real name is not William Morris. I need scarcely tell you that I am not a sailor by profession, for you are seaman enough to know that. When I came on board, you will remember I was rated in the ship's books a landsman. What will surprise you, however, is, that I am a country gentleman—or 'squire, as you call them—and that I have considerable landed property in one of the midland counties. My name is Cavendish, and the Cavendishes of ——shire

are one of the first families of that county. My
father died a few years ago, and left me, his eldest
son, heir to the entailed estates, which brought me
in an income of £7000 a year. I have two brothers
and three sisters living, and the curious fact of it is
that they are all more or less well married, and have
large families; while I, who am the head of the
family and possess the largest income, have neither
wife nor child, and, who knows, before we are out of
this war or return to England again, but that a
French bullet or cutlass will hand over to a brother
or nephew the rent-roll, which, indeed, I have turned
to precious little good account, beyond supplying myself with the enjoyments that ordinarily form the
staple amusements of an English 'squire. No, I
have passed my days in hunting, and coursing, and
shooting, and my nights in card playing and drinking; though, to do myself but justice, I must say
that I never cared for London frivolities and dis-
sipations, or indeed took any part in them during
the visits to town, unfrequent and paid at long intervals as they were."

The narrator paused a minute, and then proceeded, as if soliloquizing, and seeking to excuse to
his conscience the utterly selfish life he had led during
the few years he had enjoyed the ancestral estates;

but he was cut short by his companion, who—after the surprise occasioned by the discovery that his friend was a gentleman, and the still greater astonishment aroused at his expression of regret that he had thoroughly enjoyed himself with the means placed at his disposal—had fallen into a doze, from which he was suddenly awakened by the noise resulting from his pipe smashing to pieces as it slipped out of his relaxed jaws.   Finding his chum still descanting on his shortcomings as a country gentleman, he sprang, up, and gazing at Morris (as we will still call him) with an expression of countenance denoting an opinion that he was *non compos*, or had been at the grog bucket, he bawled out in his ear, " Paul* there now, Bill, ye've been getting the weather-gage of the purser, or, may be, it's the doctor ye want.   What's wrong o' you?" and accompanied the rousing-up process by a slap on the back, that would have made the shoulders of any man gifted with ordinary sensibility ache for a week.   It had the desired effect, and Morris moralized no more to his unsympathizing friend, whom, after his recent discreditable exhibition, he had some diffi-

* A " paul " is a stop in the capstan, and the expression, " paul there," as used above, means to cease talking.

culty in inducing to credit his narrative. Morris now resumed :—

"Nothing occurred to disturb my enjoyment until only a few days before I embarked on board the 'Melpomene,' when the circumstance took place that has changed the whole current of my life. I must tell you I hunted the county fox-hounds, and one evening, after a fine day's sport ending with a splendid spin over the country, in which I was in at the death, and carried off the brush, I asked the gentlemen of the hunt to drink the evening out and the morning in at my house, near to which the finish had taken place. They all heartily agreed to the proposal, for the greater number of them had tasted the hospitalities of the old Hall, and the remaining few knew by repute, I suppose, of the existence of the fine wines in the Hall cellars; so they all followed me to the house, and prepared to make a night of it, according to our bad bachelor habits ; for you must know, Tim Johnson, that on these occasions ladies are strictly excluded."

"Well, and quite right too," chimed in the captain of the maintop; "I never know'd a woman who didn't spoil sport when grog was to the fore. There was my owd 'oman, as has 'kicked the bucket' now this nine year, she couldn't a-bear 'a

wet night,' as me and my messmates, the boys of
the 'Hairythusa,' called our grog parties ashore;
and one night, soon after we was paid off (we got a
haul o' prize-money that commission, I tell ye), one
night she walks in, just as a lot of us starboardines
(I was on the starboard watch, ye must know, aboard
the 'Hairythusa') had brewed three buckets full of
the finest Jamaiky ye ever clapped eyes on, and she
just walks into the big cabin, or mess-room, or
whatever you call it, of the 'La Hogg' grogshop, at
which we always had our conwiwials, and she just
kicks over the bucket without a word, and sets the
place a-swimmin' with the best liquor as Ben
Bobstay ever brewed at his best, and he could mix
it, could Ben, I tell ye." At the memory of the
liquor, the honest fellow wiped his mouth with the
back of his horny hand, as if he felt very dry indeed;
but when the thought of the waste of the Jamaica
rum recurred to him, he seemed much discomposed,
and ejaculated. "It was a cruel thing, Bill, and I
never forgave her."

"What did your messmates do to your wife,
Tim?" asked his friend, who had much difficulty in
restraining his mirth at the distressed look the face
of the petty officer wore as he dwelt sorrowfully on
the painful reminiscence.

"Do, do you say ?" he asked, defiantly. "Why, they just took her up, and dropped her out of the windy. Pitched her out neck and crop, I think it was, for she was taken to the hospital with a broken leg, and serve her right too for capsizing them three poor buckets of grog mixed by Ben Bobstay, which never did her no harm."

The subject was painful as regarded the fate of the "poor" buckets of liquor, so Morris, in order to divert his friend from contemplation of this bitter recollection, proceeded with his narrative :—

"Well, we passed a jolly evening, drinking heavily, and singing songs with rattling choruses, until at length the merits of the respective hunters came on for discussion. Some of the gentlemen had sent their horses home, intending to return in their gigs, which they had ordered their grooms to bring to my house at two in the morning; while others, who were more sure of their ability to ride home on their hunters or hacks, had put them up in my stables. An adjournment to these offices was therefore proposed, to decide a question which had arisen between two of my guests regarding some trivial points in dispute—one of which was, I remember, the height of their horses. I thought these points were all satisfactorily settled by ex-

7

amination and measurement, when, on our return to table to finish the carouse with a parting glass, one of these two gentlemen renewed the discussion. I had before sought to put a stop to it, for I perceived that one of the disputants was 'half seas over,' as sailors say. This gentleman resented my effort at making peace, which he regarded in the light of an attempt at interference, and this he stated to me in the most offensive language.

"My other guests, shocked at the insult thus gratuitously levelled at their host, sought to induce him to offer an apology. Instead of doing this, however, he said that had the affair not taken place at my table, he would have called me out. Upon this I informed him that a message sent to me at Cavendish Hall, would always meet with a response; and the upshot of the whole affair was that after a few minutes' more altercation, it was agreed that the matter should be settled then and there. Duelling pistols I had in the house—no gentleman's necessaries were considered complete in those days without these instruments. They were now produced and quickly loaded, but a difficulty arose as to seconds. Without any trouble I induced a gentleman to act for me, but no one would consent to be 'the friend' of my opponent, and this, notwithstanding an earnest request addressed to several among them to act in this capacity as a personal favour. No one in fact, knew him in the room, though in the course of conversation with his neighbour at table, he stated that he had served in the army, and his manner and speech were those of a gentleman. It would never do to let the matter have an abortive conclusion, for want of a second, so as none of my guests would act in that capacity—most of them indeed saying, I ought not to go out with a fellow of whom I knew nothing and for such a paltry cause—to place my opponent on an equality in every point with myself, I called in my butler and footman, and directed them to fill the post of seconds, one to each of us. I was determined not to be baulked, or to give the man who had insulted me in my own house the opportunity of saying I had declined to resent an injury because of the difficulty of securing a second for himself, an utter stranger. On seeing my fixed determination to fight, some of my friends conjured me to pause, if only till the morning, but I persisted, and they left the house; the great number, however, although indignant with my adversary, remained to see the sport to the finish. My two domestics were dismayed at the unexpected part they were called upon to play, and at first timidly demurred; but I was accustomed to have my orders obeyed, and at length their scruples were overcome.

"The preliminaries satisfactorily settled, we retired to the opposite sides of the room, distant only some ten paces apart. The lights were put on one side so as not to obstruct our vision. The seconds having been previously instructed in their duties, took their assigned places. The dropping of a handkerchief was to be the signal. A death-like stillness pervaded the large apartment. I felt no feeling of fear, but I must own my heart beat quickly, though perhaps, this was as much due to indignation as to anxiety at the possible, and but too probable result as regarded myself; for it was evident to me as I glanced at my opponent, and marked the calm, business-like way in which he comported himself, and the experienced manner in which he handled the pistols, that this was not in all probability the first time he had been a principal in the deadly duello.

"I cast a hurried look round the well-lighted apartment, and marked the anxious or pitying expression on faces familar to me on the country side, and a pang of sorrow shot through my heart as I thought I might perhaps never more join them in the merry chase, and cheer the hounds on to the death. But I checked the thought as calculated to unnerve my hand, which must be steady, and turned away from the contemplation of the faces of friends to steel my heart by the sight of the man who had so causelessly insulted me, his host, and not content with this injury, sought to wipe out his offence against the laws of hospitality by thirsting for the blood of that host. It was enough, and my heart and hand were steady as a rock. I felt confidence in myself, though I had seldom practised with a pistol, and had never been out "before"—rather an uncommon thing for a gentleman to be able to say.

"Our eyes were fixed on the man holding the handkerchief; 'one, two,' were the words that greeted my ears. The handkerchief was dropped, and two quick, sharp reports rang out through the still apartment. I felt I was untouched, and looked eagerly at my adversary, but he also did not move a muscle or change countenance, so it appeared we had both fired ineffectively. Our seconds proceeded, under inspection of some of my friends who doubted their ability, to reload the weapons, when several of my guests stepped forward and appealed to me to express myself as satisfied. My honour and courage they argued had been placed beyond doubt, as indeed they stood before, and they hoped I would shake hands with my opponent. I merely referred them to the gentleman on the opposite side of my dining-room, who stood with a sardonic smile calmly awaiting the reloading of his pistol. To that appeal the latter contemptuously replied that he was very far from satisfied, that he did not commence the duel with the object of letting me off so cheaply, and that it was childish talking about satisfaction, when no blood had been spilt, without which his honour, at least, could not be cleansed from the imputations cast upon it. I, be it observed, had cast no imputations upon his honour, but as I saw that he regarded me as a poltroon, who would back out of the business if he could by any means, I made no observation on hearing these insulting remarks, which were delivered in a loud tone of voice, but resolved to fight it out to the bitter end.

"Again we stood opposite each other, again was heard, 'are you ready'? and on our replying in the affirmative, 'one,' 'two,' in the voice of my worthy butler—whose tones I had always associated with a cheery response on receiving my orders regarding some new bin or old vintage of port,—but which had now acquired a solemn, not to say funereal

"His right arm hung motionless by his side."

intonation as he repeated the duellist's formula. Again, almost as one report, rang out the sharp crack of our pistols; again I looked, and this time it seemed as if my fire had not been without effect.

"My antagonist's body was turned full towards me, and was leaning back towards the wall, while his face still glared at me with its former expression of malignity, though a palor was creeping over it. His right arm hung motionless by his side, but the hand yet clutched the pistol with desperate tenacity, while his left hand was convulsively clasped over his breast. Two or three gentlemen rushed towards him, but as I was not sure he was wounded, I did not move.

"Presently I heard one say, 'Lay him down,' then I knew I had not delivered my fire without effect, and I also moved hastily round the table, and bent over the wounded man. He was breathing heavily and with seeming difficulty, while with every inhalation, the thick blood slowly streamed down his closely buttoned-up coat and formed in a small pool at his side. He appeared to be in a fainting condi-tion, but on seeing me his features flushed slightly, but it was the flush of anger, not of forgiveness or sorrow. Seeing the tragic turn affairs had taken, all my guests, with the exception of three, took their departure, most of them without even taking leave of me. One of my most intimate friends merely ejaculated across the table, 'Serious business, I'm sorry for you, Cavendish,' and walked off without offering to be of any assistance, or even to shake me by the hand and express a word of sympathy.

" In the same way nearly all my friends, as they called me in the hour of my good fortune, served me, and of the three who remained, two were newly-formed acquaintances. These gentlemen had even less sympathy for the misguided wretch who lay weltering in his gore, on the carpet of my dining-room. One or two among them merely glanced at him as he lay writhing in his agony, and,—with the sympathetic exclamation of 'Poor wretch,' qualified in one instance by ' served him right, though '—they left us alone with the dying man, for dying we soon discovered him to be.

"The wound it was at once seen was mortal. The ball had passed through his right breast, of course penetrating the lung, and hence every respiration caused him intense pain. We removed his clothes from the region of the injury, and sought to staunch the flow of blood, but as we were thus employed, he gave one gasp and expired, his eyes still riveted on me with an expression of undying hate. He was, or rather had been, a decidedly handsome man, but though only two or three and thirty, his features wore a most dissipated, worn-out look. On searching his pocket for some token of his identity we found a card-case, and on the cards, were engraved the name of Captain Belmont, while on one of them was written in ink, quite recently evidently, 'late of the —— Hussars, 14, Marlborough Place, York.'

"My friends advised me strongly to fly to Holland, or at least remain in hiding until the affair was blown over, and they promised to take charge of the body of the dead man, and convey it to his people at the above address. I took the advice and started off for Portsmouth, intending to take ship for Holland, and on my arrival there to write to my friends of my whereabouts. To avoid notice, I shunned all the fashionable hotels and took up my quarters in a public house. I kept very quiet for some days, but unfortunately got drinking one night, and they say I took the King's bounty and agreed to serve in the navy, during the commission of the 'Melpomene' by Captain Gaisford. However, that may be, here I am, and here I must remain until we get back to old England. I suppose it is a punishment for my sins, and I must make the best of it; anyway, Johnson, you shall share my fortune, and if this war soon ends, we will make our escape when we touch English soil, and I will see if I can make it all right at the Admiralty, where my county influence will be of service, and you shall want for nothing the remainder of your life, old boy, not forgetting any number of buckets of the oldest Jamaiky."

On hearing this, the captain of the maintop sprang off the forecastle, and after performing a few steps of the hornpipe, so overcome was he with ecstasy at the thought of killing himself with drink, exclaimed, " By the piper that played before Moses, ye don't say so. I'd jump every week off the main-top-gallant yardarm in a gale of wind, to save your life, for one bucket of that same." Just then the officer of the watch came up, and was thunderstruck at the *pas seul* performance from one ordinarily so grave as Tim Johnson.

So it was that I learned the history of the lives of two more of the crew of the " Melpomene" who had interested me. You see my autobiography, the interest of which does not centre so much in what I myself did, as I am a passive sort of individual, but in what I saw and heard, is interspersed with episodes, which however, many of my readers will doubtless regard with greater interest than what passed under my immediate cognizance.

CHAPTER V.

THE " Melpomene " arrived at Madras Roads on the 29th of August, 1759, and found a strong fleet assembled there under the command of Vice-Admiral Pococke, who was preparing his ships with the intention of proceeding to sea forthwith, and attacking the French fleet, which was known to be somewhere off the Coromandel Coast under a distinguished officer, M. d'Apché.*

When fighting was on the tapis, Captain Gaisford was not the man to be backward, and though the British Admiral intended to sail on the 1st of September in quest of his French antagonist, the gallant commander of the frigate expressed his determination that the " Melpomene " should form part of his squadron even if she sailed without filling up with wood and water, and had to borrow these necessaries from her consorts during the voyage. However, the authorities at Fort St. George used the

* This name is also indifferently spelt by historians D'Aché.

most creditable alacrity in responding to the requisition of Captain Gaisford, and all that he indented for from every department of the local government was so quickly supplied, that at daybreak on the morning of the 1st September the " Melpomene " sailed in perfect preparation for any of those eventualities with the enemy or the elements, that befall His Majesty's ships in war time. Admiral Pococke made sail to the southward in search of the French fleet, and had not long to beat about, for on the following day the hostile squadron, consisting of fifteen sail, were sighted standing to the northward. The admiral immediately signalled the fleet to clear for action, on the supposition that the enemy being numerically superior, would at once accept the challenge ; but M. d'Apché considered discretion the better part of valour, and bore away in the contrary direction. The British Admiral now signalled the chase, and the entire fleet soon flung out to the winds all the canvas they could carry. Unfortunately the wind fell light, so that the relative distance between the squadrons did not change. How the officers and men of the " Melpomene " chafed at the delay, and whistled, and, like Shakespeare's lover, sighed " like a furnace " for a wind, but the much wooed breeze would not come. The daylight waned into night, and the sun rose in the

morning, and poured its hot rays upon the heads
of the impatient sons of Neptune, who, I am sorry
to say, after the manner of their kind, exchanged
their gentle wooings for fierce objurgations and
frequent invocations upon their eyes and limbs,
which were consigned to a place not usually considered mentionable to ears polite, or desirable as a
resting-place for those members of the human form
divine. But yet the wind refused as obstinately to
yield to threats and curses as it had previously to
blandishments and soft utterances; and so three
days succeeded the 2nd of September, on which day
the Frenchmen had commenced to tantalise their
antagonists by the sight of their hulls, and yet the
fiery tars of England were as far off the realization of
their hopes as when the foreign craft first hove in
sight. To crown the disappointment on the fourth
morning, when the looks-out cast their glances in the
direction the French fleet had hitherto occupied, they
were nowhere to be seen. The experienced seamen
employed on this duty that morning on board each
ship, rubbed their eyes, and once more scanned the
horizon, but it was only to confirm the first hasty
glance. M. d'Apché was *non est.* A slight breeze
springing up during the night, he had made sail,
and · borne aways towards Pondicherry.   Thanks

to the friendly screen of night, he succeeded in eluding the vigilance of his pertinacious enemy, and had thus successfully and incontinently "ske-daddled."

If the officers, petty officers, seamen, and marines of the British uttered curses, not loud but deep, before this unhappy event had disturbed their equanimity, the reader will not discredit me when I say that, like the "army in Flanders," they used very bad language in connection with this disappearance of the traditional foe, whom they appeared to regard as made and provided by a wise Providence, only for them to defeat and drive in confusion into their harbours. However, old Pococke was not to be done out of his fighting so easily, if it could be had under another latitude upon the same conditions, and so, craftily concluding that the French admiral had "made tracks" for Pondicherry, he bore up for that harbour under a press of sail. On the 8th of September, the French fleet were once more sighted, standing to the southward, and our fellows again prepared for action, though it was not until the 10th that they were successful in bringing on an encounter. At one o'clock on the afternoon of that day, M. d'Apché succeeded in overcoming his extreme coyness so far as to face his importunate adversaries. Throwing out the signal for the battle at that hour, he commenced the action, without further delay, by firing his guns as fast as he could bring them to bear. At the commencement of the action, the British fleet numbered nine ships, including the " Melpomene " (the only frigate), while that of the enemy consisted of eleven sail, the French admiral having detached four vessels some days previously ; but the disparity of force was much greater than this statement alone would imply. Ship for ship, the enemy carried heavier guns, and larger crews to man them.

The action at once became general, and the cannonading that ensued was very furious. The captain of the "Melpomene" singled out a 74-gun ship as his antagonist, there being no frigate, and, running up, engaged her at pistol-shot. It was about a quarter-past one that the French 74 opened fire, while the riflemen from her lofty tops kept up an incessant and well-directed fusillade, that quickly made it very hot work for every living soul on the spar-deck of the " Melpomene."

Luckily the hostile gunners being too eager to demolish our small craft, fired so rapidly that their guns were discharged before they bore on us. The 24-pound shot, therefore, ranged mostly ahead of us, and crashed into the flag-ship of Admiral Pococke, which was engaging the French commander-in-chief's ship on our beam.

Our well-trained fellows were not in such a hurry, but reserved their fire until we could bring our starboard broadside to bear well. Captain Gaisford and his lieutenants were " as cool as cucumbers," and the latter, with the junior officers in command of sections, gave the order " Fire " to the captains of their guns, as deliberately and steadily as if practising at an old tar barrel, during general quarters. The whole fleet was soon wrapped in one vast pall of smoke, out of which the incessant flashes of fire from the guns, were belched forth; occasionally a puff of wind would blow away a corner of the thick veil that thus obscured the scene of strife, but it was only for a passing moment, and soon again all was obscured. The enemy fired chiefly at our rigging, with the intention, doubtless, of rendering us unmanageable, so that she might either carry us by boarding—which she flattered herself could be easily effected with her superior numbers—or she might range ahead, and take up whatever position would enable her to rake us effectually. Captain Gaisford, on the other hand, directed the attention of his gunners almost exclusively to the hull of his gigantic opponent, and right smartly and well our brave boys

8

poured the round shot and grape into the lower deck batteries of the line-of-battle ship. The fire from these quarters visibly slackened under the "Melpomene's" efforts to silence the guns, but the main-deck batteries kept up a galling and destructive cannonade that began to tell heavily upon us, owing to our inferior weight of metal.

We had commenced the action under top-sails only, having hauled up our courses and clued up the topgallant sails. The captain being anxious to get ahead a little, out of the enemy's fire, which was cutting up his men more than he liked, sent aloft some hands to overhaul the fore and main gear. There was some delay, however, owing to the starboard main tack and sheet, with the blocks through which they were rove, having been shot away, but the riggers, under the supervision of the boatswain, took the end of the sheet up the rigging, and fitting it with clip-hooks, very soon had all ready, and let the main gear run, when it was discovered that owing to a blow from a piece of grape or bar shot, the "clew garnet" would not travel through the block in the slings of the yard. The delay in clearing this, kept the "Melpomene" still longer under the fire of her formidable antagonist; the men were falling fast at the guns, and the action had become hotter than was quite comfortable. The captain not liking this condition of affairs, ordered the " clew garnet " to be cut, and at length the gear ran freely, and the mainsail was set. This, together with the foresail caused the frigate to forge slowly ahead, when the commander of the Frenchman followed suit and overhauled his fore and main gear, in order to keep us under the terrific fire he had been pouring into us, at such short range, from his heavy main-deck guns.

" Set the top-gallant sails," shouted out the captain, anxious to secure the advantage he had almost within his grasp. Hardly had he uttered the words, when a shot from the enemy struck the end of the jibboom, carrying it away, and at the same moment a puff of wind brought clattering about our ears the foretopgallant mast, the backstays of which had early been shot away. For a moment I thought the maintop-gallant mast would follow, when we should have been without the upper sails, which are most essential, circumstanced as we now were with a light breeze, and what little there was almost driven away by the heavy cannonading. The foretop man, who had run up aloft to obey the order of his superior, was hurled down from aloft amidst the ruin of standing and running rigging, but, happily, fell overboard, and hence was enabled to regain the ship by dint of good swimming, and a handy rope's end that was trailing alongside.

Fortunately the maintop-gallant sail was set without further delay, and then the " Melpomene," under the influence of this sail, which caught the air that in the upper regions was not so subject to the deadening effects of the tempest of " villanous saltpetre " raging below, drew gradually ahead of her huge opponent. Now seizing his opportunity, Captain Gaisford ported his helm, and skilfully bringing his ship on the port bow of the Frenchman, poured into her, broadside after broadside, raking her from stem to stern. The captain of the enemy, in his turn, sought to set his top-gallant sails, so as to place himself once more on an equality with his 'puny adversary ; but the British commander, anticipating this intention, was not going to allow himself to be placed a second time, if he could help it, in the clutches of the line-of-battle ship. He sent up some young midshipmen with strict orders to the marines and riflemen in the " Melpomene's " tops to devote their attention exclusively to shooting any men engaged aloft in assisting to set the top-gallant sails, while the fire of the small swivels or wall-pieces, which in those days were fitted in the tops, as a component part of the armament of a ship-of-war, was directed at the top-gallant gear, and with such good effect that very soon those sails were rendered useless for sailing purposes.

The seamen of the " Melpomene," quickly observant of the comparative immunity from the ravages of the enemy's shot they now enjoyed, thanks to the superior seamanship of their officers, worked their guns with enthusiasm, and it appeared as if their efforts would be rewarded with success, when the French Admiral made the signal to his fleet to discontinue the action. The opponent of the " Melpomene " hauled her wind on the starboard tack, and another ship of the enemy just then making her appearance on the scene, the British frigate was robbed of the glory of having silenced the fire of her unwieldly antagonist. It was about ten minutes past four that the enemy's rear began to give way; this example was soon followed by the centre, and finally by the van-division led by M. d'Apché. Thus the whole fleet were defeated, and bore away to the S.S.E. with every stitch of canvas they could spread.

The British squadron was so much damaged in the masts, spars, and rigging that they could not pursue, so that M. d'Apaché retreated at his leisure unmolested. On counting up the losses sustained by his fleet, Admiral Pococke found that more than 300 men had been killed in the engagement, including Captain Miche who commanded the "Newcastle," Captain Gore of the Marines, with two lieutenants, a master gunner and boatswain, while more than 250 seamen and marines were wounded, among the number being Captains Somerset and Brereton. The loss of the enemy must have been much more considerable, not only on account of their ships being crowded with men, but because their fire had been directed chiefly at our vessels aloft. This they certainly did to a great extent, for many of our ships were seriously crippled, and were scarcely in a condition to renew the action.

The "Melpomene" lost twenty-nine men killed and thirty-three wounded; none of her officers were numbered in the former category, but both Captain Gaisford and his first lieutenant, Jacob Higham, were slightly wounded. The former gallant officer could not account for the singular manner in which he received his wound. It was during the heat of the action that a musket-ball struck the wrist of his right hand; luckily for him he had his sword in his grasp, for it was at a time when the enemy appeared bent upon boarding the English frigate, and the hilt of his weapon broke the force of the bullet, which

moreover, Captain Gaisford declared came from the
fore-part of his own ship. It was put down to the
clumsiness or trepidation of one of the crew, and no
more was thought of the incident. Of three seamen
whom I have more particularly described in the
earlier chapters of this work, all escaped with their
lives, but both John Mullins and Tim Johnson were
wounded—the former, slightly by the recoil of one
of the carronades which bruised and lacerated his
legs, and the latter more severely by a piece of
grape-shot which carried away three fingers of his
left hand ; however, they both recovered and returned
to their duties within three weeks, though Johnson
was shifted from his post of captain of the maintop,
for which the loss of his fingers disqualified him, to
that of quarter-master of the starboard watch.

On the 15th of September, Admiral Pococke
returned to Madras, where his fleet was placed under
repair, but such a *penchant* had the old sailor for
fighting, that he directed the captains of his fleet to
have "all ataunto" by the 26th, on which day he
expressed his determination to proceed to sea again
in search of the enemy. Sure enough, on the morn-
of the 26th, he gave the signal to weigh, and stood
towards Pondicherry. On our arrival off that city,
then the chief stronghold of the French in India, we

saw the whole of M. d'Apché's fleet in the roadstead,
lying at anchor in line of battle. The British admiral drew up his fleet, and the wind being off shore,
waited for his adversary to sally out to meet him.
At length, after a short period of doubt and uncertainty, the French commander-in-chief weighed,
and came forth, but not to battle. Instead of bearing down upon the English fleet, which had fallen
somewhat to leeward, he kept close to the wind, and
setting a press of sail stretched away to the southward. Admiral Pococke, finding him averse to
another engagement, and his own squadron being in
no condition to pursue with any chance of success,
took counsel with his captains and returned to
Madras.

The French fleet, having on board the famous
General Lally and some other military officers, made
the best of their way to the island of Mauritius, then
in their occupation, with the intention of refitting.
Thus, though superior in number and force, they left
the English undisputed masters of the Indian coast,
in which they were confirmed by the arrival in Madras Roads on the 18th of October, of a reinforcement
of four ships of the line, under Rear-Admiral
Cornish.

About the latter part of the year 1759, Colonel

(afterwards Sir Eyre) Coote arrived from England, and taking command of the British troops, captured Wandewash and other forts; defeated in the open field at Arcot, General Lally (who had returned from Mauritius) with the loss of 800 men and 22 pieces of cannon; captured the strong fort of Arcot early in February, 1760; and overran and conquered the entire province of that name in an incredibly short space of time.

Colonel Coote, after having defeated the French General Lally in the field, and reduced most of the enemy's settlements on the Coromandel Coast, at length cooped them up within the walls of Pondicherry, the principal seat of the French East India Company; this city, large, populous, and well-fortified, was held by a numerous garrison under the immediate command of Lally.

In the month of October, 1760, Admiral Stevens, who had succeeded Admiral Pococke in the command in these waters, sailed for Trincomalee in the island of Ceylon, the chief Royal naval station, in order to have his fleet refitted, and left a division of five sail of the line and the "Melpomene," under the command of Commodore Haldane, to blockade Pondicherry, and carry on the operations by sea, while Colonel Coote pressed the siege by land, which he did with all his wonted zeal and vigour. By this disposition, and the vigilance of the Commodore and the captains of the ships of his squadron, the place was so closely invested, as to be greatly distressed for want of provisions, even before the siege operations were fairly inaugurated. Heavy rains, unusually protracted this year, rendered all regular approaches impracticable. On their abatement Colonel Coote, on the 26th of November, directed the engineers to commence the formation of the batteries.

We will pass over the operations connected with the prosecution of the siege of Pondicherry, and speak of the imminent danger to which all on board the " Melpomene" were subjected about this time. On the 25th of December, Admiral Stevens, with four ships of the line, joined the blockading · squadron under Commodore Haldane, and assumed the chief command. He had a few days previously parted, in stormy weather, with Rear-Admiral Cornish and his division, though the latter rejoined the fleet at Pondicherry before the place was surrendered. But His Majesty's sailors and ships had other enemies to contend with more powerful than any number of Frenchmen ashore or afloat. On the 1st January, 1761, a violent gale broke forth, and as there is no breakwater or shelter for shipping in Madras Roads,

Admiral Stevens had to slip his cables, and with the rest of the fleet, proceed to sea, and battle against this ancient enemy where there was a "fair field and no favour," such as might be afforded to the sailors' natural enemy by the proximity of a "lee shore"— that most terrible of all allies to the cause of the "Storm Fiend." Each ship now had to fight it out alone and unaided, for so malignant was the assault of the aforesaid demon, that the entire fleet was scattered on the face of the waters, and having lost sight of each other, was driven by the fury of the tempest hither and thither—each ship striving to the utmost of her ability to weather the fury of the old yet ever new enemy.

The men of the "Melpomene" met the furious onset of the gale, with the calmness engendered by the knowledge that the gallant old frigate was prepared for eventualities at all points, like a knight clad in a suit of mail. The alarming rapidity with which the mercury fell in the barometric tube, gave ample warning of what was brewing, so that when Captain Gaisford slipped his cable, obedient to a signal from the flagship, he at once sent down his top-gallant masts, bent storm sails, close reefed his topsails, secured his guns with double lashings, had life-lines fitted on deck, "preventer braces aloft," hoisted his boats "chock up" to the davits and lashed them securely there, and in fact took every precaution that good seamanship and lengthened experience suggested as a wise provision against one of those terrible cyclones that periodically occasion not only lamentable loss of life and shipping at sea, but desolate coasts of the Indian peninsula in a manner and to an extent of which we Europeans can form no conception from experience. Notwithstanding all that could be done to mitigate the dire consequences of this visitation, for so these furious circular storms may be termed, the "Melpomene" did not come out of the encounter without signal marks of the severity of the struggle. Her starboard cutter was washed away during the night, so neatly and thoroughly, that when day dawn broke and displayed the havoc of the storm, not a chip was left on the davit heads, which stood out in the morning air like a couple of gallows. During the night the tiller ropes were also carried away, and one man received a blow on the head that fractured his skull, while a second was hurled overboard and was never seen again. For a minute or so the ship was in imminent danger of having her decks swept, and indeed of foundering with all hands on board; for, released from the restraint of the rudder, she fell off rapidly from before

the wind, and like a runaway horse that has got the
bit between his teeth, and starts off at mad speed to
dash his brains out against the first stone wall, the
frigate appeared as if now that she had " got her
head," she intended to work mischief to herself and
all concerned. But there were brave hearts among
the crew of the " Melpomene," as well as cool heads
among the officers, and before she could make away
with herself in this discreditable manner, and so not
only put an end to many valuable lives, but sink the
man-o'-war's bell in a thousand fathoms of water,
and so have prevented the recital of this veracious
autobiography,—I say, before she could do this, a
dozen hands, headed by William Morris, sprang up
the poop, and made a dash at the wheel, which was
flying round, and backward and forwards in a manner
terrible to behold. Quick as thought the quartermaster of the watch, Tim Johnson (for it was none
other than he) seized some spare rope, he had all
ready at hand to be used in the event of such or
similar accidents, and running it through the blocks
with the aid of a shipmate or two, quickly got the
wheel under control. Jamming the helm hard down,
the brave fellows brought the runaway up to the
wind again, and there she stood, dipping her bows
deep into the churning seas, and casting her crest up

again with a fierce jerk, as if, like the high mettled steed to which I have already likened her, she was champing with impotent rage the bit that had got the better of her, and tacitly owned the superior might of the "taut" hands that had gained the mastery, and had the helm well in hand.

After the cyclone a heavy gale of wind lasted for three days, and left its mark not only on the hull and rigging of the frigate, but also in the diminished crew that answered to their names at divisions on the following morning. While the forecastle-men of the port watch were flattening the sheets of the storm fore-topmast staysail, a gigantic sea came tumbling on board the fore part of the ship ; it met the frigate before she had had time to raise herself from the deep dive she made, after the previous wave had receded from under her bows. The flood burst upon her, and hurling three of the seamen who were " taking a pull " on the fore topmast staysail sheet backwards on to the spar-deck with a force that one would have thought must have broken their backs or heads, and deluging the decks with its vast volume of water, carried back into the sea over to leeward five fellows, whose gallant hearts, after a feeble and ineffectual struggle against the choking waves, soon ceased to beat for ever.

At length, after three days, Captain Gaisford was able to set sail, and make his way back to Pondicherry, when he learned a terrible tale of damage and disaster. The line-of-battle ships, "Duke of Acquitaine" and "Sunderland" had foundered in the tempest with every soul on board. The "Newcastle" and the "Queenborough," line-of-battle ships, and the "Protector," fireship, were driven ashore, and had gone to pieces, but the men were saved, together with the guns, stores, and provisions. Many, indeed all the other ships had sustained considerable damage. Notwithstanding these heavy obstacles to the proper discharge of their duties as a blockading fleet, none of the captains sought permission to retire to Trincomalee to refit, but repaired their ships as best they could, with the means at their disposal, and showing a bold front to the enemy, continued to blockade Pondicherry. So effective was the mode in which this investment was carried out by sea, that Lally was driven to the most desperate straits to procure supplies. To give an instance. One day Admiral Stevens intercepted a letter from the French General to Monsieur Raymond, the French Resident at Pullicat, the contents of which were couched in the following terms :—

"Monsieur Raymond,—The English squadron is no more, sir. Of the twelve ships they had in our road, seven are lost, crews and all; the other four dismasted; and no more than one frigate has escaped. Therefore, lose not an instant in sending chelingoes upon chelingoes laden with rice. The Dutch have nothing to fear now. Besides, according to the law of nations, they are only restricted from sending us provisions in their own bottoms, and we are no longer blockaded by sea.. The salvation of Pondicherry hath been once in your power already; if you neglect this opportunity, it will be entirely your own fault. Don't forget some small chelingoes also; offer great rewards; in four days I expect 17,000 Mahrattas. In short, risk all—attempt all—force all, and send us some rice, should it be but half a garse at a time."

On receipt of this note, so characteristic of the unfortunate Lally, Admiral Stevens immediately dispatched letters to the Dutch and Danish settlements on the coast, intimating that, notwithstanding the insinuations of the French general, he had eleven sail of the line, with two frigates, under his command, all fit for service, in Pondicherry roadstead, which was, moreover, closely invested by sea and land. He therefore declared that, as in that case it was contrary to the law of nations for any neutral power to relieve or succour the besieged, he was determined to seize any vessel that should attempt to throw provisions into the place.

The garrison and inhabitants of Pondicherry were, by the 15th of January, 1761, reduced to the utmost extremity of famine, and General Lally was driven to the necessity of sending to the British commander a colonel, attended by the chief of the Jesuits and two civilians, with proposals having for their object the surrender of the garrison as prisoners of war, and demanding a capitulation on behalf of the French East India Company, of which he was the chief. On this last head, Colonel Eyre Coote made no reply, but next morning took possession of the town and citadel, where he found a great supply of artillery, ammunition, small arms, and military stores. The garrison, amounting to two thousand Europeans, were also made prisoners of war. Thus was effected the capture of Pondicherry, and so virtually may be said to cease the existence of the French East India Company, whose power at one time exceeded that of its rival, the English Company, with which it had so long run a close race for Empire. Poor Lally, who had made such a gallant defence,

9

was treated with the utmost ignominy on his return to his native land, and was at length put to a cruel death by an enraged populace and weak government. Regarding the part taken by the fleet in the reduction of the chiefest of French strongholds in India, Smollett, in his "History of England," writes :—

"It may be doubted, however, whether Colonel Coote, with all his spirit, vigilance, and military talents, could have succeeded in this enterprise without the assistance of the squadron which co-operated with him by sea, and effectually excluded all succour from the besieged. It must be owned, for the honour of the service, that no incident interrupted the good understanding which was maintained between the land and sea officers, who vied with each other in contributing towards the success of the expedition."

Thus it was that both soldiers and sailors co-operated in the grand work of laying the foundations of that superb empire in the East India Company, which now forms the brightest jewel in the imperial diadem of Queen Victoria.

Though naturally British seamen played a subordinate part in the drama that ended in the dispersion of the French, and the reduction of the entire peninsula; though Admirals Watson and Pococke, and their brother sailors, were not in a position to undertake the roles so ably filled by Clive, Coote, Forde, and their associates, yet their great deeds, not only afloat in numberless engagements, but also ashore under Clive at Plassy, and also at Severndroog, attest the claims of the navy to no inconsiderable share of the glory of adding Hindostan, with its countless millions of inhabitants, as an appanage to that empire on which the sun never sets.

CHAPTER VI.

THE DUEL ON THE FORECASTLE.

AFTER serving on the East India station for a further period of a year, the "Melpomene" was ordered home, and sailed for England on the 5th of March, 1762. Nothing very remarkable occurred during the return voyage, until we got to the line, when an event took place, which, as it concerns Mr. James Duckworth (for he was no longer a boy, being now in his nineteenth year), I will not apologize for laying before my readers.

For some time previous to the occurrence of this incident, there had been a feud between the young officer of whom I have just spoken, and the senior mate in the gun-room. It arose, I believe, through a feeling of jealousy entertained by the latter against young Duckworth, owing to his being a favourite both with the captain and the ward-room officers. It was usually customary that the senior mate, as representative of the gun-room, should be asked to dinner by the captain on certain holidays, such as the King's birthday, and he always stood first on the list for invitations not only on board ship, but at any official entertainment or ball ashore. Henderson, the officer in question, was not a gentleman either by birth or breeding, and his appearance and bearing were altogether so vulgar and unprepossessing, that the Honourable Captain Gaisford, himself a well-bred man, recoiled from his society, and, naturally jealous of the good name of his ship as a school for gentlemen as well as seamen, made a practice of passing over the senior mate whenever he could do so with a decent pretext, or without any pretext at all, if one was not to be found. The captain did not on this account favour James Duckworth more than others of the mates and midshipmen, though he clearly preferred the society of the former, who acted as a sort of aide-de-camp, or flag-lieutenant, to that of the senior mate.

Mr. Henderson, a great burly fellow, having a sinister expression in his heavy deep-set eyes, which were shaded by a pair of overhanging eyebrows, hated Duckworth with all the force of his envious heart, but did not care openly to insult him, though greatly his superior in physical strength. But the most singular feature in the physiognomy of this gentleman was his nose. Now I take it as a well established fact, that the nasal organs of most folk are modelled on those of their parents, but in the case of Henderson, on surveying what is generally regarded as the most prominent feature in the human face divine, it was irresistibly borne home to me, that Dame Nature had been seized with a comic fit, and despairing of moulding an organ in consonance with the duplicate models set before her, had in an access of humour just incontinently dabbed [(that is the most appropriate expression as applied to the protuberance or excrescence in question) a lump of flesh "in the place where the nose ought to be."   "Not to put too fine a point upon it," it was a *lusus naturæ.* But whereas in Mr. Dickens' immortal novel of " Oliver Twist," a certain Mr. Chickweed was denominated by his familiars, " Conky," which Mr. Blathers, that shrewd Bow Street runner, was at the pains to explain, was a synonym for " Nosey ;" so Mr. Henderson, who was very unpopular with the foremast hands, went by the nickname of " Conky," though that pleasing *sobriquet* was applied in his case ironically, as his nose was of dimensions the smallest compatible with its fulfilling the requirements for which noses were made and provided.

Henderson, notwithstanding his cowardice, often

appeared inclined to pick a quarrel with Duckworth,
for his envy and malice at times seemed quite to
overpower him, though he always thought better of
it, and swallowed his spite. For a long time they
had not been on speaking terms; it was certainly
very aggravating for Henderson, and would have
been so even to a more amiable man, to watch the
calm indifference and aristocratic hauteur with which
the younger officer treated his more mature messmate. Henderson was the head of the mess, and
as such, in authority over his juniors, but Duckworth
scorned the fellow, and would have none of his bullying ways. There was a clique in the gun-room also,
who, although they hated Henderson, yet were
jealous of the favourable position in the estimation
of his officers attained by their young rival, and they
egged on the senior mate to do something either in
the way of insulting or thrashing, or keeping in his
place by any means the whilom Etonian, who
offended them mightily every hour of the day by
being handsomer, and braver, and smarter, and
altogether superior to themselves. The feeling
between the two officers grew so hostile that it was
evident it only required a spark to cause an explosion
among the combustible matter with which they were
charged. A very trivial circumstance caused the

explosion that all had foreseen, and which Duck-worth at least was anxious to have over without further delay.

One forenoon James Duckworth feeling drowsy —for he had been up half the night, owing to all hands having been turned out to shorten sail when a squall had struck the ship—turned in "all standing," or rather took a nap on the chests that were stowed in the gun-room. Now it was the peculiar privilege of the mates, and one or two senior midshipmen, to have their sea-chests in the gun-room, while there not being space in this apartment for all the huge trunks in which the juniors kept their worldly goods, these latter were ranged in the steerage, and here the owners washed and performed all their ablutions, as well as dressed. It was rather public, it must be owned, being under the eyes of the whole crew, whose messes were ranged on the same deck, but, bless you! who cared? certainly not the middies, who though perhaps when they first joined as "green-horns" just caught from school, might not have quite liked the publicity, now that they had been knocking about all the seas between Canada and the Coromandel coast, had long got used to it, and would have laughed heartily had you spoken of schoolboy modesty. There is nothing like habit in these things, and if you have been cruising about a couple of years in the tropics, and have become accustomed to seeing all hands piped " to bathe," when " Jack " and " Joey " the marine, multiplied three hundred-fold, jump overboard in the condition in which they came into the world, it certainly matters very little whether you wash in steerage or gun-room.

This forenoon, then, James Duckworth sought to avoid the noise and racket of the steerage, and the clatter of the cutlasses, for a division of the sailors were going through the sword drill on the upper deck, under the direction of the gunner, whose stentorian voice echoed through the ship as he bawled out, " Right [cheek," " Left cheek," " Right side," " Left side," " Wrist," " Parry ;" looking about then for a quiet nook, our hero laid down on a couple of chests in the gun-room—one being that of his chum, the second senior mate. The other, however, was the property of his bitter foe Henderson, and this temporary occupation of the lid of his chest aroused the ire of this individual, who, as luck would have it, came in soon after the tired midshipman had fallen into a heavy sleep, with the object of getting some article out of his box.

Henderson gazed for a minute in stupid astonishment, as if paralyzed at the audacity of the youngster, as he still persisted in calling Duckworth, when speaking of him to his messmates.

" Come," he called out, roughly; "just be good enough to move your carcase off my chest, or I'll——," and he left the sentence unfinished, as if he was undecided what he would do in the event of his orders not being complied with, which it was, indeed, very probable they would not be.

But Duckworth did not move. He was in too deep a slumber to hear the request, but had he done so, he would assuredly not have acted up to its requirements, when couched in such offensive terms, or with so menacing a manner. Henderson thought that the latter was the reason that the sleeper did not rise at his bidding, so merely ejaculating, " D'ye hear, youngster, d—— you ? " prepared to oust him from his position. At this moment a number of the seamen, with half a dozen of the members of the gun-room mess, came down below, having been released from cutlass drill, which had concluded for that day. Henderson was beside himself with rage at the idea of his junior refusing to move off his chest, and so openly insulted him before the whole mess, a thing he had before never attempted to do. Receiving no reply, and completely carried away by passion, he without further parley, roughly

raised the lid of his sea-chest, thus jamming Duckworth's legs against the bulk head that divided the
gun-room from the narrow slip that did duty as
pantry for the mess.   Thus rudely awakened from
his slumber, the young officer, raising himself, gazed
round the assembled circle of his messmates with an
expression in which unfeigned astonishment was
blended with rising indignation.   He made an
evident effort to calm himself, however, and extricated his legs from the unpleasant position in which
they still remained, owing to Henderson's keeping
the lid of his box raised with one hand, while with
the other he proceeded to ransack one of the tills
with which midshipmen's chests are always well
garnished, for the article of which he was in quest.
Springing to his feet, Duckworth calmly asked the
senior mate if he had dared to do this out of rude-
ness intentionally; though the voice in which this
question was put was not elevated beyond its ordinary pitch, there was a tremulousness in its tones
which he could not disguise.   Without lifting his
head, which was bent over the contents of his box,
Henderson, quietly putting a pipe which he had
charged with tobacco into his coat pocket, sneeringly
replied in the affirmative, adding; "What then ? "

He had barely time to conclude his sentence,

when the individual he addressed struck him straight from the shoulder, and with a speed that rivalled the lightning—a blow that took effect on the side of the face and head of the insulter, and sent him headlong into his chest, the lid of which fell on him as he lost his balance. There was an exclamation of astonishment from all the lookers-on, at the celerity and terrific force of the blow, and they fell back with the expectation of a mill. These two young men, now placed in such direct antagonism to each other, had notwithstanding the disparity in their ages, led the two cliques into which the mess was divided, for though no one liked Henderson, many rallied to his side, both because as senior he had some authority vested in him, and was feared as a ruthless bully, and on account of the jealousy with which some among them regarded his antagonist.

Henderson quickly extricated himself from his undignified position, and rushed at his opponent with the fury of a mad bull. The latter was prepared to receive him, which he did in the most artistic style by a duplicate of No. 1, on the jaw, that must have unsettled some of his " teeth." But nothing could overbear the brute strength of Henderson, and there being no space for a stand-up fight in the mess-

" He clutched him by the throat with both hands."

room, which was small and crowded with tables and boxes, Duckworth was unable to avoid his onset, as he might have done in a properly constituted ring. As it was, he was knocked over, and the pair rolled on the floor together, struggling and striking as if in mortal strife. And, truth to say, it was in mortal strife as far as one of the combatants was concerned. Henderson was so transported with fury, that when he got the upper hand, he clutched his less muscular antagonist by the throat with both hands, and sought to strangle him. At first Duckworth hit him repeatedly with his fist on the head and face to make him relax his hold, but the other disregarded the punishment he thus received, and clung to the throat of the midshipman with the tenacity of a bulldog, which not all the blows and threats of bystanders will induce to loosen its hold. The combatants rolled under the table, the senior mate uppermost now, for James Duckworth was growing faint with exhaustion, and the fell pertinacity of his enemy was doing its work. Duckworth, indeed, was fast being strangled under the very noses, if not the eyes (for they could not see him) of his friends and messmates, and not a hand was raised to save him, for the desire of fair play so characteristic of Englishmen restrained them from interfering, and, moreover, like all uneducated men (and in those days naval officers who went to sea at the age of ten might with truth be classed in this category), they were naturally cruel. The generation who could look on at all the barbarities incidental to bull-baiting, cock-fighting, and such like exciting sports, loved not less a mill—truth compels us to add, no matter who were engaged in it, for these worthy people, our ancestors, in the good old times were not chary of their own blood if they thought little of spilling, or seeing spilt, that of their friends.

But we must return to James Duckworth, whom we have left choking under the gun-room mess table. It is certain that he would have died under the iron grip of Henderson, who was at least twelve years his senior, but that one of his friends not quite comprehending the reason for the quiet under the table, that had now succeeded the previous furious struggling, and, moreover, being attracted by a convulsive twitching of the legs of his friend, which were the only members of his body that remained in view, had the curiosity to look under the table, when to his horror he found his chum lying quite still and black in the face with the agonies of suffocation, while the wretch above him was kneeling with both knees firmly planted on the chest of his antagonist, whose face, moreover, he was critically watching while it changed its hues from blue to the deepest shades of black. The chivalrous young Duckworth was almost gone; he had scorned to cry out for help while he could do so, and when he had become exhausted with his struggle to extricate himself, Henderson had continued his grip with one hand, which was enough to complete the strangling, while with the other, he covered the mouth of his helpless enemy, so that he could not make himself heard.

But it was not yet too late. In a moment the friend in need had sprung upon the would-be murderer, and by a supreme effort dragged the wretch backwards, so that he was forced to relax his hold, while he called out to his messmates that murder was being wrought. It was some time before Duckworth completely regained consciousness, but towards the afternoon he was himself again, though pale and weak. He refused to allow the surgeon to be called in to see him, and merely pleading temporary indisposition, obtained leave for a messmate to perform his ordinary duties on watch. But he had not done with the coward, Henderson, and sent word to him through the friend who had so opportunely rescued him from a fearful death, that he, Duckworth, gave him the alternative of meeting him that night in the middle watch, on the forecastle, and fighting the quarrel out with swords—the crack of the pistol rendered it an undesirable weapon to go out with—or of having the whole circumstance reported to the captain immediately; the challenger gave the other half an hour to make his decision, but there was no necessity for the concession of this indulgence, as the officer who acted as Henderson's friend, returned with the reply (a gratifying one to our hero) that he would be on the forecastle at any hour, and with any weapon he liked, and only stipulated that they did not hold their hands until one or the other lay dead, or mortally wounded.

The preliminaries were soon settled by willing seconds and kind messmates, anxious to show their friendship by this touching exhibition of unselfish devotion, and true British love for sport. The officers, it was agreed, were to fight with their regulation swords, and as Duckworth, being a midshipman, was only entitled to wear a dirk, his friend and chum, Stanley, lent him his sword; not a word was said about the projected encounter, but every one, including the principals, equally with their messmates, was in a fever of doubt and fear, lest some one among them, seized with a humane fit, or dreading the extreme probability of a fatal issue to the approaching duel, might "blow the gaff," as Henderson expressed it, in idiomatic but not choice English. However, he was mistaken; the members of the gunroom mess proved staunch "to a man" or "boy," and were far too anxious for the occurrence of an event that would pleasantly vary the monotony of this long sea voyage, to spoil sport.

The night at length closed in,—it seemed to all the mess that it would never succeed the long and dreary day,—and the first watch passed away. Few eyes were closed that night in the gun-room, though it was agreed that only the seconds were to accompany the combatants to the scene of action, in order to avoid the chance of discovery. There was a fresh breeze that night, which blowing right aft, would carry the sound of the strife away, and the foresail was out, which tended still further to deaden the noise inseparable from the use of steel weapons. Every soul in the ship, with the exception of the officers on duty (fortunately Henderson as senior mate had charge of the middle watch), the quartermaster, the helmsman, and the look-out man, was wrapped in a profound slumber. The previous night had been a fatiguing one, owing to squally weather, and all hands had turned out to shorten sail, and to secure the guns; hence, every one slept

10

particularly heavy, and the watch on deck either
wrapped themselves in their blankets, and lay down
on deck, or contrary to rule, sneaked down below,
and turned into their hammocks, " all standing," and
ready for a call.

It was half-past one a.m., when Henderson,
giving over charge of the deck temporarily to one of
the midshipmen, " until he had settled the hash of
this bumptious cabin-boy," as he said to his junior,
walked quickly forward, and springing up the ladder
that led to the topgallant forecastle, found that he
had been anticipated, and the " bumptious cabin-
boy " was already waiting for him, as calm and collected to all outward appearance, as if he had been
going to dine with the captain. Strikingly different
was the demeanour of the two duellists. Of Duckworth's bearing we have already spoken. Henderson's, on the contrary, was characteristic of the
man, bullying and offensive to a degree that was
aggravating to a sensitive nature like that of the
youth he was going to fight. He swaggered about
the confined space, and dropped ejaculations and
inuendoes expressive of his contempt for his adversary, while the seconds made the necessary preparations and agreed to certain preliminaries in a low
tone of voice. Duckworth took no notice of him,

but stripping himself to the shirt, turned back his cuffs, and testing for the last time the temper and strength of his sword for the trial it was about to undergo, quickly informed his second he was ready, and placed himself in position. His opponent also said he was prepared, garnishing the statement with an oath, and then the two messmates, without even the interchange of the customary shake of the hand, or salute of the sword, to show they bore no malice to each other, were at once and eagerly engaged in the stern ordeal of battle.

They commenced the conflict with widely different feelings and intentions as to the course proposed to adopt, though they both entertained confidence in their ability to bring it to a successful conclusion. It was Duckworth's purpose to " wing," or otherwise wound his adversary, but not to kill him; whereas the latter proposed to himself not to stay his hand until he had slain outright, or, better still, mortally wounded the young man who had been his messmate and rival for four years. Henderson was wild with passion and malignant hate, and, while in this devilish fit, cared nothing for the consequences to himself, though he knew, had he thought a moment, that they must be of the most serious character. Though a bully, and at heart a coward, as all bullies are, he entered without any misgivings into the duel, as he was assured, after the events of the morning, of his greatly superior strength, and also counted on his adversary not only being demoralized by the recent exhibition of this strength, but on his not having recovered from the weakness incidental to the desperate assault he had committed on him. He was aware of the finished swordsmanship for which Duckworth was remarkable in the ship, but he intended to force the fighting, and, by dint of sheer strength, to bear down all opposition; no uncommon thing, I may observe, in passing, to befall the most accomplished fencers if once *they lose their nerve.*

On the other hand, Duckworth relied on the superb skill he had attained. Unerring of eye, quick of hand, and bold of heart, there was no want of nerve in his breast; rather, as he dwelt on the insult and well-nigh murder to which he had been subjected, the only difficulty he experienced was to prevent his running into the other extreme, and losing himself in an access of indignation. But he calmed down when he reflected how much was at stake, and watching the line of action his formidable opponent intended to adopt, proposed to bide his time.

After a few passes and cuts, which the junior

officer easily parried, Henderson struck furiously and fast, and so occupied Duckworth with the fury of the assault, that he was forced to give ground. Having fallen back a few paces, the latter turned his head for a moment, and found that he was on the brink of the forecastle, and that another step would launch him on to the deck below. Quickly altering his tactics, he watched his opportunity, and, with a clever parry and a turn of the wrist, whirled the sword of his adversary out of his hand, and sent it flying over his shoulder into the sea. Henderson became livid with rage on discovering the deft manner in which his weapon had been whipt out of his clutch; he stamped his feet, and swore horribly that he would be avenged yet, calling at the same time for another sword. Duckworth, who, like a brave fellow, scorned to take advantage of the defenceless condition of his adversary, stood calmly waiting to renew the contest, and dropped the point of his weapon so as to recruit his strength. The seconds came forward, and sought to obtain an admission from Henderson that he was satisfied; but he replied, with a shower of oaths, that he did not come there to play at single-stick like a fencing-master, but to fight, and to fight it out, too, to the bitter end. Another sword was at hand, and was quickly supplied, and the exciting game went on— Duckworth, on his part not uttering a word nor changing a muscle; that his hand was well in, his friends saw with satisfaction.

The combat was renewed. The senior mate adopted his old tactics, though with more wariness; he used his weapon freely, cutting and slashing, but, though always considered proficient in the use of the cutlass, he had never practised with the small sword, and knew not the mysteries of carte and tierce. Duckworth, on the other hand, was, as I have said, a finished swordsman, and excelled in the use of the rapier, which he had learnt from his former friend, Mullins, whom he now surpassed in the noble art. At length, the midshipman, taking advantage of an unguarded moment, made a lunge at his adversary, which took effect on his right shoulder, and drew blood freely. Maddened with pain, and still more with the disgrace of this second contretemps, Henderson made fiercely at his foe, and pressed him back. The impetuosity of the onset was so great that the latter gave way, and it employed every energy, and "took all he knew," to parry and elude the shower of blows which almost broke down his guard. Calm and collected, he stepped back, when suddenly, in avoiding a trenchant blow, he came in contact with the structure from which the narrator of this autobiography was suspended, and was so taken up with defending himself, that he was unable to recover his equilibrium. He stumbled, and fell with one knee against me; to save himself from falling headlong on to the deck, he caught at at the woodwork from which I was slung. His cowardly opponent, heedless of the fact that he was disarmed, and forgetful of the quarter he himself only a few minutes before had extended to him, raised his weapon to cleave the head of the youth, who, wholly unsuspicious of such a cowardly advantage being taken of him, was leisurely raising himself up, and stretching forth his hand to pick up his sword. I could see a smile on the honest, handsome face of the boy I had known so many years, whom I had learnt to admire, and in whose career I had so long taken a hearty interest. I could see all this, and I could see (but he could not) his burly and merciless foe lift his sword for the foul blow, that in another moment would have laid that young head low, and deluge in a torrent of blood the fair curling locks. All this I could see, and I sickened at the sight of the imminence of the stroke I was helpless to avert.

CHAPTER VII.

AT this terrible and, to me, agonizing crisis, a figure, which for the last few minutes had, unregarded by principals and seconds, watched the course of the combat, sprang forward, and knocked up Henderson's arm with a tremendous blow that almost paralyzed that member, and, indeed, would have well-nigh shattered it had it appertained to a less robust personage than that burly warrior.

"Who the foul fiend are you?" ejaculated Henderson, turning upon this new comer with a fierce wrath; "and how dare you interfere, you infernal scoundrel?" he added, seeing it was only a seaman, being, indeed, none other than William Morris, or Cavendish. "Go below, and I'll not forget you."

"I was bound to interfere," the latter replied, "when I saw you about to take a cowardly advantage of Mr. Duckworth."

"Cowardly, do you dare to say, you blackguard?"

broke in Henderson, white with passion. " I'll remember you for this."

Morris took no notice of this ebullition, but,
turning to the seconds, said, with the air and manner
of a polished man of the world, " Excuse me, gentlemen, I regret extremely that I interfered with you
in the execution of your duties as seconds, but
I saw that murder, and not justifiable homicide,
would have been the inevitable result. I have been
myself——" But he stopped, and added, " I like,
as does every Englishman, to see fair play."

The seconds, colouring with vexation, stepped
forward and thanked him; Duckworth's friend
adding that he did not anticipate that Henderson
would have taken such an unmanly advantage of his
friend, and was not therefore prompt enough in
warding off what he now saw would have been a
foul blow.

The two principals once more stood facing each
other. Henderson had regained his weapon, and
looked more malignant than ever at thus having
been twice baffled in taking the life of his enemy;
while the latter, on whose mind began to dawn a
faint perception of the narrow escape he had just
had, looked from one to the other for an explanation
of this interruption. His second, Stanley, a good

and brave officer, and very much attached to Duckworth, but who was as unprepared for such treachery
as his principal, did not care to enlighten him, as it
would reflect upon the careless way in which he had
discharged his duties, though he inwardly promised
to take care that there should not be a repetition of
the act.   No such compunction worked in the mind
of Morris, who stepped up to the young officer
whose life he had saved, and whispered in his ear,
" For God's sake, take care, sir; that murdering
ruffian wants your heart's blood, and will have
nothing less."

James Duckworth started, looked hard at the
sailor, and replied slowly, as if weighing every
word,, " Will he ?   Then, by the living God, I
will have his !"

Again the duel was renewed; and this time it
was patent to all lookers-on that the end was not
far off.   Henderson was beside himself in his fury,
and even Duckworth, hitherto so calm, was roused;
his blood was up, and it portended a " short shrift "
for one of them, when the latter met his antagonist's
furious onslaught, not with his ordinary passiveness,
but with an·eagerness which showed that he was
only waiting his first opportunity to end that scene
of treachery and blood; and it soon came.   More

impetuous than ever, Henderson gave repeated chances, until a blow he aimed at his adversary having been evaded rather than parried—for the young midshipman 'merely sprung on one side—his whole body was left defenceless. His sword, missing its object, had struck the narrator with the full force of a blow that would have cleft the skull of any living man, even had he the pate of a negro, causing an indent, and making my metal emit a sharp sound. It was his own funeral knell that he thus unconsciously rang with his weapon. Before he could recover himself, young James Duckworth moved lightly, but swiftly, up again towards him, and drawing his sword arm back until his hand touched his shoulder, delivered the point, and drove the weapon with resistless force through the body of his opponent. The latter stood still for a moment; a shudder swept through his frame as the cold steel was drawn reeking from his body, and with a single groan he fell dead at the feet of his victorious, adversary. The thick, dark gore rushed in a hot flood from the breast of the dead man, who had been run through the heart—the sword's point having been only checked from passing out at the back by the shoulder-blade, against which the extreme point of the weapon had broken off,

with such force had the fatal thrust been delivered.

It was all over now. To the fury and fell passions that animated the combatants, and the fever
of anxiety that filled the breasts of the lookers-on,
succeeded the awe inspired by the presence of death,
and the chilling thought of what was in store on the
morrow for them all, principal and seconds, for the
latter would be regarded as abettors, and called to
account for thus breaking through the bonds of discipline, and turning the deck of His Majesty's ship
into an arena for the adjustment of a private quarrel.
They were now joined by some of their messmates;
one or two bent over the dead officer—out of whose
body the blood still poured, gathering into a pool at
the break of the forecastle, and thence trickling,
drop by drop, on to the deck beneath, with a chill,
heavy splash, that sounded loud and measured in
the stillness that reigned around—and heedless of
the futility of what they were doing, sought to
staunch the flow of the life stream, as if they could
thereby bring the soul back into the tenement out
of which it had been reft with violence scarce one
minute before. These officers had been accustomed
to death in all its most horrid forms, and though in
its consequences this business might cost them their

commissions, and close the naval career for ever to them, yet they were not the sort of men to waste time in vain lamentations, but rousing up the first lieutenant and surgeon, informed the one of all that had taken place, and brought the latter to the body of the late senior mate.

Duckworth retained his composure throughout the subsequent trying scene. He went aft, yielded up his sword to Lieutenant Higham, and was placed under arrest. The captain was informed in the morning of what had occurred, and sending for the unfortunate young officer on to the quarter deck, upbraided him for the gross breach of discipline in fighting a duel on board his ship, accused him of ingratitude, and ended by the announcement that he would be tried for his life on the arrival of the ship at Plymouth.

James Duckworth said not a word until charged with ingratitude, when his face flushed up, and he was about to speak, but was stopped by Captain Gaisford, who thundered out, " Silence, sir; go below, under close arrest."

The first lieutenant lost no time in learning all the particulars of the quarrel, and when the captain had calmed down a little towards the evening, sought him out, and laid before him the gross provocation his favourite had received, and the cowardly conduct of his aggressor, whom he maintained had been properly served. Captain Gaisford was somewhat mollified on hearing all that his executive officer had said to him; but he replied that he cared nothing for the fate of Henderson, who was a brute and a bad officer, and he would not forgive the breach of discipline; but he said the martial law that governed the Navy must take its course, and he could not depart from his word.

Now-a-days, the articles of war are very severe, and award death as a punishment for what are considered very trivial offences; but in the times of which we write, it may be said with truth that the code was written in characters of blood. Death, therefore, would certainly be the sentence that would be meted out to Duckworth by any court-martial that sat to hear the charges preferred against him; and, notwithstanding every plea put forward in his defence by Lieut. Jacob Higham, the captain remained inflexible, and persisted that justice must be carried out. So matters stood.

Sailors are notorious for their love of story-telling or "spinning yarns;" and in those days of wars, I have heard many most thrilling accounts of

adventures in the battle and the breeze; of cutting-
out affairs, and other desperate deeds in which the
narrators—no boasters, as the scars they bore testi-
fied—had taken prominent parts; of lengthened
confinement in French prisons, with hard fare and
harder treatment; of adventures in uninhabited
islands on which they had been shipwrecked; and
of numberless hair-breadth escapes in " battle, fire,
and wreck."   It was during the pleasant evenings,
while running for "the line" with the "south-east
trades," that a knot of old salts and youngsters
would assemble in a favourite spot close to me;.
here sitting on the break of the forecastle, with
their legs dangling over the deck or seated on the
rail, but always with pipes in their mouths, the
" watch below would listen by the hour to some
yarn, " tough " as the " old horse " they had for
dinner that day, while the younger hands of the
watch on duty, when not engaged, would swallow
with equal eagerness the stories of " antres vast and
deserts idle."   This the latter were enabled to
do almost without interruption during those jolly
tropical evenings, for the south-east trade, when once
you get fairly into it, will carry you nearly from the
latitude of the Cape to within a few degrees of the
line, without you having to " touch a rope-yarn."

After all the stormy weather we had experienced, and the hard actions we had been engaged in, it was a great relief even to the most fire-eating tar on board, to have for a brief space neither Frenchmen to fight nor "stormy winds to blow" and harass them night as well as day in trimming sails, reefing topsails, sending masts and yards down, and securing the guns. Among stories that impressed themselves on my memory, was one told by the master-at-arms.*

The sea is full of mysteries and unrevealed secrets; but no man can have followed a sailor's life for many years without encountering incidents that appeared inexplicable. Often have we passed, and perhaps picked up, floating on the wide expanse of sea, articles, valueless in themselves, but once cherished by warm hearts. These waifs of the sea were, doubtless, relics of human passions, and links in a chain of human interest now snapped for ever, and have never been traced; though, perhaps,

---

* The title of this petty officer is a relic of the old days when there was no regular navy, but merchant ships were hired, fitted with guns, and manned by the king's soldiers, the ship being worked by her own crew, under their master. It was only in Henry the Eighth's reign that the first regular man-o'-war was built and retained in the service of the country for fighting purposes only.

some heart mourned long and faithfully the owner who never more returned.

The master-at-arms' tale partakes of this character of mystery, and has the merit of truth still further to recommend it :—

"We had been knocking about the Indian seas for some weeks seeking to make Trincomalee, for soon after leaving Madras Roads, a heavy westerly gale drove us far out of our course, and for days we were unable to take observations, owing to the sun being obscured. I was then serving on board a brig-of-war, an old tub that had long seen her day, and ought by rights to have been in the ship-breaker's yard, instead of knocking about the high seas. However, we managed to weather the gale, and tried to patch the brig up and refit aloft, for the state of the barometer showed only too plainly that we had in all likelihood not seen the last of the bad weather. That evening we sighted something that looked like the hull of a vessel floating about. On nearing her we found that all her masts and the bowsprit had gone by the board. We hailed her, but got no answer; but to make sure that none of her crew were still on board, the captain lowered a boat, and as I was one of the crew—holding the rating of ordinary seaman in the books of the 'Thalia'—I proceeded in the boat. The lieutenant commanding the cutter hailed the derelict as we approached her, but received no answer. In another minute we were alongside, and swinging ourselves on board the best way we could, with the aid of a rope's end or two hanging over the ship's side, half a dozen of us were soon standing on the decks of the silent ship. The cause of this quiet soon became apparent. A more dismal scene than that presented on board that vessel I have never seen during my forty-four years' service afloat. Splintered spars entangled in canvas and rigging were scattered around in confusion; the decks were lumbered up with the debris of gear, while the planks and fittings of a boat—probably the launch, which had been stowed amidships—were lying about. The wind and the waves had worked sad havoc; but more terrible than the destruction of a once noble ship were the scenes which further investigation brought to light. Below a heap of rigging, and broken by the weight of a spar which lay across it, were the bones of a human being. It was an entire skeleton, the skull and ribs of which had been crushed almost on a level with the deck.

" Further search revealed a more hideous spectacle: five other skeletons were discovered; and on four of these there yet remained a slight covering of crisp flesh, showing that they had died more recently than the other two. Many pots and cooking vessels were found on board, but not one of them contained the least particle of food. This circumstance seemed to denote that these wretched men had all died by the most agonizing and lingering of human deaths, and proportionately excited our pity.

"The vessel, which bore no name over the taffrail, as merchant ships do, had been brig-rigged, but all her spars were gone. The foremast had been cut away to save her from foundering—a step only taken as a last resort ; the mainmast had gone by the board, and the bowsprit close by the ' gammoning.' Altogether the ship was as complete a wreck as ever floated on the waters, and so she was pronounced by the most experienced among us.

"We now continued our researches. A most overpowering stench assailed us as we prepared to enter the forecastle, which was filled with water ; it was only with some difficulty that two of us, I being one, consented to enter, and remain long enough inside to report on its contents. There were two corpses on the floor, and one stretched across a ' bunk,' partially covered with bed clothes—all three bodies being in the most digusting stage of decom-

position.   Proceeding aft, we found the wheel-house
had been carried away, no doubt by a tremendous
sea which had swept the decks; and looking over the
taffrail, the rudder was seen to be no longer in its
place.   The brig was flush, having no poop, but we
proceeded down the companion leading into the
cabin, for the purpose of continuing our investiga-
tions below.   At the bottom of the companion was
a pool of fetid water, through which we had to wade
in order to search every portion of the interior.   On
passing into the cabin, a foul odour was discovered,
but not so bad as assailed us while investigating the
secrets of the forecastle, and we were all able to
enter.   The following was the scene that met our
gaze :—

   " Between a stationary table and a couch, the
head of a corpse protruded from a sleeping-berth in
the bulkhead, in a state of decay, and presenting the
most ghastly spectacle.   A buttoned jacket of good
material, blue serge pantaloons, a flannel shirt,
marked J. F., and one boot, formed the clothing of
the corpse, which lay outside the bed.   The chrono-
meter in the cabin pointed to half-past four o'clock,
and on the table was an open Bible turned down-
ward, a pair of loaded pistols in a case, as if placed
ready for use, and a small bottle.   On taking it up,

we found that it contained a piece of paper, on which was scrawled in scarcly legible characters, ' Lord, guide us to some helper!   Merciful God! why let us perish ?'   The words, irrespective of their meaning, expressed in the most pathetic manner the extremity of human suffering and earnest supplication; they were written in a detached form, and a hiatus occurred between every two or three words, evidently showing that the ill-fated writer must have been either in the lowest stage of debility, or driven to madness by hunger.   Proceeding into the cabin beyond, evidently that of the captain, we came upon his corpse.   There it lay on the floor, mouldering and doubled up as if he had fallen from weakness, and died where he fell.   This completed the ghastly remains of the gallant men once forming the crew of the nameless derelict now floating unheeded on the troubled waters of that distant eastern sea.

" On making search we soon found some articles, by which we hoped to trace the identity of the brig and her late crew.   On the captain's bed were scattered books and papers, but one sheet attracted particular notice.   It was dated—' At sea, 14th January, 1731,' and ran as follows : ' Dear Emma—I will post this letter on arriving at Madras, to assure you of my well-being, and that though so many years have elapsed since we parted in Old England, that my affection for you remains undimmed, indeed, is perhaps increased by time and absence. I have got on famously, and have at length reached the summit of my ambition. I am my own master, and the master, too, of a fine brig, which though old and rather cranky for these seas, will, I daresay, last my time and enable me to make enough money in three voyages to return to England, when I hope we shall never part again. Your father will not turn me away from his door when I show him a bag of £2000, which I hope to clear before I return home. I have kept all my promises to you in spite of a thousand temptations, and many bad, drinking shipmates. Your picture and letters I keep always beside me; scarcely a day passes but I look at them and read a letter. Direct to Mr. Haver's at Madras, as before, when you can find opportunity to write a few lines. Good-bye, and God bless you. Yours for ever and ever.—JAMES H. HOLLAND.'

"There was no address on the letter; the ship's regular papers were not found, but there was a writing-desk, which, as it was locked, the lieutenant in charge of the boat took with him unopened on board the brig. There was a slate on the table in the cabin, which was, no doubt, used for taking down the log in rough, but we could decipher only blurred figures, the writing being totally illegible. The table was covered by guards, such as are used in rough weather to prevent the dishes and plates from being carried away, and which are known at sea as 'fiddles.' In the captain's trunk, which was un-locked, were found numerous letters, but they and everything portable that was of any value or interest, were removed into the boat for the purpose of being taken on board the brig. Having hailed the latter, which lay-to close by, the lieutenant received permission to perform the last sad offices for the remains of our unfortunate countrymen.

" The boat was sent on board the ' Thalia,' and returned with the sail-maker and his tools, a prayer-book, and some other necessaries ; and as night was closing in, and the weather looked threatening, we quickly made the necessary preparations for a 'funeral at sea.' A quantity of old canvas lying about the decks was cut up and sewn into bags, which formed coffins for the dead. A long board was laid upon a sound portion of the bulwarks, and round shot were attached to the bags ; the service for the Burial of the Dead at Sea was now reverently performed by the uncertain light of two lanthorns, held one on each side of the officer by a sailor—for it was now dark ; and as the plank was tilted upward, one by one the skeletons in their shotted bags fell with a dull splash into the sea. The ceremony concluded, we all, almost without exchanging a word, for the sad duty had struck a chill to the hearts of the most careless of us, returned to the cutter, and pulled back to the 'Thalia.'

"Although the conduct of all engaged in the performance of these last melancholy offices to our fellow-seamen was marked with an unusual degree of solemnity, little did any of my messmates think that no friendly hand would ever consign them to the grave, and no voice repeat over their remains the consolitory words from Holy Writ, selected by the Church for this most solemn of all the ceremonies in which we can take part.

"But the tragic fate that was to overtake the crew of the 'Thalia' was even now pursuing them, and before another night fell, the sea had engulfed another holocaust of Britain's best and bravest seamen.

"Hardly had we placed our feet on the deck of the brig, and the boats were hoisted up, than the storm which had been brewing, was upon us. Warned by the distant mutterings of the thunder and the vivid flashes on the horizon, which portended what is called in those seas a 'Sumatra,' from their usually coming off the island of that name, our captain shortened sail, and made all preparations for the tempest. Everything was secured below and aloft, and all hands would have been quite at their ease had we had a sound plank under our feet. Sailors care not how hard it blows, if they have plenty of sea-room and a tight ship; but a lee-shore appals the bravest heart, and a leak is the most terrible spectre that can haunt the breast of poor Jack. Unhappily, we all knew that we had grave cause for anxiety as regarded the condition of the 'Thalia' on the latter point; but our worst fears were soon more than realized, and we found that the brig had sustained so much damage in the recent bad weather, that she was little better than a sieve.

" Before midnight the wind was blowing a strong gale, and the sea had risen with surprising rapidity. Early in the gale a sea broke on board abaft, and carried away the mainsail, which we had set reefed; soon another sea tumbled on board at the waist, and shattered the pinnace, which was secured on the chocks, carrying away with it, as it receded to leeward, three hands, who were busy over some job amidships.

" The brig began to strain heavily, and made

water fast; strong gangs were put on to the pumps, but all their efforts were fruitless, and the water gained on us—slowly at first, but quicker the longer the ship remained exposed to the fury of the storm. A little after midnight, a strong squall split the foresail. We unbent it, and bent another, but it also was carried away while we were setting it. The brig now lay-to under a foretopmast-staysail and close-reefed foretopsail, but the wind at times blew with such intensity and suddenness, that momentarily we thought every rag would be blown away. To lighten the vessel and enable her to ride more buoyantly, the guns were, one after another, thrown overboard, until only two six-pounders (boat-guns) were left. This sensibly relieved the brig, and she appeared more easy; but unless the storm decreased, we began to see there was little hope of her weathering it, for the leak gained on us with alarming rapidity. All efforts to reduce the water were fruitless, and the captain determined to have recourse to baling as well. Accordingly, the tarpaulins and gratings were removed, a barrel was rigged, and a party told off to bale the ship; but a terrible mishap soon put a stop to this. A huge 'green sea' was seen to rear itself on our quarter; a cry of warning was raised by the officer on duty, and all hands on deck rushed for protection and shelter where they could, clinging to the bulwarks, to ropes, to anything that afforded a hold; but vain was any help against such an enemy. The vast volume of water burst on board with a mighty roar, and the decks were in a moment deluged with the flood. Smiting down the puny form of every man on the deck, it swept off every living soul, and poured down the open hatch in a cataract. The brig-of-war shook and groaned in every timber, and fell over almost on her beam ends, and would certainly have gone down there and then, had not the foremast snapped off short by the deck, and gone over the side, thus relieving her in a measure from the pressure of the wind.

"I was down on the lower deck at the time, it being my watch below, but, in common with everybody, rushed up the fore-hatch, as I thought the ship was going down. Merciful Heaven! what a scene met my gaze. The ship was a wreck, like the ill-fated vessel we had boarded the previous day, while the sea ran literally mountains high. I can use no other expression to describe the enormous masses of water heaving around, and under us, as if impelled by the forces of a submarine earthquake. A dreadful sight caught my eye to leeward: the receding wave was carrying off on its angry crest half the ship's company, and in the last hurried glimpse I caught sight of many a well-known face which had beamed with light-hearted jollity on Saturday evenings—when some of us would have our song and rattling chorus, and others call upon the ship's fiddler to strike up 'Jack's the lad,' or some other tune, while we footed it smartly on the deck. The captain was also gone, and half the officers; while alone on the deck stood the helmsman—two seamen who were assisting him and the quartermaster having disappeared. Still the bonds of discipline were not relaxed.

" The first lieutenant gave the necessary orders, and when the ship slowly righted herself, we secured the hatches, and battened them down. Nothing could be done in the way of baling, and though a party stuck manfully to the pumps, we could not be blind to the fact that our peril from foundering was most imminent, and that, unless the tempest speedily abated, all hope of the brig weathering the gale must be abandoned. She had fallen off the wind, but we managed to lay her to again, though her water-logged condition and the loss of the foremast rendered her unmanageable.

" Drenched through, and almost without hope,

we continued to work the pumps, though, with five feet of water on board and the desperate condition of affairs, it was like combating against the inevitable. The sea raged around us with unabated fury, and swept away the bowsprit; and soon afterwards the ship giving a fearful lurch, the mainmast went by the board, killing one or two poor fellows. The brig tossed and surged on her spars with great violence, and it seemed as if they would knock holes in her sides. At length, with some difficulty, we were able to cut the rigging, and disengage the wreck, which floated clear. The brig now lay helpless on the water, dismasted, and with the rudderhead disabled. We wedged the rudder, and repaired damages as well as possible; and the brig was kept with her head to wind by some tarpaulins spread abaft. So the night passed away; but when the morning broke, so far from the light bringing us any hope, it only plunged us into a deeper abyss of despair.

"By the grey streaks of dawn we could discern, within a mile or so of the ship, the shore of a low-lying island on which could be seen some palm-trees. All hope of safety now vanished, for the sea was raging so violently that we knew we could not pass through the white line of breakers without being dashed lifeless on the strand. Our boats were all gone; the ship was drifting helplessly towards the land, and we could not tack while we had not room to wear. Thus we watched and waited for the minutes now fast approaching, when, the brig having stranded and gone to pieces, we should be precipitated into the boiling surf, and left to fight, each man as best he might, his way to the unknown shore we were approaching.

"I will pass over the few minutes that intervened, all the more agonizing as we could make no effort to avert the fate that was reserved for us. A heavier wave than almost any before, and the ill-fated 'Thalia' was hurled on the beach, but, owing to the shallow water, too far out for an attempt to land being made with any chance of success. A few men in desperation jumped overboard to swim to land with lines round them, so that we might haul them back if unsuccessful; but they were killed or drowned almost immediately, and the lines parted. Some were dashed back against the ship, others were overtaken by the gigantic rollers, and were cast about like corks, and seen no more. The rest of us remained aboard, but it was only for death to meet us instead of our going forward to seek him. The brig was overwhelmed by wave after wave, three following in rapid succession; and at the last she parted with a crash, and went into a thousand pieces, like matchwood.

"I saw nothing more of my companions, and found myself battling wildly with the surf. I was a powerful swimmer, but all my efforts to reach the shore appeared vain. One moment, indeed, owing to superhuman exertions and my being forced forward by the advancing sea, I felt my feet tread *terra firma;* but then, as the receding wave carried me back, I was swept out again. But my hour had not yet come. I had struggled thus desperately for some minutes for dear life, and had escaped, as by a miracle, death or injury from the heavy spars and timbers which were washing about, when once again I was borne on the crest of a great wave, and dashed half-senseless and bleeding on the beach. I tried eagerly to rise, but felt one of my legs give way under me. A feeling of despair took possession of me, and I gave myself up for lost; and so I should have been, but that the boot on my right leg had caught in a crevice between some large boulders lying on the beach, and the receding wave was thus prevented from dragging me back. At this moment occurred one of those periodical lulls which may often be noted in the severest gales. I was thus enabled to drag this boot off—the other one had been washed away already; and having thus disengaged my leg, I raised myself, and managed to crawl high enough up the beach to be out of the reach of the sea, which in a minute or so roared more fiercely than ever, as if furious at having allowed a single victim to escape.

" I looked round to see if any of my shipmates were saved, but I could not see a living soul. Some few bodies were washing about hither and thither amongst the wreckage, and one—it was that of a ship's boy—was flung by a sea at my feet, as if in exultation at the destruction wrought ; not one of the gallant hearts, recently instinct with life and hope, but now lay cold and pulseless. I cried out the names of some of them, but the howling wind only answered my voice. I was alone, the sole survivor of 115 officers and men. All were gone to their rest, with no one to mourn over them, while the wind and sea sang their *requiem* :—

'There's on the lone, lone sea,
    A spot unmarked, but holy,
For there the gallant and the free
    In their ocean bed lie lowly.

'Down, down beneath the deep,
    That oft to triumph bore them,
They sleep a calm and peaceful sleep,
    The salt waves dashing o'er them.

'And though no stone may tell
   Their name, their work, their glory,
They rest in hearts that loved them well,
   They grace Britannia's story.'

"After recovering from the condition of extreme exhaustion into which my efforts at escape had brought me, I began to look about me, but the prospect was drear indeed. I had been cast upon a small, and, as appeared, an uninhabited island, the entire extent of which was apparent at the first glance. It could not be more than about one mile across, and the highest point scarcely exceeded an elevation of twenty feet above the level of the sea. There were no animals, and the only living things, besides shellfish in a small group of rocks, were sea birds, which, in countless myriads, made this desert island their home. The only vegetation, in addition to short scrubby-looking grass, was a few clumps of palm-trees.

"Before nightfall, I had walked round my new domain, and though, unhappily, I was lord of all I surveyed, the prospect before me, and the condition of my kingdom were equally dismal and unpromising. The ground inland was covered with sea birds' nests, and I had eggs in abundance to eat. The birds themselves were so tame, owing to never before having

seen one of my species, that I was easily able to
knock over as many as I wanted. I determined not
to frighten them, however, by useless slaughter, but
having killed one, lit a fire with a flint and some dried
sticks, and cooked him upon it. I found the flavour
of what was to be my staple article of diet anything
but agreeable to the palate; the eggs were better,
and altogether, after all I had gone through, I felt
deeply thankful that I had even this hard fare. It
might have been worse, and my home might have
been a coral reef, when it would speedily have been
transformed into my grave. Here life could be supported, for there was spring water in abundance in
one of the groves, and plenty of food, such as it was.

" I will not give details of my solitary life in this
spot, which I afterwards found was one of the Cocos,
a group of islands in the Bay of Bengal, about forty
miles from the Andamans. Luckily, I was not cast
upon one of the latter, or I should have been speedily
consigned to the cannibal's pot, and transformed into
black man; indeed, the same dreadful fate would
have awaited me on some of the Cocos group, of
which the larger, I believe, are inhabited. Week
after week passed away, but there appeared no prospect whatever of my being rescued and brought
back to civilization. I only sighted one vessel

during all that time, and she passed so far from the island, that though I set fire to a great stack of dried wood I had raised, neither the flame nor the dense volume of smoke attracted the notice of the crew. At all events, if it did, they doubtless thought it was raised by the aborigines, and, sailing away, left me alone. I shall never forget the sensations of despair and grief with which I watched the ship growing smaller and smaller on the distant horizon, then saw the setting sun just bringing the white speck into prominence for a brief moment, only to disappear in the darkness of night.

" I had often thought of building for myself a hut from the wreckage of the old 'Thalia' still strewing the beach, but owing to want of energy, had deferred commencing it from day to day, now intending to wait for fine weather, and then putting it off because the sun was too hot. The temperature was so uniformly warm that I could sleep in the open air without discomfort, but as it might get colder, I resolved to set about constructing some sort of a house. At length, one day I determined to begin on the morrow, but when that morrow dawned, I felt so indisposed that I once more put off commencing operations till the next day. It was, indeed, providential that I had been so undecided, or rather lazy, for when I awoke on the following morning, I descried, making for the island, a small canoe under sail, and manned by three men. The wind was blowing fresh on to the island, and probably they had been fishing, and were driven by the stress of weather to shelter here. Had I built a hut they would have seen it easily from any part of the beach, as the groves of palms, with their tall trunks devoid of leaves, except at the top, afforded no concealment. Still my position became most perilous, as I could only conceal myself in a clump of these palms, and any search among them would lead to my detection. Luckily, the savages, who were perfectly naked and appeared of short stature, did not commence an exploration, but, lighting a fire, proceeded to cook their dinners. All that day I remained hid in the grove in a state of trepidation, and praying earnestly for fair weather, that I might get rid of my objectionable visitors. The wind fell with the setting sun, and to my unspeakable joy the savages launched their canoe soon after, and paddled off by the light of the moon. They must have come some distance, though the land whence they came, if low-lying, might have been nearer than I had imagined.

"On the following morning, I climbed up one of the tall palms, cutting notches in the stem with a hatchet that had been washed ashore ; and looking in the direction the canoe had taken, easily made out two islands lying close together, and certainly not distant more than about fifteen or twenty miles.

" I now gave up my design of building myself a house, and as I occasionally saw canoes with natives in them, fishing not many miles distant, I considered it prudent to avoid lighting fires to attract the attention of passing ships. This proximity of savages not only rendered my safety extremely precarious, but took away all hope of my ever being rescued. As I recognized my real position, my heart for the first time gave way to feelings of utter despair. For days I scarcely ate anything, but roamed about my small domain in a purposeless sort of way. I bitterly regretted now that I had not perished with my ship-mates, instead of being permitted to linger on here without hope of ever returning to my native country and friends, and tortured with the never ceasing danger of being discovered by savages, and put to a cruel death. But my rescue was nearer than I expected, or could for a moment have hoped.

"On waking one morning and taking my first glance around the horizon for a sail—which I did every morning, from habit, I could hardly believe my eyes when I saw anchored within half a mile of the shore, a large " country " barque, as the native

owned and manned vessels of the Eastern seas are
called. I could not credit my senses, but stood as
one transfixed. My brain appeared to reel, and I
momentarily lost the use of my eyesight. Making
an effort, I aroused myself, rubbed my eyes to make
sure I was not dreaming, or subject to an hallucina-
tion, and looked round me to see if nature wore its
ordinary aspect. Everything looked as usual, and I
turned again quickly towards the direction in which
the ship lay. There she was, sure enough, at her
anchorage, rising and falling on the long swell, and
with her sails not furled, but hanging in the buntlines.

" It was true, then, and I was neither dreaming
nor mad. *It meant that I was saved.* The next
moment, however, I found myself screaming out
something, and running down to the beach very
much like a maniac. I took off the sorry rags clothing my body, the sole remnant I had saved or picked
up from the wreck, and waved them in the breeze,
hallooing at the top of my voice. Some minutes
passed, but no one appeared attracted by the sound
of my voice. Strange to say, I was not noticed,
and, to my dismay, I saw two or three men slowly
making their way up the rigging, as if to overhaul the
buntlines previous to making sail. I looked on

aghast, and my ear caught the distant click of the windlass, as the anchor was being hove up. Seized with despair, and resolved not to be forsaken, I determined to make one last effort to escape the fearful fate awaiting me on that desert island. I plunged into the sea for the purpose of swimming off to the ship. This was not beyond my powers when in health, for I had often swam even longer distances; but I was weakened by privations, and the mental sufferings I had latterly endured had affected my strength, equally with the want of proper nourishment. I found I could swim with difficulty, and with none of that buoyant elasticity I had often prided myself upon. I felt I was totally unequal to the effort, but yet resolved to persevere or perish in the attempt. I screamed out as loud as I could. I was seen, for a boat which was astern of the barque was pulled alongside, and some men jumped into it.

" Oh, what happiness ! The prospect of succour nerved my arm, and I struck out with redoubled energy; but my strength was already spent. Though full of hope, I felt my head every now and then sinking beneath the surface; making strenuous exertions, I breathed again freely. Again my head was below the wave, and I felt half-choked. I struck out wildly over my head and around; a moment more, and my arm appeared as if paralyzed. I felt myself going; the water closed over me; one final effort more, but it was ineffectual. The bitter thought coursed rapidly though my brain that my rescuers would, after all, come too late, and I should die. I remember it was the last effort of the mind, as consciousness was leaving me. But I was mistaken.

"I learned afterwards that, as I was sinking for the third time, the bowman in the 'dingey' that had put off from the country ship, plunged his hand beneath the surface of the water, and seized the hair of my head. I was ill a long time, and recovered but slowly, for my health and strength had been sapped by the bad diet and the terrible anxiety of mind I had gone through during the past eight weeks.

"I learned from my preservers that the barque was bound from Manilla to Bombay, between which ports she traded. I received every kindness from the captain—who was a half-caste, and could speak English fluently—and from his officers, and felt very grateful for all their attentions. I was too weak to crawl up to the deck for a long time, and a few days after I made my first appearance there, to inhale the fresh breezes after sunset, the high land about Carinja was sighted. My troubles were now at an end.

We arrived at Bombay on the following day, when I landed, and reported myself as the sole survivor of the crew of the 'Thalia.' I was subjected to many examinations, and at length proceeded to England in the first of His Majesty's ships homeward bound."

CHAPTER VIII.

The Captain of the Forecastle gave us some experiences of his life, which, as actual occurrences in our naval history, speak of the matchless hardihood of British seamen. Napoleon used to laud as the rarest description of bravery what he called, "Two-o'clock-in-the-morning courage," alluding to an anecdote related of a gentleman of Avignon, named Grillon, who sustained his reputation for coolness and resolution during a sudden surprise at that early hour of the morning.* The stories we are about to tell are good examples of this "Two-o'clock-in-the-morning courage."

"In one of my voyages from Glasgow to America," said the Captain of the Forecastle, "I had a narrow escape from experiencing the hardships of the interior of a French prison. I was a foremast-hand on board the 'Euphemia,' a small merchant

---

* The anecdote is told in "Sully's Memoirs," vol. iii. p. 409 ; note. See edition of 1812.

brig, and at daylight one morning, when nearing the
latitude of Gibraltar, was the first to sight a large
ship astern, close-hauled on the starboard tack,
standing to the southward. Soon after I reported
the circumstance to our captain, a young man of
twenty-two, it was observed that the stranger had
bore up, and was making sail in chase. As we were
running before the wind, and the stranger was a considerable distance astern, plenty of time was given
for anxious consideration of the course we should
adopt. We ' took stock ' of our strength, and
hazarded guesses at that of the enemy, who, it was
evident, even at that great distance, was a ship-of-
war; for the practised eye of a sailor can tell the
difference by the cut of the canvas, and other pecu-
liarities. Our means of defence were very limited.
The crew of the ' Euphemia,' including boys and
officers, mustered 25 hands, and her armament consisted of eight 12-pounder carronades, and two
3-pounders, most diminutive pieces of ordnance.

" At 11 a.m., when the stranger was about two
miles distant, she hoisted an English ensign and
pendant, which only increased the suspicion previously existing, that she was an enemy. In another
hour, when she was within pistol-shot range, she
threw off the mask, and, showing French colours,

fired a gun athwart our fore-foot. She appeared to be a large corvette, mounting 22 guns, with her decks and tops crowded with men.

"On board the 'Euphemia' we had made every preparation for resistance; and now, notwithstanding the overpowering force of the enemy, the crew, true to the character of British seamen, stood to their guns, resolved not to strike without a fight for it. Our young captain, a regular fire-eater, who I believe cared for nothing above ground, or, for the matter of that, 'in the waters under the earth,' coolly examined his huge antagonist, and having satisfied himself that there was no chance of successful resistance, but that we must strike sooner or later in the conflict, called out to his men, 'Now, lads, you see exactly the enemy's force. What do you say? Shall we fight her, or haul the colours down?'

"One strapping big Irishman, the captain of one of the guns, took upon himself to answer for the crew, and sang out in reply, 'We'll stand by you, sir, every man of us; and we'll go down with you.' It was like the cheek of this fellow, who was not remarkable for the possession of the virtue of modesty."

"Ah!" broke in one of the auditors of the

Captain of the Forecastle, " I'll go bail I know who that same chap was. It was Bob Lyde, cap'n of the fo'castle aboard the ' Melpomene.' "

The narrator blushed like a " bread-and-butter " school-girl, and did not deny the soft impeachment. After two or three queries from his listeners, he proceeded with his narrative.

" The crew, though gallant fellows enough, evidently did not relish the idea of an encounter with so strong an opponent; but no man liked to put himself forward as the spokesman. The captain looked at his handful of men, who were all at their stations under his eyes; but there was no further response. Our flag still fluttered aloft, and every moment we expected a broadside to be poured into us. At last, after a few moments of painful suspense, the man at the wheel, who, from his station, and the sheer of the deck, was very much exposed, pointed out the hopelessness of the contest, and conjured the captain not to expose his crew to certain destruction. The remainder of the men now plucked up heart to speak, and expressed their willingness to fight when there was any chance of success, but considered themselves overmatched in the present instance.

" I can say now, that the men of the ' Euphemia '

were perfectly right in the course they pursued; and no sane man would have been justified in engaging a regular ship-of-war with such a disparity of force. Where success is *hopeless*, there is no disgrace in yielding to the fortune of war.

"The captain, seeing that he could do nothing with a crew who were opposed to fighting, ordered the colours to be hauled down, and we became the prize of the ' Saint Louis,' of 22 guns, and a crew of 220 men.

"A couple of boats were sent to take possession of us, and we laid down our arms at the dictation of the officer commanding the prize crew. By the same token, I threw my cutlass down in a transport of rage, and drew down upon myself the abuse of the French lieutenant; at least, I am told that the shower of ' *sacrés* ' was intended for such.. I was directed by this officer (through a French sailor, who acted as interpreter) to pick up my weapon, and give it into his hands, but I refused, and returned the compliment of the ' *sacrés* ' by a volley of the choicest Billingsgate. I was in a terrible rage, and gave him all I knew; indeed, I couldn't have kept my hands off him, but that our captain seized me round the waist, and held me by main force.

"First telling me that if I had struck him, he

would have shot me like a dog, Johnny Crapeaud ordered his men to seize me up to the rigging, and give me fifty lashes with the cat. I resisted; but most certainly I should have been either flogged or brained, had it not been for our captain, who indignantly pointed out to the French officer that he was violating the law of nations, as regarded prisoners of war, by inflicting corporal punishment on me, and that the act would bring eternal disgrace on himself and his nation, whom the English hitherto regarded as a chivalrous enemy. At the same time, the captain conjured me to be calm; and at length matters were compromised by my permitting myself to be put in irons.

"All the ship's company were now removed to the Frenchman, and also the carronades and three-pounders; only small arms were left on board, sufficient for a prize crew of eleven men and a boy, who were sent to navigate the 'Euphemia.' I should have said that there were three of us who were not sent on board the Frenchman, and these were the captain, an old man who had been cook, and was allowed to remain as his servant, and I; the two former were suffered to move about the ship unmolested, but I was kept in close confinement as a dangerous character.

" The boats having been hoisted up, both vessels shaped their course for Brest. The following day proved stormy, with the wind westerly, as before; gradually the wind increased until it blew a strong gale of wind. We burned lights and threw up rockets during the night, so as to keep together, but when the morning dawned there was no sign of the 'Saint Louis.' In order that I might assist in working the vessel, the French prize-master—not *my* friend, who had returned to his ship—offered me my liberty, which I gladly accepted. No sooner were the captain and I together, and we saw that the 'Saint Louis' had parted company, than we began to plot means of recapturing the 'Euphemia.' It was a most hazardous, not to say harebrained, project, but this recommended it perhaps all the more to our attention.

" The firearms were kept on deck in racks round the masts; but we knew that the prize-master had stowed away, somewhere, two brace of pistols and a sword, and to obtain possession of these became our primary object. The magazine being, as is usual in this class of vessel, below the cabin floor, to which access was had through a hatch under the table, we anticipated little trouble in providing ammunition.

The great difficulty was to ascertain the exact position of the concealed arms.

" As it was manifest that the successful termination of the enterprise depended solely on the advantage taken of the first moments of panic, it was desirable that the enemy should have no time for consideration, and that the surprise should be complete.   Fortunately, we could mature our plans with little chance of detection, as we knew only one man on board was conversant with English.   While one of us during favourable opportunities searched for the hidden arms, another kept watch above without exciting observation.   This was rendered easy in consequence of an opening over the cabin door, large enough for a person sitting on the lockers in the cabin to see the companion ladder; this opening had been made after the vessel was a prize, by a pet parrot, which had worked away with its bill, thus constituting itself a valuable auxiliary to its master's enemies.

"At length the arms were found concealed beneath the mattrass in the prize-master's bunk. They were taken possession of in the morning, and we then resolved to carry out our enterprise immediately, before their loss could be discovered.   As the captain thought it better not to load all the pistols

13

with ball cartridge, one pistol of each brace was charged with slugs, made of a pair of pewter tea-spoons, broken up hastily just when they were wanted. We each took a brace, intending to make use of the slug-loaded pistols first, and the others if absolutely required. After having loaded them and seen that they were in an efficient state, as far as we could without firing them off, the captain concealed them in the bed-clothes in his berth, which was on the starboard side of the cabin. Opposite him, on the port side, slept either the prize-master or his mate. The crew's quarters were partly forward in the forecastle and partly abaft in the steerage, where I also slept; the passage to this was through the companion, in consequence of the steerage hatch being kept closely battened down on account of the cold.

"At length the hour, 4 p.m., at which we had resolved to make the attempt to regain our liberty, was struck on the ship's bells. I confess I felt a little nervous, and I think the captain did so too, for he looked pale, and his fingers and mouth worked convulsively. Not for a moment did either of us think of giving up the project, although it was as desperate a one as men could well be engaged in. Two against twelve were long odds, for we had not taken into our confidence the old cook, who had neither enterprise nor strength to be of any use, while the fewer confidents we had the better chance we had of ever making the trial. No sooner had the hour struck than we commenced operations. Three of the crew were known to be in the steerage, and the prize-master had just turned in; thus eight only, including the boy, formed the watch on deck. At a preconcerted signal, we made our way quickly down to get our arms. The prize-master was asleep, and we left him to his slumbers, locking the cabin door upon him, while the captain remained below at the companion to warn the watch off duty against making any resistance. I sprang up the ladder, and on reaching the deck, shouted out that the ship was English property again, and discharged the pistol at the helmsman, followed it up by a blow from my cutlass which laid him low. At this time all the people on deck appeared to be collected on the port side of the quarter-deck, talking with the man at the helm. They immediately ran round the opposite side of the companion on their way forward, and I pursued, discharging the remaining charge of slugs among them.

"On reaching the windlass, I found the mate, a tall, muscular man, with a boarding pike in his hand.

On perceiving me, he instantly charged, but I knocked the weapon on one side with my cutlass, and placing the muzzle of a pistol to his head—it was not loaded, for had it been I should have blown his brains out without further palaver—I ordered him instantly below, on pain of sudden death. Thinking himself wholly in my power, and, doubtless, blessing me for my clemency, he promptly obeyed. His countrymen thereupon quickly followed suit, tumbling down the hatchway one on top of the other in hot haste, to the manifest danger of their limbs.

"I now drew the hatch over, and secured it from the possibility of removal. Coming aft, I found that the watch below were inclined to be obstreperous, so, having loaded my pistols again, I showed myself to them, and warned them that the brig was ours, and any attempt at mutiny would meet with instant death to those concerned. The prize-master, who had woke up and was thundering at his door, which had been locked, I brought out with a pistol at his head, and having marched him round the deck just to satisfy him that he and I had changed places, I marched him back again. After a short consultation, the captain, commander once more of the brig 'Euphemia,' offered him his choice of being locked

up where he was or regaining his liberty, provided he
gave his parole, as a French officer, not to make any
attempt at recapture. He spoke a good deal of his
honour, so we locked him up to consider the matter,
as if it was a matter of perfect indifference to us;
but the captain knew his man when he declared to
me that he was only a boaster, and would be only too
glad of an excuse to pledge his honour not to trust
himself to the perilous chances of a recourse to arms.
Within an hour's time, he called out that he was
willing to accept his freedom on the stipulated terms;
but so strangely constituted was this man, that he
prayed us not to insist on his giving the required
bond in the presence of one of his own men. This,
however, we insisted upon, for the word of a gentleman of such a pusillanimous spirit could not be
relied upon. This precaution was a very politic
movement on the part of the captain, for on the
shameful compact entered into by their superior
officer becoming known to the crew, they expressed
their disgust, and appeared inclined to think they had
no choice but to obey. The only one to dissent was
the mate, who showed a fine spirit, and bitterly de-
plored the conduct of the prize-master, which he said
nothing should induce him to follow; his liberty of
action he declared he would reserve, and would, like

ourselves, make a blow for freedom the first favourable opportunity.

"Our position was, truth to tell, a very critical
one, for we must have sleep, and, as we were only
mortal, one of us might fall ill, and then what could
the other do ?

"Our first considerations were the navigation of
the ship and the care of the wounded men, for I was
certain a man had been wounded by my second pistol-
shot, as I had heard an exclamation of pain.   On
examining the helmsman, I found he had been
seriously, but not mortally, wounded, and would
probably recover with care.   The other wounded man
was called up, and we found that the slug-shot had
entered his arm, but the injury was of little consequence.   After dressing his wound, we sent him
down again to the forecastle, to which all the three
men in the steerage were likewise transferred.   The
prize-master was allowed to remain with us in the
cabin, in which also a bed was made up for the
wounded helmsman.   The whole of the small arms
were thrown overboard, with the exception of the two
brace of pistols and the cutlasses we wore.

The weather had been nearly calm all day, but as
it could not be expected to remain so long, for the
sky looked lowering, and a swell had set in portend-

ing strong winds in no very distant quarter, we called up from below a man and a boy to assist in reefing topsails and working the ship. When, with these inadequate means, everything aloft was made secure, the captain examined the log-book, whence the ship's present position on the chart could be approximately marked out. As no observations had been taken for several days, we had to trust to dead reckoning alone. The prize-master, when questioned, knew, or professed to know, nothing, and very little confidence could be placed on the conjecture we formed, as we could not ascertain the course the ship had been steered during our incarceration below in the early part of our captivity. A course was, however, shaped for Gibralter, as the most convenient port. During the night it came on to blow heavily from the north-east, and for some days the weather was as unpropitious and trying for men in our precarious position as could be imagined. It became exceedingly cold, and the spray washing over the deck kept us continually wet to the skin. We tried at first to work the brig with the assistance of only two extra hands, but we became tired out with the constant watching and hard work this involved. At length we found it absolutely necessary to have six of the enemy to assist us, three being on deck at a time to work the ship. Daily, nay hourly, we expected the French seamen would overpower us, and re-capture the ship; and that they did not do so showed extraordinary lack of enterprise, though I think the chief reason was, as I have before said, owing to their disgust at the conduct of their superior.

"We were now in the extremity of misery. Worn out with want of rest,—for that could be hardly called sleep which consisted of a hasty doze snatched at odd times with pistols in one's belt, and one's fingers clutching the cutlass by one's side,— more than once we thought seriously of surrendering the ship back into the hands of the enemy, on the single stipulation that our liberty should be assured us; and indeed without conditions at all, for it became evident that the least effort at resistance on their part must be successful. However, we were ashamed to make the proposal and held on, hoping for we knew not what. But at length our long-suffering, or whatever you may call it, was rewarded.

"Owing to the requisitions made on the brig's stores by the 'Saint Louis,' the wine and spirits were soon exhausted after she left us; the oil for the binnacles was all expended, and we had to use lights made from the cook's skimmings. The sea washed the galley fires out, and we had been unable to cook any food for days, and altogether, what with the want of the common necessaries of life, and the hardships we endured from want of sleep and anxiety, we were plunged into the extremity of despair, when we found ourselves, not less unexpectedly than suddenly, delivered from all our troubles. A shift of wind occurred one night, and on the following morning a large fleet of merchantmen was seen under convoy of one of His Majesty's ships, from whose mizen-peak was flying the flag of 'Old England.' We immediately hoisted the Ensign, Union down, as a signal of distress, and firing a gun bore up for the man-of-war, which proved to be the 'Alert,' 38-gun frigate. Very soon she had lowered a boat, and a smart young officer leapt on board, and asked what we wanted. All we required was that he should take possession, and this he did, and relieved us of further anxiety. We requested permission to be taken on board the 'Alert,' which was granted. We were received on board with the utmost kindness by all hands, from the captain downwards. I immediately entered my name on her books as A.B.; and as soon as the rules of the service permitted, the captain promoted me to petty officer. This was the way I entered the navy, and from that day to this I have always been rated as a first-

class petty officer.   A few words will conclude
my tale.

"The captain of the 'Euphemia' was landed at
Gibraltar, and made his way to England by the first
opportunity; and as for the old brig, it was lucky
indeed that we asked to be taken out of her, for
after parting company with us on her way home, she
was captured off Cape La Hogue by a French man-
of-war, and her prize crew of ten men, with the smart
dandy of a lieutenant in command, soon found
themselves in a French prison, where they remained
till peace was concluded."

"Well done, Bob," chimed in a chorus of voices,
when the Captain of the Forecastle had finished his
yarn; "That was as plucky a thing as we have yet
heard."

"Well, I suppose," replied Bob aforesaid, "it
runs in the blood of my family to hate Frenchmen,
and think a Briton is a match for any three of them.
At least I was told so when a boy, and by hearing
the thing so often dinned into my ears, I believed it,
and, what is more, I believe it still.   I was saying it
runs in the blood, and you would agree with me if I
was to tell you a circumstance that occurred to my
grandfather, and which is as true as gospel."

"Let's hear it," sang out a dozen voices.   "It's

only three bells yet, and lots of time for another twister!"

"Twister," broke in the petty officer; "I tell you it's as true as gospel. A book was published about it, and I have a copy down below in my toggery, though perhaps you would rather I told the adventure than that it should be read to you, for half of you would *not* understand it, and the other half would get tired before I had finished. You see you chaps don't understand French, which my grandfather, who had been in a French prison, spoke, and used in his book as naturally as 'Bermuda Jack' there"—pointing to a negro, who grinned and nodded in response, proud of being so pointedly referred to—"patters his broken lingo."

This he said in a contemptuous and self-complacent tone that was highly diverting, but which did not appear to offend any of his auditory, except the individual who had cast a doubt on its authenticity, by speaking of the incident as a "twister," and who now expressed further doubts as to the elder Lyde having spoken French, or the younger scion of the family understanding it better than any of his shipmates. This ignorance will perhaps be shared by the reader of the following narrative, even though he may be familiar with the purest Parisian ;

and we feel ourselves bound to express an opinion
that his admiration for the linguistic attainments of
this gifted Lyde family, which formed so pleasing a
subject for reflection to Bob of " that ilk," will not
be increased by a perusal of the specimens now to
be laid before him.

A few recriminations, couched in expressive but
unparliamentary language, passed between Bob and
his interlocutor, and it was not until the exchange of
mutual explanations, to the effect that the opprobrious
epithets and playful expletives were applied in a
strictly " Pickwickian " sense, that the equanimity
of the Captain of the Forecastle was restored, and
harmony once more reigned in the assemblage
centred round the Man-o'-war's Bell.

It was carried, *nem. con.*, that Bob should narrate
in his own unsophisticated vernacular the adventure
that befell his grandfather, and which brought about
the contempt for " frog-eating Frenchmen," which
formed one of the idiosyncrasies of the Lyde family,
and that the book referred to should be brought up
and placed in the hands of one of the quartermasters
—who was pronounced a "scholard"—for reference,
and in corroboration of the truth of the narrative.

As my readers, however, would prefer to peruse
the incidents in the quaint phraseology of the gallant

seaman himself, garnished with his amusing French, I will give an extract from the book in question. After perusal, they will not wonder that Bob held our neighbours across the channel in such cheap estimation; that one Englishman was equal to three Frenchmen, was an article in the creed of all the members of his glorious profession, including Lord Nelson himself, who not only asserted, but proved, its truth on a hundred occasions.

CHAPTER IX.

THE following narrative will be found fully detailed
in a very rare pamphlet,* published about 1692, by
"Richard Baldwin, near the Oxford Arms, in War-
wick Lane," and entitled, "A true and exact account
of the retaking a ship called the 'Friends' Adventure,' of Topsham, from the French, after she had
been taken six days, and they were upon the coasts
of France with it four days. Where one Englishman and a boy set upon seven Frenchmen, killed
two of them, took the other five prisoners, and
brought the ship and them safe to England. Performed and written by Robert Lyde, mate of the
same ship."

"In the month of February, 1689," says this
seaman, "I shipped myself on board of a Pink, in
Topsham, burthen 80 tons, Mr. Isaac Stoneham,

* We believe only two or three copies of this pamphlet
are extant. One, of course, exists in the library of the
British Museum.

master, bound for Virginia, and from thence to
Topsham again; and on the 18th May following we
arrived there, and, after we had taken in our lading,
we set sail homewards-bound, with 100 sail of
merchantmen, under the convoy of two men-of-war;
and about a fortnight after the wind separated us
from our convoy, so that our ship, with several
others, made the best of our way for England, but
soon left each other's company; and on the 19th
October following, we came up with two Plymouth
vessels that were of our said fleet, being then about
40 leagues to the westward of Scilly, having the
wind easterly; and on the 21st of the same month,
we saw four other ships to leeward of us, which we
took to be some of our said fleet; but one of them
proved to be a French privateer, who came up under
our lee quarter, and went ahead of us, and took a
Virgineaman of our former fleet, belonging to London,
which gave us three an opportunity to make our
escape from the said privateer; but the two Plymouth-
men being in great want of provisions, and an easterly
wind like to continue, they bore away for Galicia, in
Spain.

" But our ship kept on her way for England;
and the mate of our ship and I made an agreement
(in case we should be taken by the French, and left

on board our own ship), although they should put ten men on board with us, to carry the ship and us to France, yet (if we lost sight of the privateer) to stand by each other and attack them (and if it did please God that we should overcome them), and carry home the ship.

"On the 24th of this month we were (as I feared) taken by a privateer of St. Malo, of twenty-two guns, eight pattereroes, and one hundred and odd men. But the mate's design and mine were spoiled; for we were put on board the privateer with three more of our men, and the master with four men and a boy left on board, and eight Frenchmen were put on board to navigate the prize to St. Malo. On the 26th, we had as much wind as could well blow at south-south-west, that the privateer could not take care of the prize, and so left her, and in some time after she arrived at Havre-de-Grace. Then I made it my endeavour to persuade our mate and the other prisoners to attack the Frenchmen on board the privateer, being very positive (with the assistance of God and theirs) to overcome them, and carry home the ship (with less trouble to my share than I found in this which I have done). But they concluded it impossible, and so we continued attempting no resistance at all.

"On the 28th of October we arrived at St. Malo, and were carried on shore and imprisoned; and in all respect during the space of seventeen days were used with such inhumanity and cruelty, that if we had been taken by the Turks, we could not have been used worse. For bread we had six pounds and one cheek of a bullock for every twenty-five men for a day; and it fell out that he that had half of a bullock's eye (for his lot) had the greatest share. This makes me wish that I could be the prison-keeper, and have my liberty to do the Frenchmen that are brought in, their justice; they daily adding to our number, until the prison was so full that swarms of vermine increased amongst us (not only here at St. Malo, but also at Dinan, whereunto we were removed); insomuch that many of our fellow-prisoners died, three of which were our mates, and two more out of the five of our company, and all that did survive were become mere skeletons. I was so weak that I could not put my hand to my head; and there died out of 600 men upwards of 400 through their cruelty in three months' time. They plundered us of our clothes when we were taken, and some of us that had money purchased rugs to cover our rags by day and keep us warm by night; but upon our return home from France, the Deputy-

14

Governor of Dinan (in hopes either to kill us with cold or to disable us for their Majesties' service at our return) was so cruel as to order our said rugs to be taken from us, and staid himself and saw it performed. And when some of our fellow-prisoners lay a-dying, they inhumanly stript off some of their clothes three or four days before they were quite dead. These and other barbarities made so great an impression upon me, that I did then· resolve never to go a prisoner there again; and this resolution I did ever since continue in, and by the assistance of God always will.

"And so I was released, and through the goodness of God got to England; and after I had been at home so long as to recover my health and strength, fit to go to sea again, I shipt myself as a mate of a vessel of Topsham, burthen 80 tons, Roger Briant, master, bound from thence to Oporto, in Portugal, and from thence to London; and accordingly, on the 30th day of September, 1691, we began our voyage, and on the 27th day of December following we arrived at Oporto, and on the 24th of February following we set sail from thence to London; and on the 29th day, being then about 25 leagues north-west from Cape Finisterre, about six in the morning, we saw a ship, which came up with us at a great pace. At ten in the morning he was within half a league of us, and then put out French colours and fired a gun, whereby we knew he was a Frenchman.

"Then I took a rope-yarn, and seized two parts of the topsail-hilliers together, that our men might not lower the topsail, for I was desirous to have as much time as possible I could to hide some necessaries to attack the Frenchmen; at which the master (perceiving and knowing my intention) said, ' Mate, are you in the same mind now as you have been in all the voyage?' (for I had often been saying what I would do towards the retaking of our ship.) I answered, ' Yes,' and said that I did not question but with God's assistance to perform what I had said. The master said he believed I could not do it; but if I should he thought it was impossible for me to carry home the ship. Notwithstanding all this, I was not discouraged, but desired him to pray for a strong gale of wind after we were taken, that we might be separated from the privateer, and be out of sight of her.

"Then I went down in the forecastle, and hid a blunderbuss and ammunition betwixt decks amongst the pipes of wine, and before I went aft again the topsails were lowered; and I, perceiving that it would not be long before the enemy would be on board us, took a five-gallon vessel of my own wine, and with a hammer beat in one head, and put several pounds of sugar in it, and then drank to the master, and said that I designed that I would drink my fill of it while I had the command of it; and if it should p'ease God that I should be continued on board, I hoped that I should not be long dispossest of the rest.

"Between ten and eleven o'clock, by the privateer's command, we haul'd up the coasts, and brac't to; then the privateer's boat full of men came on board us, and I stept over the side, with my hat under my arm, handing the French gentlemen in, till one of them took hold of my coat, and, I not daring to resist him, helpt it off, and ran aft into the cabin, and saved myself from further damage.

"After they had taken away almost all our clothes, and what else they pleased, the lieutenant ordered me and a boy to stay on board, which I was very glad of, but could heartily have wished they had left a man in the boy's room. Before the master and I parted (for he and four of our men and a boy were carried on board the privateer), I asked him privately what he had done with the money he had in a bag? He told me he had given it to the lieutenant, and withal would know of me why I made that inquiry; I answered, because I did not question but that I should secure that on board by retaking our ship. But the master said it was an impossible thing to be done; but I replied, although it seemed to him to be so, yet nothing was impossible to be effected by God, in whom I put my trust.

" Soon after, the lieutenant and our men returned aboard the privateer, having left seven of his men on board our ship to navigate her to St. Malo, who in three hours' time was out of our sight, which I was very glad of, and askt the master if I should fetch a barrel of wine up, in hopes to make them drunk, and then I should command them with the less trouble. He said I might if I could find one; then I fetched a barrel of five gallons of sweet strong wine, and kept it tapt in the steerage, and I drank freely of it, hoping that they thereby would be induced to do the like, and to drink to excess; but that strata-gem failed me (for they never were the worse for drinking all the time I was their prisoner), and then I acquainted the boy with my intent, and persuaded him to assist me in overcoming them, and I would, with the assistance of God, carry the ship to Galicia, in Spain. I continued soliciting him for his compli-ance in that, and spoke to him of England, but could not prevail with him.

" On the 3rd of March we saw Ushant in the night, we being within two ships' length of the

Fern Rock, and in great danger of being lost. They called up me and the boy to save our lives; and when I came up and saw that the Frenchmen had got the tackle in the boat, and going to hoist her out, I told the boy to stay aft, for when the boat is overboard they may all go in her if they will, but they shall not come aboard again; for I will not leave the ship, because I shall get the ship off presently, for the wind was west-north-west, and the Frenchmen never minded to trim the sails close by the wind. And I could not tell them of it (because I would get them out of the ship) till I saw that they did not get out the boat, but gaz'd at the rock, and some cry'd and others call'd to saints for deliverance, then I desir'd (and helpt) them to trim the sails, and got the ship soon off again. On Friday at noon, we being about ten leagues to the eastward of Brest, with the wind easterly, they bore away for Portbean (or some such name they call'd it), which was about four or five leagues to the eastward of Brest; then I call'd the boy down betwix't decks, and read two or three chapters in the Bible, and then used all my endeavour to persuade him to assist me; but, by all the arguments I could use, I could not prevail at this time. Then I took a brick, and wet my knife upon it, and told the boy I would not use my knife upon any account until I was carried into France, except it were to cut the throats of the Frenchmen; at which words the boy startled as if his own throat had been cut, and then left me, and went upon deck.

"At four in the afternoon, we were within half a mile of the aforesaid harbour; then the Frenchmen fired a pattereroe for a pilot to come off, whereupon I went upon deck, with a sorrowful heart, to see how near we were to the shore (but the Frenchmen were as joyful as I was melancholy); and then, considering the inhuman usage I formerly had in France, and how near I was to it again, struck me with such terror that I could stay no longer upon deck, but went down betwixt decks, and prayed to God for a southerly wind to prevent her going into that harbour, which God was graciously pleased immediately to grant me, for which I returned my unfeigned thanks.

"Friday night the wind was westerly, and Saturday southerly, so that in the evening I heard the Frenchmen say that they saw Cape Farril. At eight on the Saturday night I prayed again for a south-west wind, that we might not be near the shore in the morning, and immediately I heard them put the helm a-lee, and put her about, and get the larboard tacks aboard. The boy then lying by my side,

I bid him go up and see if the wind was not south-west; which he accordingly did, and at his return told me it was, and that the ship lay off north-north-west. Then I rejoiced and gave God thanks for this second signal providence.

"The nearer we came to St. Malo, the surlier the Frenchmen were to me. At twelve o'clock on Saturday night they call'd me to the pump (as they had done several times before); although I never went but when I pleased; nor would I do anything else for them, thinking it much inferior for an English-man to do anything for a Frenchman. But they calling on me several times, at last I turned out, and stood in the gun-room scuttle, and told the master that I had served two years for the French already; and if I went to France again I should serve three years. 'That's *bien*!' said the master. Then I told him I had nothing in the ship to lose, and if they would not pump themselves, the ship should sink for me. Then I went and laid myself down again, fully resolved that if they came to hawl me out by force, that I would make resistance, and kill or wound as many of them as I could before I died myself; but they let me alone, and all that night when the boy was awake I endeavoured to persuade him to assist me, but still could not pervail, though I used (as I had done ever since we were taken) many arguments; so that that night I slept but very little, and when I did slumber at all I dreamt that I was attacking the Frenchmen; for, s'eeping or waking, my mind ran upon the attacking of them.

" Sunday, at seven in the morning, we being then about five leagues off from Cape Farril, I then prayed heartily for a south-east wind, and immediately I heard them take in their topsails and hauld up the foresail, and brac't them aback, and lash't the helm a-lee, and let the ship drive off with her head to the westward. Then I sent the boy up again to see if the wind was not come at south-south-east, and he brought me word it was. Then I gave God thanks, and rejoiced at His signal providential mercy on me, and for so immediately strengthening my faith, and confirming my hopes of redeeming myself from slavery; and then I renewed my solicitation to the boy to yield to me, but still he would not consent, which made me think of attempting it myself. And then I went and took a pint of wine and half a pint of oil, and drank it to make me more fit for action.

" At eight in the morning all the Frenchmen sat round the table at breakfast, and they called me to eat with them; and, accordingly, I accepted of their invitation; but the sight of the Frenchmen did immediately take away my stomach, and made me sweat as if I had been in a stove, and was ready to faint with eagerness to encounter them ; which the master perceiving, and, seeing me in that condition, asked me (in French) if I were sick, and because he should not mistrust anything I answered, 'Yes.'   But I could stay no longer in sight of them, and so went immediately down betwixt decks to the boy, and did earnestly entreat him to go up presently with me into the cabin, and to stand behind me, and knock down but one man in case two laid hold on me, and I would kill and command all the rest presently. For now, I told him, was the best time for me to attack them while they be all round the table ; for now I shall have them all before me purely, and it may be never the like opportunity again.

"After many importunities, the boy asked me after what manner I intended to encounter with them.   I told him I would take the crow of iron, and hold it on to the middle with both hands, and I would go to the cabin and knock down him that stood at the end of the table on my right hand, and stick the point of the crow into him that sat at the end of the table on my left hand, and then for the other five that sat behind the table.   But still he not consenting, I had second thoughts of under-

taking it without him; but the cabin was so low
that I could not stand upright in it by a foot, which
made me at that time desist.

" By this time they had eaten their breakfast.
I went out upon the deck; then I told the boy, with
much trouble, we had lost a brave opportunity, for by
this time I had had the ship under my command.

" ' Nay,' says the boy, ' I rather believe that by
this time you and I should have both been killed.'

" In a little time after they had been upon deck
they separated from each other; viz., the master lay
down in his cabin, two of the men lay down in the
great cabin, one in a cabin between decks, another
sat down upon a low stool by the helm to look after
the glass, to call to pump (which they were forced to
do every half-hour, by reason of the leakiness of the
ship), and the other two men walked upon the decks.
Then, hoping I should prevail with the boy to stand
by me (if not, resolved to attack them by myself), I
immediately applied myself to prayer; and then I
endeavoured again to persuade the boy, telling him
that we should bring a great deal of honour to our
native country, besides the particular honour that
would accrue to ourselves. But all this, and much
more, would not prevail with him to consent.

" Then the glass was out, it being half-an-hour

after eight, and the two men that were upon deck went to pump out the water. Then I also went up on deck again to see whether the wind and weather were like to favour my enterprise, and casting my eyes to windward, I lik'd the weather, and hoped the wind would stand. I begged of the boy again to stand by me while two of the men were at the pump, but I could by no persuasions prevail upon the boy, so that by that time the men had done pumping; whereupon, losing this opportunity caused me again to be a little angry with the boy for not yielding to me, telling him that I had prayed three times for the change of the wind, and Heaven was pleased to hear my prayer, and to grant my request, and thereupon I had a firm belief wrought in me that I should not be carried a prisoner again into France, where I had suffered great hardship and misery; our allowance of food at St. Malo, where we were kept prisoners for seventeen days, was only one cheek of a bullock, and eight pounds weight of bread, for twenty-five men a day, and only water to drink; and at Dinan, where we were kept close prisoners for three months and ten days, our allowance was three pounds weight of old cow beef, without any salt to savour it with, for seven men a day; but I think we had two pounds of bread for each man, but it was so bad that dogs would not eat it, neither could we eat but very little, and that we did eat did us more hurt than good, for 'twas more oats than bread, so we gave some of it to the hogs, and made pillows of the rest to lay our heads on, for they allow'd us fresh straw but once every five weeks, so that we bred such swarms of vermin in our rags, that one man had a great hole eaten through his throat by them, which was not perceived till after his death; and I myself was so weak that it was fourteen weeks after my releasement before I recovered any tolerable measure of strength again. And all this through their cruel tyranny in not allowing us as their men are allowed in England.

"Said the boy, ' If I find it so bad as you do say when I am in France, I will go along with them in a privateer.'

"These words of his struck me to the heart, which made me say, ' You dog; what, will you go with them against your king and country, and father and mother?' Sirrah, I was in France a prisoner four months, and my tongue cannot express what I endured there, yet I would not give up my country and go with them; yet they came daily, persuading me and others to go out, and the time that I was there I think seventeen did so, and were kept in a room by themselves; but Heaven was pleased to make an example of them, for I think twelve of them died while I was there. And if thou dost turn traitor, thou may't fare as they did, and if thou or any of them that be turn'd be ever taken again, you will certainly be hanged in England by the law ; but if I had the command of a privateer, and should take my brother in a French privateer after he had sail'd willingly with them, I would hang him immediately.'

" Seeing the boy seem'd to be reconcil'd, I told him that he should not go into France, if he would do as I would have him to do. The boy ask't what I would have him to do. I told him to knock down that man at the helm, and I will kill and command all the rest presently.

" Saith the boy, 'If you be-sure to overcome them, how many do you count to kill ?'

" I answered that I intended to kill three of them.

" Then the boy replied, ' Why three, and no more ?'

" I answered, that I would kill three for three of our men that died in prison when I was there. And if it should please God that I should get home safe to England, I would, if I could, go in a man-of-war or fire-ship, and endeavour to revenge on the enemy,

for the death of those four hundred men that died in
the same prison of Dinan.

"'But,' the boy said, 'four alive would be too
many.'

"I then replied, 'I would kill but three, but I
would break the legs and arms of the rest, if they
won't take quarter, and be quiet without it.' Then
the boy asked which three I designed to kill? I told
him I designed to kill those three that I judged to be
the strongest, which were those that carried themselves most surly towards me; but if any one of the
rest did take hold on me, and that my life were in
danger, I would then endeavour to kill a fourth, and
not otherwise. I told him I would take the crow of
iron, and go into the cabin and knock down one with
the claws, and strike the point into the other that
lay by his side in his cabin, and I would wound
the master in his cabin; and so then take the
drivebolt, and be sure to knock down the man at
the helm, so soon as you hear me strike the first
blow, for otherwise if he should hear the blow he
may come into the cabin, and lay hold on me before
I shall overcome them three.

"Then the boy asked what he should do when he
had knock't down the man at the helm? I told him
he should stand without the cabin door, and not stir

from thence, but to have his eye upon the two Frenchmen that were upon deck, and not to come into the cabin to me, unless he observed them coming towards the cabin, and then he should tell me of it, and come into the cabin.

"At nine in the morning, the two men upon deck went to pumping; then I turned out from the sail, where the boy and I then lay'd, and pull'd off my coat that I might be the more to the action; and having little hair, I haul'd off my cap, that if they had the fortune to knock me in the head, they might kill me with it. Having fitted myself for the action, I went up the gun-room scuttle into the steerage to see what posture they were in, and being satisfied therein, I leapt down the scuttle, and went to the boy (who seeing me resolv'd upon the action) with an earnest entreaty to him to join with me; he at last did consent.

"Then the boy coming to me, I leapt up the gun-room scuttle, and prayed for help and strength; and I told the boy that the drivebolt was by the scuttle, in the steerage, and then I went softly aft into the cabin, and put my back against the bulke-head, and took the iron crow (it lying without the cabin door), and held it with both my hands in the middle of it, and put my legs abroad to shorten myself (because the cabin was very low). But he that lay nighest to me, hearing me, opened his eyes, and perceiving my intent, and upon what account I was coming, he endeavoured to rise, to make resistance against me; but I prevented him by a blow upon his forehead, which mortally wounded him, and the other man, which lay with his back to the dying man's side, hearing the blow, turned about and faced me, and as he was rising with his left elbow upon the deck, very fiercely endeavouring to come against me, I struck at him, and he let himself fall from his left arm, and held his arm for a guard, whereby he did keep off a great part of the blow, but still his head receiv'd a great part of the blow.

"The master lying in his cabin on my right hand, hearing the two blows, rose, and sate in his cabin, and seeing what I had done, he called me *Boogra* and *Footra*, but I having my eyes every way, I push't at at his ear betwixt the turn-pins with the claws of the crow, but he falling back for fear thereof, it seem'd afterwards that I struck him a severe blow which made him lie still, as if he had been dead; and while I struck at the master, the fellow that fended off the blow with his arm rose upon his legs, and, running towards me, with his head low, for I suppose he intended to run his head against my breast to overset me; but I push't the point at his

15

head, and stuck it an inch and a half into his forehead (as it appeared since by the chirurgeon that
searched the wound), and as he was falling down I
took hold of him by the back, and turn'd him into
the steerage.

"I heard the boy strike the man at the helm two
blows after I knock'd down the first man, which two
blows made him lie very still; and as soon as I
turn'd the man out of the cabin, I struck one more
blow at him that I struck first (thinking to leave no
man alive further aft than myself), and killed him
outright.

"The master all this time did not stir, which
made me conclude that I had killed him with the
blow I had struck him. Then I went out to attack
the two men that were at the pump, where they continued pumping, without hearing or knowing what I
had done; and as I was going to them I saw that
man that I had turn'd out of the cabin into the
steerage crawling out upon his hands and knees
upon the deck, beating his hands upon the deck to
make a noise that the men at the pump might hear
(for he could not cry out nor speak), and when they
heard him they came running aft to me, grinding
their teeth as if they would have eaten me; but we
met them as they came within the steerage door, and

struck at them, but the steerage being not above four
feet high, I could not have a full blow at them,
whereupon they fended off the blow, and took hold
of the crow with both their hands close to mine,
striving to haul it from me; then the boy might have
knock'd them down with much ease while they were
contending with me, but that his heart failed him, so
that he stood like a statue at a distance on their left
side, and two foot's lengths off the crow being behind
their hands, on their left side. I call'd to the boy to
take hold of it, and haul as they did, and I would let
it all go at once; which the boy accordingly doing, I
push'd the crow towards them and let it go, and was
taking out my knife, to traverse amongst them, but
they seeing me put my right hand into my pocket,
fearing what would follow, they both let go the crow
to the boy, and took hold of my right arm with both
their hands, grinding their teeth at me.

"The master that I had thought I had killed in
his cabin coming to himself, and hearing they had
hold of me, seized me with both his hands round my
middle. Then one of the men that had hold of my
right arm let go, and put his back to my breast, and
took hold of my left hand and arm, and held it close
to his breast, and strove to cast me upon my back;
and the master let go from my middle, and took hold

of my right arm, and he, with the other that had
hold of my right arm, did strive to turn me over
from the other's back, thinking to get me off from
my legs; but I, knowing that I should not be long
in one piece if they got me down, I put my left foot
against the ship side, on the deck, for a supporter,
and, with a great effort, I kept upon my feet, when
they three and one more did strive to throw me
down (for the man that the boy knock't down at the
helm rose up, and put his hands about my middle,
and strove to haul me down).   The boy, seeing that
man rise and take hold of me, cried out, fearing then
that I should be overcome by them, but did not
come to help me, nor did not strike one blow at any
of them, neither did they touch him all the time.

   " When I heard the boy cry out, I said, ' Do you
cry, you villain, now I am in such a condition ?
Come quickly, and knock this man on the head that
hath hold on my left arm.'   'The boy, perceiving that
my heart did not fail me, he took some courage from
thence, and endeavoured to give that man a blow on
his head with the drivebolt, but struck so faintly that
he mist his blow, which greatly enraged me against
him ; and I feeling the Frenchman that held about
my middle hang very heavy, I said to the boy, ' Do
you miss the blow, and I in such a position !   Go

round the binnacle, and knock down that man that hangeth upon my back, which was the same man the boy knock't down at the helm. So the boy did strike him one blow upon the head, which made him fall, but he rose up again immediately; but being uncapable of doing any further resistance, he went out upon deck staggering to and fro, without any further protestance from the boy. Then I look't about the beams for a marlin-speek, or anything else, to strike them withal; but seeing nothing, I said to myself, 'What shall I do?' and then casting my eye upon my left side, and seeing a marlin-speek hanging with a strap to a nail on the larboard side, I jerk't my right arm forth and back, which cleared the two men's hands from my right arm, and took hold of the marlin-speek, and struck the point four times about a quarter of an inch deep into the skull of that man that had hold of my left arm, before they took hold of my right arm again; but I struck the marlin-speek into his head three times after they had hold of me, which caused him to screech out. But they having hold of me, took off much of the three last blows, and he being a strong-hearted man, he would not let go his hold of me, and the two men, finding that my right arm was stronger than their four arms were, and observing the strap of the marlin-speek to fall up and down upon the back of my hand, as struck him that had his hands nearest to mine, he let go his right hand, and took hold of the strap, and hauled the marlin-speek out of my hand; and I, fearing what in all likelihood would follow, I put my right hand before my head for a guard, although three hands had hold of that arm, for I concluded that he would knock me on the head with it, or else throw it at my head; but (through the help of a wonderful providence) it either fell out of his hand or else he threw it down, for it did fall so close to the ship side that he could not reach it again, without letting go his other hand from mine, so he did not attempt the reaching of it, but took hold of my arm with his other hand again.

"At this time I gained strength enough to take one man in one hand and push at the other's head, and looking about again to see for anything to strike them withal; but seeing nothing, I said to myself, 'What shall I do now?' And then the thought suddenly came into my mind of my knife in my pocket, and, although two of the men had hold of my right arm, yet I felt so strengthened that I put my right hand into my right pocket, and took out my knife and sheath, holding it behind my hand that they should not see it, but I could not draw it

out of the sheath with my left hand, because the
man that I struck in the head with the marlin-
speek had still hold of it, with his back to my breast;
so I put it between my legs, and drew it out, and
then killed the man that had his back to my breast,
and he immediately dropt down, and scarce ever
stirred after. Then, with my left arm, I gave both
the men a push from me, and hauled my right arm
with a jerk to me, and so cleared it of both of them,
and fetching a stroke with an intent to put an end
to them both at once. They, immediately appre-
hending the danger they were in, both put their
hands together, and held them up, saying, ' Cortè,
cortè, monsieur, moy allay pur Angleterre si vous
plea.' With that I stopt my hand, and said, ' Good
quarter you shall have, *alle a pro;*' and then I put
up my knife into the sheath again, but they not
obeying my command, but standing still, I concluded they had a mind to have the other bout with
me; but I drew out my knife again, but then their
countenances immediately changed, and they put off
their hats and said, ' Moy alle pro, monsieur, moy
travallay pur Angleterre, si vous plea.' Then I stopt
my hand again, and they went out upon deck, and
went forwards.

" Then I held fast the steerage door, and ordered

the boy to stand by it, and to look out through the blunderbuss holes, and if he did see any man coming towards the door with anything in his hand to open the door, he should tell me of it, and come into the cabin for the blunderbuss and ammunition, which I hid away before we were taken. The Frenchmen had found and kept it in the cabin, which, after I had loaded, I came out with it into the steerage, and look't forward (out the companion) to see if any man did lie over the steerage-door with a bait of a rope to throw over me, or any other thing that might prejudice me, as I should go out; but seeing no man there, I went out upon deck, and lookt up to the maintop, for fear the two wounded men were there, and should throw down anything upon my head to do me an injury; but seeing no man there, I asked the boy if he could tell what was become of the two wounded men that came to themselves, and went out upon the deck while I was engaged with the three men in the steerage. The boy told me they scrambled overboard, for he said he lookt through the blunderbuss-holes in the bulkehead, and saw them staggering to and fro like men that were drunk; but I thought it very strange that they should be accessory to their own deaths.

"Then I ordered the boy to stand by the steerage-door to see if that man betwixt decks did come up, and if he did to tell me of it, and come forward to me, which he promised me to do. Then I went forward to the two men that cried for quarter, who stood by the boat side, but they being afraid ran forwards, and were going up in the fore-shrouds; but I held up the blunderbuss at them, and said, 'Veni aban et monte à cuttelia, et ally aban;' and they then put off their hats, and said, 'Monsieur, moy travalli pur Angleterre, si vous plea;' but I answered, 'Alle aban, for I don't want your help;' and then they said, 'Oui, monsieur,' and undid the scuttle, and went down. Then I went forward, and as I came before the foot of the mainsail, I look't up to the foretop, and seeing no man there I went and look't down in the forecastle, and showed the two men a scuttle on the larboard side that went down into the fore-peak, and said, 'Le monte cuttelia, et ally aban.' They answered, 'Oui, monsieur,' and then undid the scuttle, and put off their hats, and went down, giving me great thanks for my mercy towards them, and giving them a longer life.

"Then I called down to them, and asked them if they saw any men betwixt decks before they went down, and they answered no. Then I called forward the boy, and gave him the blunderbuss, and bid him present it down the forecastle, and if he saw any men take hold of me, so that I could not get clear of them, or if I called on him for his help, then he should be sure to discharge the blunderbuss at us, and kill us altogether, if he could not shoot them without me. The boy promised he would, but he would not shoot me.

"Then I took the boy's bolt, and put my head down the scuttle, and look't all round, and seeing no man there I leapt down in the forecastle, and look't that round also; but seeing no man betwixt decks, I laid the scuttle and nailed it fast, and thought myself safe, seeing two men killed and two secured. Then I went upon deck, and took the blunderbuss from the boy, and gave him the bolt, and went aft and ordered the boy as before to stand by the steerage-door, and give me an account if he saw any man come towards him with a hand-spike; and then I went aft into the cabin, and cut two candles in four pieces, and lighted them; one I left burning upon the table, the other three I carried in my left hand, and the blunderbuss in my right hand; and I put my head down the gun-room scuttle and look'd round, and, seeing no man there, I leapt down, and went to the man that lay all this time asleep in a cabin

betwixt decks, and took him by the shoulder with
my left hand and wakened him, and presented the
blunderbuss at him with my right hand, and commanded him out of his cabin, and made him stand
still till I got up into the steerage; then I call'd the
man, and he standing in the scuttle, and seeing the
man that had been killed on deck, he wrung his
hands, crying out and calling upon some saints. I
told him I had nothing to do with them, 'Monte,
monte et ally a pro;' then he came up, and went
forward, looking round to see for his companions;
but I followed him, and made him go down into the
forecastle, and stand on the starboard side. Then I
gave the boy the blunderbuss, and ordered him to
present it at the man, and if he perceived him either
to come towards me, or to take anything to throw at
me while I was opening the scuttle, then to shoot
him.

"Then I took the crow of iron, and leapt down
with it into the forecastle, and drew the spikes, and
opened the scuttle, and went upon deck, and bid the
man go down, which he readily did, and rejoic'd
when he had found two of his companions there;
and after I had nailed down the scuttle again I went
aft and ordered the boy to stand by the steerage-door
again, and I took the candles and the blunderbuss,

and went down betwixt decks, and went forward and aft, and look't in all the holes and corners for the two wounded men, but found them not; and finding the gun-room scuttle open that went down into the hold, I call'd down, but hearing none make answer I laid the scuttle; and there being about twenty bags of Shumack in the gun-room, I rolled two of them upon the scuttle of six hundredweight, and rolled more close to them, that if the men were there and did lift up one side of the scuttle the bags might not roll off. Then I went upon deck, and told the boy I could not find the two men betwixt decks, and he said they were certainly overboard. I told him I would know what was become of them before I made sail.

"Then I told the boy I would go up into the maintop and see if they were there, and then I should be sure to see them if they were in the foretop. So I gave him the blunderbuss, and bid him present it at the maintop, and if he saw any man look out over the top with anything in his hand to throw at me, he should shoot him. Then I took the boy's bolt and went up; and when I was got to the puddick-shrouds I look't forwards to the foretop; I saw the two men there, covered with the foretopsail, and their sashes bound about their heads to stanch their wounds and keep their heads warm. Then I call'd to them, and they turned out, and went down upon their knees, and wrung their hands, and cried, ' O, cortè, cortè, mounsieur; moy allay pur Angleterre, si vous plea.'

"Then I said, 'Good quarter you shall have,' and I went down, and call'd to them to come down; and he that the boy wounded came down and kist my hand over and over, and went down into the forecastle very willingly. But the other man was one of the three that I designed to kill, and the same that I struck the crow into his forehead; and he knew that he had said ill-things of the Prince of Orange—meaning our gracious King, and that an English man-of-war was unfit for a man, and did always call me up to pump; these things, I suppose, he thought I had not forgot, and that, therefore, I would not give him quarter, notwithstanding I intended to do; but I suspected him to be an English or Irishman, and I resolved if he proved so, that I would hang him myself when I was fortunate enough to have help coming aboard from England. So I call'd him down, but he, being unwilling, delayed his coming. I took the blunderbuss, and said that I would shoot him down, and then he came a little way, and stood still, and begged me to give quarter, and if I would, he then would 'trevally pur Angle-terre,' and also pump the water. I told him if he would come down he should have quarter, and I pre-sented the blunderbuss at him again; and then he came a little lower, and said, 'O mounsieur, vou battera moy.' I told him that I would not beat him, and withal I would discourse with him no longer. If he would come down, he might; if not, I would shoot him down. And then he came down, and I gave the boy the blunderbuss, and the Frenchman took up my hand and wrung it, and kist it over and over, and call'd me his 'boon mounsieur,' and told me he would help me to carry the ship for England. I told him I did not want his help, and commanded him down in the forecastle. Then I made them both stand on the starboard side, and ordered the boy to shoot them if they offered to throw anything at me, or come near to me, while I went down in the forecastle to unnail the scuttle.

"Then I took the crow of iron, and leapt down into the forecastle and unnailed the scuttle, and commanded the two Frenchmen down into the hold, and I call'd one of the men up that cried first for quarter, to help me to sail the ship for England. This man was not wounded at all, and was not above twenty-four years of age, and I had least fear of him, because he was indifferent kind to me while I was their prisoner ; but he was very unwilling to come up, but with much importunity I prevailed with him to come up, and I sent him aft, and then laid the scuttle, and nailed a piece of oaken plank to each beam with spikes over it, and I bid them get from under the scuttle, and I split the scuttle with the crow, and drove it down into the hold to give them air.

" Then I went aft, and commanded the man to help haul out the two men that were dead, which he accordingly did, and so we threw them overboard ; but before I threw them both, I took a sash from one of them because it was red, on purpose to make fast about the white antient,* which the Frenchman put on board, and put it out for a whiff,† when occasion should require it, and I searched his pocket for a steel and flint, but found none ; for want whereof, I was forced to keep two candles always burning in the cabin till I got the pilots on board from Topsham. Having secured all the men, I ordered the boy to put the blunderbuss in the boat, for him to command the Frenchman withal, when I was doing anything. Then I sent the Frenchman to loose the helm and

* Ensign.
† A whiff is a long, narrow flag, like a streamer.

put him a-weather, and wared the ship, and then, almost without assistance, I had three topsails, the spritsail and mizen trimm'd in less than an hour's time, to make the most of a fair wind.

" Then I gave down to them in the hold a basket of bread and butter, and a gimlet and spikes, and ordered them to draw and drink of one of my own casks of wine which I had there, because if they should draw out a pipe, they might not find the hole in the dark, and so spill a great deal of wine, and I gave them down their clothes, and some old sails to lie upon; I gave them likewise a bottle of brandy to wash their wounds, and salve which they brought on board, and candles to see to dress their wounds, and having no more necessaries for them, I was sorry to receive him that the boy wounded, because he was very bad of his wounds."

The gallant fellow then details how he worked the ship. The wind was fair at first, but got round to the westward, and then two points to the westward of north. At six on the following morning, he says, the wind " blew hard in showers (squalls); and I let three or four showers pass without lowering either of the topsails. At eight it blew very hard, but still I kept up the topsail, till at last the wind in the showers did put the gunwale of the ship in the

water, and then I hauled down the topsail, and
clewed up the sheets, and brac'd them aback, till
each shower was over, and then haul'd home the
sheet, and up with the topsail again. At nine the
wind blew harder; then I took in the two topsails,
and the wind increasing, I hauled down the mizen,
and after we had pumpt out the water we sat down
and eat some bread, and drank a glass of wine to
refresh ourselves, and I took brandy and butter and
rubbed it into my hands, and especially into my left
thumb, which was strained by the man that had his
throat cut, and bruised by the boy when he mist his
blow at the man's head, so that it was much swell'd
and inrag'd."

At two in the afternoon land was sighted, which
Lyde made out to be the Start, and the wind not
being so squally he set more sail, but it freshened again
on the following morning, and he was compelled to
furl both his topsails. So passed the third day, the
wind falling and rising, and at six in the evening he
says he fired "a pattercroe* three times, which spent
all the powder I had on board, and the French
antient tied in a red sash I put out for a whiff, for
the pilots to come off; but by all the sail that I

* Small piece of swivel ordnance fitted on the ship's
gunwale.

could make, I got no nearer than a mile to Topsham
Bar in the dimness of the night.   Then I went up to
the topmast head to see if I could perceive the pilots'
boat coming off, but because I could not show an
English antient they were afraid to come out, but lay
upon their oars near the bar."

He thereupon made sail, intending to go into
Torbay, but he altered his purpose because the sheet
cable having been carried away by the French privateer, the small bower was " not fit for ocam "
(oakum), and he was afraid he might go ashore, for
it was now blowing a " reef-topsail gale."   So he
" kept her along with two coasts* and a mizen,"
and made three ineffectual attempts during the night
to tack, but could not make the ship stay.   At
length he got her round, and at one in the morning,
putting the Frenchman to the wheel, he went aloft
with the boy, and was an hour taking two reefs in
the maintopsail.

At ten o'clock he neared the Bar at Topsham,
and the pilots were coming on board, but when they
saw no colours, and only one man and a boy on
deck, sheered off, fearing foul play.   Lyde then called
to them, and they hearing the English tongue, laid

* The fore and main-sails, or "courses." ·

on their oars until he neared them, when on recognizing the features of an old friend, they came on board. Then he recounts how the pilots would not credit the story he told them, of the manner in which he had recaptured the ship, at which we cannot wonder, though he speedily dissipated all doubt, by showing them his five prisoners. On casting anchor he sent ashore for help, and also dispatched a man to post to Exeter with a letter to the owners of the " Friend's Adventure," detailing how he had saved their property, but they gave the messenger only "a French half-crown and a shilling" for carrying the news a distance of eleven miles; for, he significantly adds, "they did not much regard the news, having insured £560 upon the ship, and a man since appraised her but at £170."

This circumstance shows how little the inferior class of shipowners are changed, now-a-days, from what their predecessors were 200 years ago. Those who take an interest in shipping matters know how, in this latter half of this enlightened century, the owners of our colliers and traders send to sea, to face the storms of winter, miserable unseaworthy vessels insured to their full value, so that it is a subject of indifference to them whether they sink or swim, though the alternative is a matter of life and death to their gallant crews; thus it happens that every year scores of women are made widows and children fatherless through the greed for extra profits of the proprietors, who trade upon the well-known recklessness of our maritime population.*

At five o'clock in the afternoon, the ship was brought to an anchor at Staircross, and crowds of people came on board. The gallant seaman sent the prisoners ashore to Topsham, and an hour later he followed, and proceeded thither, when he says—

"I found my prisoners with a doctor dressing their wounds. Upon searching he concluded two of them could not live a week. But as soon as I came in, those that were clear of the doctor put off their hats, and kist my hands, and shew'd a great deal of love to me outwardly. After I had seen them drest and good lodging provided for them, I went home to refresh myself with sleep; and the next day I marcht my prisoners to Exeter, and carried them to one of the owners' houses, and afterwards delivered them to the Mayor."

Lyde then details the shabbly manner in which

---

* This was written before the publication of the now famous "Appeal" of Mr. Plimsoll, M.P., which has roused the attention of the British public to a subject of such momentous interest to our mercantile marine.

he was treated by the owners of the cargo, who lived in London. He weighed anchor on the 5th of April, on his way to London, but was driven back by head-winds, and returned to Topsham on the 7th, luckily for his own safety and that of his ship, for he had not been "three hours at an anchor before there came two French privateers, from the eastward, with English colours, supposed to be King James's priva-teers, because they were for the most part man'd with Irishmen; and they went along about a league from the Bar, and went into Torbay, and took and carried away with them two English ships, which came from Oporto; and my owners hearing thereof, and that I was in safety, were very angry with me, and hurt at me, because I did not stay to be a prey to the enemy."

On the 19th April he weighed again, " with the wind west-south-west a topsail gale," and on the 26th arrived in London. "And (he continues) when I came ashore to the fraighters, they had 115 pipes of wine on board, they not so much as bid me wel-come, but bid me go to the Custom-house and enter the cargo, for they said they would unlaid the ship forthwith. Then I asked them for money to pay the men that helpt to bring the ship to London; but they denied to give me any. There was, besides the merchant's wine, two pipes of the master's, (that was in all 117 pipes), eight tuns of shumack and cork, which paid the King in duties £1,000. Then I asked the merchants again for money to pay the men (who belonged to men-of-war), which they again refused to pay."

The brave seaman who had saved all the cargo could not induce the "fraighters" to return to him an equal quantity of wine to that which the privateersman had carried away, and as he had served out to his prisoners all of his own that remained, the poor man was a loser of all his venture, while, the Frenchman having taken only one pipe of the merchants' wine, they had escaped almost all loss. To his remonstrances the only reply he could get was, "Tush! all the reason is, your's is carried away, and mine is left; and if mine had been carried away, and your's left, I could not have helped it." Thus he would have lost everything, for he says, "I have more adventure money to pay than my wages will come to."

In this strait, he met a gentleman, who took up his case, and, "entred an action in the High Court of Admiralty for £1,000 upon ship and cargo, and by the assistance of an honourable person, I brought it to a trial, and overthrew the owners and fraighters

for half the ship and cargo; but they appeal'd to
the High Court of Chancery, and, having nothing of
truth, disgrac'd me; withall they informed the Lords
Commissioners that I took a bag of money out of
the ship belonging to the owners, which the master
told me he deliver'd to the lieutenant of the privateer.
But I having no proof against the same, this did
me a great unkindness. Yet I overthrew them there
for the moiety of the ship and cargo, and had a
decree for the same, which decree is enrolled, and so
is become a precedent in that court, which will be
an advantage to anyone that shall hereafter retake
their ship from the enemy: if they sue them in
Chancery or the High Court of Admiralty for
salvage, they will be allowed as much as if it were
taken by a privateer."

But though the unfortunate seaman consoled
himself with the reflection that his Chancery suits
were productive of public good, in that they created
precedents guiding the courts in awarding salvage to
gallant fellows like himself, he had nothing more
substantial to show for all the dangers and hardships
he had undergone. He tells how the implacable
freighters pursued him with a false charge—that he
had run into and sunk a ship moored in the Thames,
while beating up the river. He was arrested on the

19th June, and though he managed to find bail, contrary to their expectations, was obliged to remain on shore till Michaelmas term following. He gained the case by the evidence of five witnesses; but he pathetically adds—" And so I ended my law and the greatest part of my money together."

However, he gained the support of a powerful Court noble; and the Marquis of Carmarthen recommending his case to the Queen, "Her Majesty was pleased, as a token of her extraordinary favour, to order me a gold medal and chain, and recommended me to the Right Honourable the Lords of the Admiralty for preferment in the Fleet, which I am now attending the Honourable Board for."

In concluding his book, he says : "Thus I have endeavoured to give an impartial account of the whole matter of fact, from first to last, ascribing all my success therein to the Omnipotent Power of the great God, who was with me, and protected me throughout the whole action, and made me capable of performing this piece of service for my King and country, in whose defence I am still willing to serve, and shall as long as I remain to be—R. L."

With all his readiness to cut throats, our hero professed great piety, and had ever the name of his Maker on his lips, displaying the spirit of the

Israelites in their dealings with the Philistines, whom they smote hip and thigh. This constant recourse to prayer, and "reading two or three chapters of the Bible" to the boy, before imbruing his hands in the blood of his enemies, rather detracts than otherwise from our favourable estimate of the gallant seaman. It was with some misgiving we laid before the reader the somewhat revolting details of the manner in which he slaughtered his enemies, with the same breath exulting over the ghastly wounds he inflicted with the "crow," and praising God, who "strengthened his right arm." However, if he prayed at all times as earnestly as during the dreadful moments when he was contending single-handed with so many foes, he would have made a fervent member of the "Church Militant. Such a minister would have compared the "marlin speck" which delivered his enemies into his hand to the "sword of the Lord and of Gideon."

Remarkable as was the feat performed by this Englishman, it was not unique, for in the "Advertisement," or what we should call the preface, to his book, he mentions that a man and boy of another ship, "called the 'Trial,' of 50 tuns," fell upon the the prize-crew of five Frenchmen, "and overcame them, and brought their ship into Falmouth, for which the master was immediately made commander of the 'Mary' galley*; and I, that had used the sea thirteen years, did but desire the command of a fire-ship."

No wonder, with these examples before them, our seamen held their neighbours across the Channel in contempt, and considered themselves individually equal to three Frenchmen !

* Galley, a sort of gunboat, propelled by oars.

CHAPTER X

THE captain of the mast told a yarn which time has not effaced from my memory. Hastings was one of those smart, handsome fellows, of whom during my service afloat I have come across not a few, and went by the name of the "lady-killer." He was not only exceedingly good-looking, but was well-mannered and well-spoken, and indeed whatever his birth may have been, was, in appearance at least, one of Nature's gentlemen. The rules of the service, which require men to be scrupulously clean in person and attire, were so far from being irksome to him, that "blow high or blow low," Phil Hastings always looked fresh and clean, and was pointed out to the slovens by the officers as an example for their imitation. No matter whether it was the middle watch at night, or a sudden turn-out during his watch below to reef topsails in a heavy breeze, his fine, dark, curly hair was always clustering in smooth ringlets about his frank, handsome face, while his well-knit, graceful figure looked well in any rig. Like many salts of the old Benbow school, he wore earrings, which had been given him—so the story went—by the daughter of an admiral whose life he once saved when she fell overboard from the quarter-gallery of her father's flag-ship. It was also said, and I believe with truth, that the young lady fell desperately in love with him, upon perceiving which the admiral removed him to another ship. They had been thrown together a great deal, for Hastings, being rated coxswain of the admiral's barge, used to attend upon them when they went ashore, and carried articles for the admiral or his daughter, or conveyed messages to the captain from the admiral's residence on shore. The attachment, of course, ended un-happily, as far as the young girl was concerned, and the gallant old admiral made a great mistake when he concluded he could cure his daughter, whom he loved tenderly, of her unhappy attachment by banish-ing its object. This course had the contrary effect, and in her case " absence made the heart grow fonder." She pined, fell into a state of melancholy, and died within six months. There was always a romantic story current in the fleet that at her earnest request, Hastings was permitted to pay her a last visit as she lay dying, and that the scene was most distressing. He never alluded to it, or any of the circumstances attending the love affair, and by his reticence showed himself a true gentleman, for the admiral never did anything for him after his daughter's death. These circumstances occurred a short time before the " Melpomene " was commissioned, and Hastings, who for a long time was grave and abstracted in his demeanour, only gradually recovered his habitual gaiety of manner. Towards the latter part of the commission, he had, however, quite regained his spirits, and was now one of the wildest, most rollicking fellows on board.

Talking about Phil Hastings' earrings reminds me of a good story about Sir Samuel Hood, which is mentioned by Captain Basil Hall, in his " Fragments of Voyages and Travels." Sir Samuel Hood was a stern disciplinarian, and hated everything that appeared to him foreign or effeminate, but he was loved and respected by every man in the fleet as a true and gallant seaman. The two brothers, Lords Hood and Bridport, were worthy of each other, and the noble service whose annals they enriched by their brilliant achievements.

" I remember," said Captain Hall, " once witnessing on the beach of Madras, an amusing scene between Sir Samuel Hood, then Commander-in-chief in India, and the newly-promoted boatswain of a sloop-of-war belonging to the squadron. The admiral, who was one of the bravest, and kindest and truest-hearted seamen that ever trod a ship's deck, was a sworn foe to all trickery in dress-work. The eye of the veteran officer was directed earnestly towards the yeast of waves, which, in immense double rows of surf, fringe and guard the whole of that flat coast. He was watching the progress of a mussullah boat, alternately lost in the foam, and raised in very uncertain balance across the swell, which though just on the break, brought her swiftly towards the shore. He felt more anxious than usual about the fate of this particular boat, from having ordered on board the person alluded to, with whom he wished to have some conversation previous to their parting company. This boatswain was a young man, who had been for some years a follower of the admiral in different ships, and to whom he had just given a warrant. The poor fellow, unexpectedly promoted from before the mast to the rank of an officer, was rigged up in his newly-bought, but marvellously ill-cut uniform, shining like a dollar, and making its wearer, who for the first time in his life put on a long coat, feel not a little awkward.

" As soon as the boat was partly driven up the

beach by the surf, and partly dragged beyond the
dash of the breakers by the crowd on shore, this
happiest of warrant officers leaped out on the sand,
and seeing the admiral standing on the crest of the
natural glacis which lined the shore, he took off his
hat, smoothed down the hair on his forehead, sailor
fashion, and stood uncovered, in spite of the roasting
sun flaming in the zenith.

" The admiral, of course, made a motion with
his hand for the boatswain to put his hat on; but
the other, not perceiving the motion, stood stock
still.

" ' I say, put on your hat,' called the commander-
in-chief, in a tone which made the newly-created
warrant officer start. In his agitation he shook a
bunch of well-trimmed ringlets a little on one side,
and betrayed to the flashing eyes of the admiral a
pair of small, round, silver earrings, the parting gift,
doubtless, of some favoured and favouring Poll or
Bess of dear, old, blackguard Point Beach, the very
ninth heaven of all light-hearted sailors.

" Be this as it may, the admiral, first stepping on
one side, and then holding his head forward, as if to
re-establish the doubting evidence of his horrified
senses, and forcibly keeping down the astonished
seaman's hat with his hand, roared out—

" ' Who the devil are you ?.'

" ' John Marline, sir,' replied the bewildered boat-wain, beginning to suspect the scrape he had got himself into.

" ' Oh ! ' cried the flag-officer, with a scornful laugh ? ' oh ! I beg your pardon ; I took you for a Portuguese.'

" ' No,' instinctively faltered out the other, seeing the admiral expected some reply.

" ' No. Then if you are not a foreigner, why do you hoist false colours? What business has an English sailor with these machines in his ears ?'

" ' I don't know, sir,' said Poor Marline ; ' I put them in only this morning when I rigged myself in my new togs, to answer the signal on shore.'

" ' Then,' said Sir Samuel, softened by the contrite look of his old shipmate, and having got rid of the greater portion of his bile by the first explosion, ' you will now proceed to unrig yourself of this top hamper as fast as you can ; pitch them into the surf, if you like, but never, as you respect the warrant in your pocket, let me see you in that disguise again.' "

Well, to my story.

Hastings told the following veracious narrative of the capture of some pirates, in which he was engaged a few years before.

"His Majesty's sloop 'Zebra,' on board of which I was an A. B., happened in May, 17—, to visit Port Antonio in Prince's Island, on the west coast of Africa, a place seldom resorted to by British men-of-war, and Captain Howson learnt from a merchant residing there, that in the local paper of Salem, a port on the American seaboard, there had appeared an account of the seizure and plunder at sea, by a piratical schooner, of a brig named the 'Briton,' hailing from that port. Some particulars of the transaction were given, and also a tolerably minute description of the schooner, which agreed with that of a Spanish vessel named the 'Castille,' which had sailed from Port Antonio only a few days before for Africa. On our arrival these particulars were communicated to Captain Howson, whó hearing that the 'Castille' was supposed to be lying in the river Nazareth, immediately proceeded in search of her.

"The account of the capture of the 'Briton,' as stated in the Salem paper, was briefly as follows :—At daylight on the 20th September previous, the watch on deck discovered about a mile off, and standing across the brig's bow, a low-lying, rakish-looking schooner. At first she appeared to be standing from the 'Briton' on her weather quarter, but she soon

17

tacked, and was observed to be in chase of her. The captain of the latter resolved to make all sail away from the unwelcome stranger, which was accordingly done, but without avail, as it was soon found that the schooner gained fast on them, and was already within gunshot. Another interval passed, when the signal of a round shot that nearly struck the mainmast, warned them of the futility of attempting to escape. The brig accordingly threw her maintopsail aback, and awaited the approach of her pursuer.

" ' Where are you from? ' hailed a voice from the schooner's forecastle, as she ranged up to within pistol-shot of the brig's stern.

" ' From Salem,' was the captain's reply, while he and his crew anticipated no gentle treatment from the ill-looking fellows in red caps crowded about the speaker, who had a foreign accent.

" ' Where are you bound to ? and what is your cargo ? ' These questions were concluded with the order, ' Bring your boat on board,' on which the schooner sheered off, and took up a commanding position on the brig's weather beam. The captain at first demurred, excusing himself on the ground that the boat was leaky, but a second and more peremptory summons caused him to overcome his scruples, and he proceeded on board with a crew of four men. The captain steered for the gangway, but on his approach was ordered to the forechains; and no sooner had he reached them than five ruffianly fellows, armed with long Spanish knives, sprang into her, and ordered him to steer for the brig.

"On reaching the 'Briton,' the pirates, drawing their knives, ordered the captain to deliver up any money he had on board, on pain of instant death. Seeing that a refusal would result fatally for him, the captain directed the mate to bring up all the money from the cabin. The pirates finding that the work was not progressing as fast as they wished, used threats towards the captain, and at length all the boxes, containing some twenty thousand dollars, were gradually brought up on deck, and immediately transferred to a boat from the schooner, whither it was taken. The pirates now began to rob the mate and crew of the brig, whom they threatened with death unless more booty was given up to them. Fearful of a sail heaving in sight, they hurried about ransacking every place, and smashing open boxes and lockers in the search for more money or articles of value. Finding themselves disappointed, the pirates took possession of coils of rope, leather, and almost everything they could lay their hands on; having thrust the mate into the cabin with the captain, they went on board the schooner to consult on further measures. Soon they returned, with hatchets in their hands, and having closed the fore-scuttle and after-hatchway, commenced hacking every article in the most wantonly mischievous manner conceivable. The compasses were broken, the rigging, tiller-ropes, braces, and running and standing gear cut to pieces; spars, and other neces-sary things were thrown overboard, and to complete their atrocious designs, they set fire to a quantity of tarred rope yarn in the caboose. Then taking the brig's colours and scuttling her only boat, they proceeded to their ship; hoisting the launch, she made sail and left her victims to their fate.

"Fortunately, in their hurry, a ship having hove in sight, they had neglected to secure the cabin sky-light, and the mate creeping through was just in time to prevent the fire spreading, and causing the destruction of the brig and all on board. By his exertions and those of the crew, whom he speedily released, the flames were extinguished, and they managed to bring the 'Briton' in safety into Salem.

"While the schooner was at Prince's Island, after visiting the African coast, a vessel came from Salem with the news of the outrage committed on the brig, and suspicion which was immediately directed to her was increased by the lavish manner in which the crew were spending their dollars. However, she put to sea, and no one knew whither she had gone.

"Soon after her departure the 'Zebra' accidentally arrived, and Captain Howson, hearing of the outrage committed on the brig 'Briton,' made inquiries about the schooner. He learned that a vessel answering the description of the pirate had sailed from Havana on the 20th of August. No one knew there anything of her purpose and intended course, for she had evaded the last visit of the Spanish authorities, although she bore their flag. It was known she had a crew of thirty-one men, and carried a cargo of goods for the African coast. After gaining all the information he could regarding her, Captain Howson followed her, as we have said, to her suspected hiding-place, the river Nazareth.

"On the 4th of June, the 'Zebra' arrived off the mouth of this river, and immediately her three boats, manned and armed with forty men, of whom I was one, under the immediate command of the captain, proceeded in quest of the pirates. After pulling all night, the boats got sight of the object of their pursuit lying at anchor, and in order to effect her capture they kept in shore, and only displayed their colours when close to her. Immediately they were seen by the pirates in the schooner, the latter took to their boats, and hurried ashore, with the exception of one man, who was seen to follow soon after in a canoe. Captain Howson made straight for the boats, but they were too far ahead of him, and he soon altered his course for the schooner. Smoke was seen issuing from her, and on our fellows getting on board, she was found to be on fire near the magazine, in which, below the cabin floor, were sixteen casks of powder. A train had been laid from the caboose which in a few minutes would have communicated with the magazine, when the schooner and all on board would have been blown up. This, then, was what the last individual, who quitted the vessel in the canoe, was busy about, but he had his trouble for nothing, for our captain anticipated the nature of the warm reception kindly intended for him.

"By our exertions the fire was extinguished; search was then made for her papers, but without success, nor could any valuable property be discovered. A few private letters were, however, found with the signature of the captain, Pedro Gibert, and addressed to the boatswain and carpenter of the 'Castille,' so that we knew that this was the same schooner that had sailed from Havana and Prince's Island. There was one important document found on board, and that was a letter of instructions (without signature) for Pedro Gibert. These instructions were most craftily worded, and, without referring specifically to the nature of the cargo she was to bring over from the African coast, it was made manifest she was engaged in the African slave trade, and the captain had further a general licence to pick up any 'unconsidered trifles,' such as peaceful traders on the high seas, on which he might cast an envious eye. A quantity of foreign national flags were found on board, to be employed, doubtless, to disguise herself, and avoid the right of search, which might carry with it unpleasant consequences. Captain Howson determined to get possession of Pedro Gibert and his crew, and was successful in securing five of the crew who had joined her at Prince's Island, but whom he decided to retain as prisoners. The 'Castille' was then removed to the mouth of the river, where the 'Zebra' had been left.

"Captain Howson used every endeavour to induce the native chief of the district to deliver over to him the commander and crew of the pirate, but in vain. At length he proceeded in the 'Castille' up

the river, and, anchoring off the chief's town, proceeded on shore, and explained to him that, unless
his demands were complied with, he would destroy
the place.   The native potentate still continuing obdurate, Captain Howson opened fire; but almost
after the first shot a serious accident occurred,
putting an end for a time to further operations.
A spark from a 12-pounder gun ignited some loose
powder lying on the deck, and communicating with
the magazine, the after part of the ' Castille ' was
blown to pieces.   Two officers and three men were
killed, and the captain was blown overboard, but
happily without being much injured.   I was in one
of the boats at the time, and so escaped.   The
' Castille ' went down soon after, and the expedition
having returned to the ' Zebra,' she proceeded on the
20th of June to the Gaboon, in quest of the second
mate of the pirate, from whom the captain wished to
get some information.   On arriving there, he was
again foiled, for it was found that this man had left
for Havana.   We then sailed for Port Antonio, in
Prince's Island, where we accidentally learned that
two Spaniards who had quitted the ' Castille ' when
she was there, were at Whidah.   Our indefatigable
captain, with the determination to succeed so characteristic of him and the service to which he belonged,

proceeded first to Cape Coast Castle to pick up a prize crew of our men, and to meet a brig-of-war he hoped to find there. He was, however, disappointed in both his expectations, and set sail for Whidah, after leaving on shore an officer and one of the five prisoners of the ' Castille's ' crew, in order that they might recognize any of their late shipmates should they turn up. Arrived at Whidah, the captain learned that one of the two men after whom he had come, had gone to Bahia, and the other, on the appearance of the ' Zebra,' had given himself up to the King of Dahomey as a slave. The ' Zebra,' after cruising about for a few days, sailed for Fernando Po, arriving there on the 15th of August. Here Captain Howson was seized with fever, the result of disappointment, and of the exposure to the sun he had undergone in boarding suspicious vessels, and prosecuting his search for the crew of the pirate. But an accident once more put him on the right trail, and he had the satisfaction of successfully completing the task he had undertaken. Captain B——, one of the officers of the establishment at Fernando Po, happened to be at Bimbia, at the mouth of the Cameroons River, where he met five Spaniards, who requested him to give them a passage to the Old Calabar River. Captain B—— informed them he

could not do so, as he was going to Fernando Po,
but offered to take them there with him, and then
they could find their way to Calabar. They accordingly proceeded to Fernando Po, and were about to
sail for Calabar, when Captain B—— received from
his agent at Bimbia a quantity of Spanish dollars,
with information that they had been picked up at
low-water mark, and were supposed to have been
lost from the canoe in which the Spaniards had
arrived there. Captain B—— immediately came to
the conclusion that these dollars had been plundered
from some vessel, and had been thrown away to
escape detection, and detained the men. We were
at Fernando Po, and on the matter coming to the
ears of Captain Howson, who had now recovered
from his illness, he had them confronted with the
prisoners he had taken at the Nazareth River. This
was no sooner done than they were recognized as
part of the crew of the late pirate schooner. One of
them was admitted as king's evidence, and his statement of the piracies committed by the 'Castille'
appears in an old number of the 'Nautical Magazine.' Regarding the movements of himself and his
shipmates after the capture of the 'Castille' at
Nazareth River, he says he ran away into the bush,
and when the schooner returned all the remainder of

the crew fled except the captain, who was secreted by the native chief, or king.

"Four days after the 'Zebra' sailed, the schooner 'Esperanza' arrived, and some of his shipmates went on board of her. He and five men got a canoe, and having secured their share of the plunder from the captain, they first went to the Cameroons River, and then to Bimbia, where they heard an English schooner was lying. To prevent suspicion, they threw away most of the dollars in their possession, retaining only a few. The singular circumstance of the finding of these dollars at low-water led to suspicions which resulted in their conviction, owing to the 'Zebra' being at the time in Fernando Po with some of their shipmates. One of the six men still remained at Bimbia, but a vessel was despatched for him, and he was brought to Fernando Po. All the piratical crew in the hands of Captain Howson were committed under separate warrants, to await a favourable opportunity for despatch to England. But our captain could not rest satisfied until he had secured the commander of the 'Castille,' and as the cruisers on the station were scattered about, so that he could not do much by force, he had recourse to a stratagem to effect his purpose.

"The captain of a British barque at Fernando

Po having offered the gratuitous use of his vessel, it was resolved, after a consultation, that she should proceed to the river Nazareth as on a trading voyage, and that an officer and twelve of the ' Zebra's ' men should reinforce her crew.   Mr. Adams, mate, commanded the party, of which I was one.   Having got his instructions, Mr. Adams sailed on his hazardous mission, and no better officer could have been selected, for he was not only bold and dashing, but had a good head on his shoulders wherewith to encounter the cunning crew with whom he had to deal.   It was arranged that the ' Zebra,' which was to be disguised, was to follow, and that their rendezvous should be Cape Lopez, about thirty miles west of the Nazareth.   Acting in the capacity of a trader, Mr. Adams was to entice the king and his principal men on board the barque, and then seize them until the arrival of the ' Zebra.'   On his arrival at Cape Lopez on the 24th of September, the young officer addressed a communication to Captain Howson, requesting him not to risk any lives in the attempt to rescue or avenge him should he fall, and then proceeded to the Nazareth.   Arrived here, he landed alone in disguise, and the first person he encountered was the captain of the pirate.   Pedro Gibert saluted Mr. Adams, who, not knowing that he had his anticipated prey within his grasp, merely returned his salute, and passed on to the house of the native chief. Don Pedro's suspicions were excited by the appearance of the officer, who he thought looked too much of a gentleman to be a common trader, and he avowed his opinions to his sable majesty. But the latter thought only of the unlimited supply of rum he hoped to get drunk upon, with muskets and powder to triumph over his enemies, and he eagerly closed with the offer of the supposed trader, and permitted his son and some of his principal officers to return with Mr. Adams to the barque. On their arrival on board, they were regaled sumptuously, and permitted to indulge in such copious libations of their favourite ardent spirit, that they were soon all under the cabin table.

" In the meantime, the 'Zebra,' on her way to join the barque at Cape Lopez, as agreed upon, touched at St. Thomas's Island, and the Portuguese prisoner retained on board her recognized a man he accidentally saw as one of the 'Castille's' crew. A merchant also stated confidently that four more of the pirate's men were on the island, and that a Portuguese vessel, the 'Esperanza,' then lying in the harbour, had brought them from Cape Lopez. The

Portuguese governor of the island, which was a possession of the crown of Portugal, indignantly denied
this assertion, stating that no one could land on the
island without his permission, and, further, that the
' Esperanza ' had not come from Cape Lopez. · This
statement was also made to the officer who searched
that vessel; but Captain Howson knew sufficient of
the duplicity of the Portuguese authorities, and their
notorious complicity in the then legal traffic of slaves,
to doubt the word of his Excellency. As, however,
he had to join the barque at the rendezvous at Cape
Lopez, he considered it best not to excite the suspicion of the governor, but requested him to institute
a strict search for these four men.

"On the arrival of the ' Zebra ' at midnight at
Cape Lopez, Mr. Adams immediately proceeded on
board, and reported his success in having secured
the persons of the prince and others. After their
meeting, Captain Howson stood out to sea again,
having agreed to enter the river in company with the
barque on the following day. Accordingly, the next
afternoon, both vessels ran into the river under easy
sail with Portuguese colours, and came to an anchor.
The ' Zebra ' was so well disguised that the natives,
taking her for a slaving vessel, flocked on board,
though immediately on their arrival their minds were

undeceived by the long line of guns. Escape was, however, now impossible, and they were made prisoners. The king had been leading the way for the vessel in his canoe, when suddenly the thought came into his head that all was not right. Turning his canoe towards the shore, he made his escape, and, so far as he was concerned, Captain Howson's plans were frustrated. The sudden flight of the king opened the eyes of the young prince, who soon found that he and all his boon companions were prisoners. The greatest consternation reigned on board the barque, where all before had been jollity and mirth, and the native chiefs expected instant death.

" Having thus secured substantial hostages, Captain Howson now threw off all disguise, and demanded the captain and the remainder of the crew of the ' Castille ' in exchange for his prisoners. Much delay and lengthened negociation took place, but at length terms were agreed upon, and on the following morning Captain Howson proceeded ashore with an armed boat's crew, and received Don Pedro Gibert, the commander of the late pirate. Soon afterwards three of the crew were sent on board the ' Zebra,' upon which Captain Howson released the hostages; and now, amid manifestations of popular rejoicing and the expression of the king's best wishes, the two ships got under way, and sailed for St. Thomas to look after the remainder of the crew. He had learnt at the Nazareth river that the 'Esperanza' had really conveyed away the mate, carpenter, and other men belonging to the 'Castille,' with the sum of two thousand dollars to buy a new vessel at St. Thomas; but, notwithstanding, on his arrival at this island, the governor had the effrontery to re-iterate his previous denials. After a fortnight's delay, the merchant who had informed him of their being concealed on the island secretly gave informa-tion that the 'Esperanza,' which had sailed during the 'Zebra's' absence, had arrived on the previous evening at another part of the island, that she was hovering off the shore to receive the four Spaniards in question, and that they had started for the nearest point of embarkation. Captain Howson thereupon immediately sent the boats of the 'Zebra,' manned and armed, to seize the 'Esperanza,' and, after a long and tedious pull, this was done; but unfortunately, on search being made, it was found that the pirates had not arrived on board. At length the patience and pertinacity of the captain of the man-of-war wore out the governor, who, to rid himself of the presence of the obnoxious foreigner, sent word that he had heard some Spaniards were concealed in a distant part of the island, and he had given directions that they should be taken into custody. On the following day they were examined, and it was found that they were the men of whom Captain Howson had been in search; they were accordingly sent on board the 'Zebra,' and joined their companions in guilt.

"The British man-of-war, accompanied by the 'Esperanza,' now sailed for England, where she arrived in June, exactly eleven months after the seizure of the 'Castille.' The crew of the latter were sent to Salem, and arrived, curiously enough, just as the brig 'Briton,' with her old captain, mate, and cook on board, were going to sea. These men confronted and recognized the gang as the miscreants who, exactly two years before, had plundered and half-burnt the 'Briton.' The chain of evidence was complete, and, after a long trial, six of them were condemned to death. Of these, five were executed, and the sixth, the mate, was reprieved, owing to his having some few years before, when in command of a brig, gallantly rescued from a foundering ship no less than seventy-four souls, the crew and passengers. Such pertinacity, judgment, and ability as was displayed by Captain Howson is happily not rare in the annals of the noble service to which he belonged, and it is gratifying to record that both he and Mr. Adams were promoted by the Admiralty."

The officers of the Navy regard as only inferior to the sacred duty of defending the honour and interests of their country, assuaging the evils to which nautical suffering humanity is exposed by the brutalities of the slaver and the pirate. To exterminate these pests, whenever and wherever encountered, is an obligation which our gallant seamen carry out with the single-minded devotion for which the race is famous :—

> " Ye heroes of ocean ! whose blood and whose breath
> Are cheerfully spent in the battle of death,
> Go forth at humanity's noblest call,
> For the pirate—the tyrant—the despot must fall."

To return to the doings of the " Melpomene " and her crew, from which we have so long been detained by the relation of these episodes in the lives of some of them.

CHAPTER XI.

THE "Melpomene" experienced favourable winds, and running to the northward was soon in the latitude of Brest, and about to enter the Channel. Duckworth was still under close, and his accomplices under open, arrest, and officers and men were speculating with singular anxiety upon what would be the result of the trial that would now in all likelihood come off in the course of a few days, though there was only one opinion as to the certainty of capital punishment being awarded, when a circumstance occurred that altered the whole course of events. Never was the truth of the maxim, "Man proposes but God disposes," more signally verified.

One morning the pipe went for all hands to "scrub and wash clothes." It was to be the last time before reaching Plymouth Sound, in which every one counted upon anchoring within fifty hours. The crew were busy making preparations for the final clean up; the hammocks and blankets, as well as body linen, were to be thoroughly well scoured that day, so that the old frigate might look as clean as a new pin, as well as all hands aboard her. Suddenly the look-out man hailed the deck with the announcement of a sail having hove in sight in the direction of the island of Ushant, near the French coast. She appeared to have just come out of Brest and steered for us direct, crowding all sail. The captain of the " Melpomene," on his part nothing loth to try conclusions, even now, provided the disparity of force was not too great, stood in under easy sail, and awaited the approach of the stranger. Within an hour's time she was near enough for us to make her out to be a 60-gun frigate, nearly double our size, and seemingly fresh from port. The private signals to test whether she was an English man-o'-war, or one hailing from a friendly power, not being answered, her nationality stood confessed. At eleven o'clock we hauled up, bringing the wind on our starboard quarter, took in studding sails, and prepared for action. The enemy's ship still continued standing towards us, and about twelve, when some four miles distant, hoisted her private signal, and finding it unanswered, set her mainsail and royals, which she had previously taken in,

The " Melpomene " made sail in a parallel

direction, and soon afterwards Captain Gaisford
hoisted his colours, and having shortened sail to
topgallant sails, jib, and spanker, stood towards the
stranger, then bearing about three points on our lee
bow, who on her part also hoisted French colours,
and putting herself under the same sail, luffed up to
the wind. At ten minutes past two, when the
"Melpomene" had approached the enemy,—who
was seen to be a most formidable opponent, being
both considerably larger, and carrying a heavier
battery than the British frigate—the distance being
then about half a mile,—she opened a fire from her
larboard guns, which were so well aimed at this long
range, that the round shot splashed the water against
the "Melpomene's" starboard quarter. At this
time, when our officers and men were at their
quarters, with the exception of James Duckworth
and the two seconds, the former characteristically
wrote a few lines to the captain, and implored him,
as the last favour he would ever ask, to be permitted
to repair to his station and take part in the
approaching conflict, at the conclusion of which he
would return to his cabin as prisoner. Captain
Gaisford, chivalrous as he was, could not refuse such
a request, coming from a man whose life he considered was as good as forfeited, and sending for the

young officer, shook him warmly by the hand, without saying a word, for his heart was too full to speak, and motioned him to repair to his post.

Not being so close as he could wish, the captain of the " Melpomene " stood on until within pistol-shot on the Frenchman's weather or port bow; then having received a second broadside which passed over her—inasmuch as the guns were elevated too much as before they had been too little—fired a broadside in return; almost every shot of this, we subsequently learned, took effect. The Frenchman had his wheel shot away, besides receiving other damage, and lost six men killed and ten wounded by this discharge alone. The enemy, doubtless dreading a repetition of this warm salute, having fired her third broadside without much effect, wore ship in the smoke to get farther to leeward, so as to work her guns at long bowls. On our part, the captain, as soon as he discovered that his wary antagonist was running before the wind, made sail after her, and at twenty-five minutes past two the enemy, and then ourselves, having come round on the starboard tack, the two frigates exchanged broadsides. Again the Frenchman wore to get away. The " Melpomene " wore also, and passing slowly under the former's stern, prepared to rake her. At this time the vastly superior size of the hostile ship became apparent as she towered over our taffrail. By some means the fire we poured in at this critical moment of the action was not so effective as it might have been, and no very considerable damage was done. After raking her, the " Melpomene" stood on, and by this means the enemy secured the weather gauge. This did not, however, suit her long-shot tactics, and she therefore made sail on the port tack, the wind being free, followed by the British frigate, which, luffing up, crossed the Frenchman's stern again, and let her have her starboard broadside once more. At a quarter to three, the enemy, probably ashamed of the tactics she had hitherto adopted of shunning a close en-counter with a ship so much her inferior in size and weight of metal, as she had discovered us to be by the effect of our repeated broadsides, seemed deter-mined to change her plan of action, and close with us. We had stood on in chase, but the enemy now shortened sail, and for a few minutes engaged at close quarters. Again, however, she repeated her favourite manœuvre, and wearing in the smoke was not perceived until nearly round on the starboard tack.

We would have followed suit, but having had our jib-boom and the head of the bowsprit shot away,

must have experienced some difficulty in wearing
ship with the requisite alacrity, so the " Melpomene"
hove in stays, hoping to do so in time to avoid being
raked, but from the same cause that had brought
her so readily to the wind, the loss of her head sails,
she paid off very slowly.   The French frigate luffing
up, poured in a heavy and destructive fire, though at
the distance of five hundred yards, a range at which
our guns, being of so much lighter calibre, were
comparatively harmless.   As the " Melpomene " fell
off the wind, she returned the fire with her larboard
guns.   Immediately on receiving our broadside the
enemy wore round on the port tack; we followed
suit, and then as quickly as he could the Honourable
Captain Gaisford ranged up alongside his powerful
adversary.   It was a desperate venture, but then it
was a choice of evils; whether to be knocked "into
a cocked hat" at long bowls, or engage within half-
pistol shot, and if he could not force his huge
antagonist to fly, at least to fight out to the bitter
end the unequal battle.   I was filled with the sin-
cerest feelings of admiration and pity for our noble
captain and his gallant crew.   They were now only
combating for barren honour, for unless some un-
foreseen accident occurred, or the advent of a friendly
sail, it was absolutely impossible that they could

escape capture, while it was melancholy indeed that after four years' meritorious service in America and India, in which countries they had so well upheld the ancient renown of their noble service—it was hard indeed that after all this they should have to succumb to superior force, and, when in sight of their native land, be captured and borne off to experience the horrors of a French prison. It was hard, but I saw it was well nigh irremediable.

The French frigate having reduced the "Melpomene" almost to a wreck, had her completely at her mercy, and being enabled to engage at whatever point she liked best, came up abreast of her at three o'clock within pistol-shot distance, and the battle raged more furiously than ever. The havoc wrought in a few minutes was so terrible that Captain Gaisford, who did not even now dream of surrender, determined to adopt the last resource at his disposal. Desperate though the expedient was, he resolved to board. At this time, besides the loss of her bowsprit and mizenmast, the fore and mainmasts had been badly wounded, and were tottering to their fall; it was desirable, therefore, that no time should be lost.

Calling his men together, to board with him the moment the ships touched, Captain Gaisford stood on the quarter-deck, sword in hand. He looked the

personification of the indomitable pluck and daring
for which the name of the British sailor, all the
world over, is a synonym. Pale he was, and his
teeth were clenched, and his lips pressed close to one
another, while his hand closed with a convulsive
clutch over his trusty weapon. I thought he seemed
like a martyr; for though, no doubt, it was an exaggerated sense of what was due to his country that
induced him to protract the hopeless conflict, yet
it was a noble error that thus sacrificed all in this
world, so that he might retain that will-o'-the-wisp
honour. It was equally grand and inspiriting to see
how every officer and man responded to the desperate
scheme of boarding an enemy superior in numbers
and filled with ardour at the imminent realization of
victory.

With alacrity they crowded round him, and when
at that moment, the ensign having been shot away,
he ordered another to be "seized" to the mizen
rigging, a dozen sprang forward to obey.

Foremost among them all was James Duckworth, who, with a boat's ensign in his hand,
jumped up the ratlines torn with shot, and spun-
yarn in hand, lashed the emblem of England's
glory to the mizen shrouds with all his old smartness.

He was amply rewarded when on his regaining the deck, his old commanding officer, forgetting all the recent unhappy business, shook him warmly by the hand, and in a choking voice said, "Well done, boy? I'll not forget you when all is over;" adding in loud and inspiriting tone to his men, "And now, lads, follow me."

The "Melpomene," which had bore up, would have laid the French frigate aboard at her larboard main chains, had not the foremast at that instant fallen, and by its weight and the direction of its fall crushed the forecastle, killing and maiming several men, and encumbering the principal part of the deck. But misfortune dogged the brave sailors to their ruin in spite of every effort. The remains of her bowsprit, now passing over the Frenchman's stern, caught in her starboard mizen rigging, and brought the ship up in the wind, whereby the opportunity to rake as well as to board was lost. All this time a terrible fire, not only from the enemy's guns, but from the small-arm men stationed in her tops and elsewhere, swept the deck, lessening the gallant band assembled together to board, and who formed so prominent a mark for the sharpshooters.

The master and second lieutenant had already been killed, and the captain was making his way to the scene of the wreck, when a musket-ball struck him in the right leg, shattering it below the knee. Hardly had he expressed to the seaman who lifted him up his intention to remain on deck, when another bullet passed through his temple. He had only time to exclaim, " My God ! " and sank back and died. Thus surrounded with every element of disaster and defeat, but with untarnished honour, departed the spirit of the gallant captain of His Majesty's ship " Melpomene."

But there was a foul deed done when this tragedy was consummated, and I, from my elevated post, was a silent witness to the fact that the unfortunate officer had not expired in fair fight, but had fallen by the treacherous hand of one of his own men. But one other eye saw this amid the turmoil and confusion of the battle. As James Duckworth headed a party of men who, directed by the captain, sought to remove the wreck from the guns, which could not be used while it lay across them, he happened to cast his eye on Mullins, who had left his gun, then disabled, and who, crouching on the forecastle, took a deliberate aim at Captain Gaisford, as he lay half supported in the arms of a couple of seamen. Duckworth's cheeks blanched with horror, but before he had time to interfere the pistol was discharged, with the fatal result I have already named.

"Now I'm avenged," whispered Mullins in a suppressed voice, for he thought no one had witnessed the foul deed. But he erred. Duckworth sprang forward to seize the assassin, when a mightier arm than his arrested the wretch, upon whom, at one and the same moment, a murderer's doom was pronounced and a murderer's doom inflicted. Hardly had the words of triumph passed his lips when a round-shot from the enemy struck Mullins full in the body, as he rose from his crouching attitude, and regularly disembowelled him. He fell over the forecastle a mangled and hideous corpse, amidst all that scene of slaughter the most terrible object to gaze upon.

The manœuvre of boarding having thus failed, the "Melpomene" was left a wreck at the mercy of her antagonist; but Jacob Higham, the first lieutenant, was a worthy successor of his honoured chief, and would not yet even strike his flag. The Frenchman, once again wearing across her antagonist's bows, raked her with a heavy fire, and shot away her maintopmast, which still further encumbered our guns. Running to leeward, past her unmanageable and now almost defenceless opponent, the enemy, at

a few minutes past three, luffed up and raked her
on the starboard quarter, then wore round on the
port tack, and, resuming her position, fired her port
broadside with most destructive effect. All this
time our brave fellows worked the maindeck guns
with bull-dog obstinacy; but the tactics adopted
by the French frigate of wearing at her leisure and
raking her adversary, wrought such fearful havoc,
that even Lieutenant Higham began to think it was
all useless bloodshed, and after receiving a tremendous discharge of round-shot, grape, and musketry,
and seeing that the enemy had taken up a judicious
position close athwart our bows, for the purpose of
sinking us at her leisure, he struck his flag at thirty-
five minutes past three, and surrendered the wreck he
had fought so nobly.

It was about time, for besides the loss of her
bowsprit and all the masts, as already mentioned,
except the mainmast, which was even now
tottering to its fall, six of her quarterdeck,
four of her forecastle, and several of her main-
deck, guns were disabled, all her boats had
been shot away, her hull shattered, and the ship
rendered a perfect wreck. Out of our crew, forty-
eight officers and men had been killed, and one
hundred and twenty-three wounded. Among the

former were the master, one mate, three midshipmen, and the boatswain; whilst the list of wounded included the first and fourth lieutenants, two midshipmen, and the gunner. But the saddest loss of all was the death of Captain Gaisford. James Duckworth said not a word to any one of the hand by whom this gallant officer fell, but he often secretly upbraided himself for not having warned the captain, and remembered the circumstance of the shot the latter received on his sword-hilt in Admiral Pocock's action. When Duckworth had been a boy before the mast, and Mullins' chum and messmate, the latter had often expressed a similar hatred of his commander, which seemed to point to an old grudge. He had sought to wean him from these bad thoughts, but all his efforts had been vain. Duckworth, therefore, had long since ceased to regard him as a friend, and they had been estranged from each other, a coolness which, moreover, the change in their relative positions—the one having become an officer and the other remaining before the mast—had tended to increase.

There was one little circumstance I should perhaps mention, as it may throw some light on the terrible deed. I had often noticed on Captain Gaisford's finger a handsome ring, containing a lock of hair and a tiny miniature, which opened by means of a spring, and which was the gift of his wife, a lady sprung of a noble family. When Mullins fell before me, his body rent with a 24-pound shot, there was found round his neck, and concealed beneath his clothes, a locket, and in this was a portrait bearing the initials "L. M.," surmounted by a coronet. It was at once apparent to the most careless observer that the portrait was a likeness of none other than the captain's wife· This singular fact escaped the eyes and vigilance of all except James Duckworth, who, with Lieutenant Higham's sanction, took possession of both the ring and locket, intending to forward the former to the widow of his friend, and retain the latter with the object of instituting inquiries when he regained his freedom. There was a strange mystery which puzzled me long, and I do not doubt that those of my readers who love mysteries will, like myself, give reins to their imagination in at· tempting to account for this singular circumstance, which there can be no manner of doubt was connected with the savage deed of murder that has so tragically closed the history of Captain Gaisford's commission of H.M.S. "Melpomene."

CHAPTER XII.

Soon after the flag of the "Melpomene" had been hauled down, or rather torn from the mizen rigging to which it was lashed, a boat from the French frigate came on board, and the officer in charge received the sword of the acting captain, Jacob Higham, and took over charge of the ship. Upon the French officer asking the late first lieutenant if he was captain, the latter, without replying—for this brave sailor, rough though he was, had a tender heart—pointed to the mangled, but still warm corpse of his old friend and superior, and with difficulty restrained the tears, though he was, like Othello, "not given to the melting mood." All the officers and men of the British frigate were transferred to the Frenchman, and a prize crew were put on board. It was with a feeling of indignation, unmixed with any gentler emotion, that the majority of the seamen took leave of the ship they had navigated for so many years through storm and sun-

19

shine, and in which they had fought so many glorious actions.

"By ——," said Tim Johnson, the old quartermaster, as he limped over the side into the cutter alongside, " I never thought it would come to this."

"But we'll live, most of us, I dare say, to fight another day, and then—look out for squalls," he added, glaring on the French boat's crew as if he had not had yet half a bellyfull of fighting, and would like to go throught it all again.

The officers took leave of the old frigate, that had been their home for four years, without breaking silence.   Most of them were filled with thoughts too bitter to find utterance in words, and, like brave men, they took their seats in the stern sheets of the capacious pinnace that was despatched to bring them off first, and were rowed in silence to their prison. The, captain of the " Richelieu," of 60 guns, was a man of aristocratic family, like most of the officers of the French navy of the days of the Louises, and he received his prisoners with the studied politeness and ease of a polished courtier. The officers were treated in every sense like gentlemen, and messed with those of their own rank, while they were placed each one on his *parole d'honneur*. The men were treated with much greater rigour, and upon Lieutenant Higham giving his word that no attempt should be made at recapture, the captain of the "Richelieu" replied that the ship would probably arrive at Brest the following day, so that the confinement would not be of sufficient length to render it irksome.

A good "topgallant breeze sprung up, and the "Richelieu," a fine new ship, quickly beat back to Brest, and on the evening of the day following their capture, the crew of the "Melpomene" found themselves in port. The English frigate was worked in by her prize crew, and was moored alongside her victorious adversary. In looking at the two ships as they lay so close to each other, all wonder at the disastrous termination of the conflict was quickly dispelled, and one was more inclined to censure the temerity that could have induced the English commander to engage in so desperate an encounter.

Not only had the "Richelieu" 60 guns, most of them of heavier calibre than those of the "Melpomene," but she was considerably larger, her superior in sailing qualities, and carried 250 more men than the "Melpomene," whose crew, owing to death in battle and by disease, had been wofully reduced from the total they had mustered on sailing from Plymouth two years before. Notwithstanding all these advantages possessed by their champion, the good people of Brest were transported with joy at the capture, and, I suppose, on the principle of not looking " a gift horse in the mouth," especially when the gift is of a description rarely bestowed, they made no invidious comparisons between the ships, but were duly thankful for the very small mercy vouchsafed to them, and manifested their exultation by the performance of Te Deums and other rejoicings usual among our Gallic neighbours on such occasions. Pursuing the events of my own biography, or such as fall under my own observation, I must now leave the officers and crew late of his Majesty's ship " Mel pomene " to their fate in a French prison, with the expression of a sincere hope that a speedy peace or an exchange of captives soon effected the opening of their gloomy and inhospitable prison doors.

The naval authorities at Brest lost no time in refitting the " Melpomene," and having decided to send her once more to the East Indies, there was a probability of my visiting former scenes, and reviving recollections of happy days when under my own country's flag, which, as a good patriot, I devoutly hoped might soon float over me again. I never could reconcile myself to the chattering conversation of French sailors, for whom, whether owing to the finikin nature of the language, or to the appearance and conduct of the individuals who expressed themselves through its medium, I have always had a contempt, and yet, like all Frenchmen, they are brave, and struck me as being certainly more patient than our tars, who, when thwarted or out of temper, swear at everything and everybody but their own officers.

Well, we put to sea, and arrived in Eastern waters without the occurrence of any circumstance of note, except that we were chased by the frigates of an English fleet soon after we lost sight of land, though we easily eluded our pursuers. We had been ordered to put in at the island of Bourbon, now known as Reunion, and which, with Mauritius (which the English subsequently captured), formed the two chief French naval stations in the Indian Ocean. Reunion belongs to the Mascarene group of islands lying within the southern tropic, about 400 miles east of Madagascar, and is about 40 miles long by 30 broad, and of an oval shape. In times of subterranean disturbance, Reunion cannot be considered a very desirable or safe residence. It was discovered by the Portuguese in 1545, and must have been regarded by them as a most unpromising place to colonize, for the whole island was little more than a rock with inaccessible peaks, while its inhospitable shores were covered with huge boulders. It was uninhabited, though the sea birds resorted to it in countless myriads, and the only animals discovered within its limits were hedgehogs and flying foxes. In spite of all these disadvantages, those clever fellows, the French, have transformed it into an earthly paradise. There is, however, a drawback attaching to a residence on its shores, for an eminent French savant has declared "that the island of Bourbon appears to have been created by volcanoes," and is in a fair way of being destroyed by volcanic irruption.

The "Melpomene," under her new masters, having despatches for the governor, made her way to the town of St. Denis, which is the seat of government, and is conveniently situated on the north side of the island. There is, however, no harbour, and we had to anchor in an open roadstead. A new comer can hardly feel very pleased by the manner in which he first makes the acquaintance of the islanders. A heavy sea beats upon the shore, and, as there are no harbours, jetties have been run out having cranes at the end of them, and on the arrival of the boat a tub is lowered, into which the passenger is stowed, and after being hoisted thirty or forty feet into the air, is landed in Reunion.

The "Melpomene," after only a few days' stay, left for Mauritius, or Isle de France, as it was then called, and hardly had she got well clear of the land when two ships were observed in the distance. Captain Boulnois was at first inclined to return to St. Denis, as he had no wish to engage so disproportionate a force; but after a short inspection he resolved to stand on, as he came to the conclusion that they were traders belonging to the British East India Company. However, he at once cleared for action, for these vessels generally also carried heavy armaments, and on more than one occasion had beaten off French frigates of equal size. As the cargoes they carried were in every instance of considerable value, Captain Boulnois determined to challenge them to battle, for if successful he would make such a haul of booty as to achieve his fortune at a stroke. It was about five o'clock in the evening that we first sighted the English ships, and Captain Boulnois at once gave chase. He made sail to topgallant sails, and stood close on a wind on the starboard tack, the same as that on which the English ships were standing. The "Melpomene," true to her good sailing qualities, overhauled the chase as impartially as in the days when she carried the flag now borne by the fugitives. The weathermost English ship, finding the French frigate approaching fast, bore up to join her consort. At half-past seven, the " Melpomene " was about two and a-half miles on the weather quarter of the two, with such a decided superiority of sailing as to hold her own with them under topsails and courses only, while they were carrying topgallant sails ! Captain Boulnois' object in not making more sail was to avoid engaging at night-time (it was already getting dark), and yet so to place himself that, when morning broke, he might be in a position to range up and commence the action. Darkness now closed in, and the chase went on during the early part of the night, the Frenchman guided in his course by an occasional signal between the English ships. Suddenly, at about ten minutes past two, in the midst of a fresh squall, the latter bore up. The word was passed over the French frigate that the English ships proposed to engage. There was a bustle through the crowded decks of the " Melpomene," while preparations were made for battle. The hammocks were lashed up and stowed in the nettings, the magazines thrown open, the guns cast loose and loaded, while the sail-trimmers attended at their stations ready for any call. All these preparations were made without confusion or a relaxation of the ties of discipline, but not as smartly, I thought, as they would have been on board the same ship only one short year before.

Immediately the English vessels bore up, Captain Boulnois, fearing their intention might be to run or wear, bore up also, and manned his starboard guns. In about ten minutes the former again hauled to the wind on the same tack, and the "Melpomene," having repeated the manœuvre, found herself within less than musket-shot distance on the weather quarter of one of the strangers. Captain Boulnois, having previously manned his guns on both sides, discharged his larboard broadside at this ship, which she, nothing daunted, returned with a similar salute. Thus, at about twenty minutes past two o'clock in the morning, the action began. The French sailors worked their guns with creditable precision, and their courage no one could doubt ; but they appeared too excited and flurried, contrasting in this respect unfavourably with their predecessors on board the frigate. At about half-past two the English ship we had engaged, having had her jibboom and the weather clew of her foretopsail shot away, ranged ahead clear of the "Melpomene's" guns. The lightness of the breeze, which had been gradually falling since the action commenced, would have deprived us of our former advantage in point of sailing, even had the East Indiaman's fire not cut away the greater part of our running rigging. Hence the "Melpomene" had scarcely steerage way through the water. The second English ship had meanwhile bore up, and now taking a station on the lee quarter of her consort, commenced her share in the action. The breeze freshening a little at this time, the "Melpomene" made sail, and, running alongside this latter vessel to windward, poured a broadside into her. At this time the first Indiaman, owing to a sudden fall of wind, was enabled to retain her station close on our weather bow, a most advantageous position, as while she raked us with a most destructive fire, her consort lay within half-pistol-shot on our larboard beam, and, with her guns manned by a fresh crew, poured in terrible broadsides of round shot, grape, and langridge that cut up the "Melpomene's" rigging in most merciless style. At this critical juncture, Captain Boulnois fell mortally wounded, and the command devolved upon his first lieutenant, an officer who possessed neither the energy nor resource of his superior, though he formed no exception to the gallantry of his nation, and did not shirk from exposing himself freely to the storm of projectiles that now swept our decks. It soon became manifest that the action would have a disas-

" Her guns poured in terrible broadsides."

trous termination as regarded the "Melpomene." Within an hour of its commencement her jibboom and foretopmast were shot away, and shortly after her mizen-topmast went by the board. Still she continued an animated fire, but it gradually grew more and more feeble. About half-past four o'clock, when daylight broke, she presented a sad spectacle. Her two remaining masts were tottering to their fall, her hull was pierced in all directions—in fact, almost riddled; her quarterdeck had been nearly cleared of officers and men, while the guns were disabled, and her maindeck quarters so thinned that only nine carronades could be manned. There was no hope of escape either, for a dead calm brooded over the sea, rendering the unfortunate ship a target, into which every shot from the Indiamen plumped with fatal precision. There was nothing to be done to avoid total destruction but to surrender; and accordingly, at a quarter to five, the French frigate hauled down her colours, and once more reverted to the nation that had launched and fitted her out.

The "butcher's bill" was even more formidable in its dimensions than on the memorable occasion when Captain Gaisford fought and lost her. Of the crew of 380 men she carried, no less than 42 were killed and 127 wounded; among the former, besides the captain, who before his ship surrendered expired of the terrible grape-shot wound he had received, were three other officers, while the wounded included the first lieutenant, who received a musket-ball through his neck and another through his hand, from both of which, however, he recovered, and five officers, among whom were the surgeon and a colonel of regulars on his passage to Mauritius. The loss of the Indiaman was, in comparison, trifling, and consisted of two officers, and seven men killed and thirty-two wounded. A ¹prize crew now came on board and took possession, and soon again the " meteor flag " of England waved over the shattered and war-worn hull of the old frigate.

It made me warm up to my very core (I suppose that my readers will not allow that I have a heart) to hear the old familiar tongue once more. I would listen for the cheery order to " Strike the bell eight, and pipe to grog," and watch the jolly English face of the ship's boy or some one of the crew, who nearly always at this time happened to be handy, as he sprang forward to "make it eight bells," and thereafter cut a broad joke or smartly danced a few steps of the hornpipe (so transported would the honest fellow be at the very idea of a tot of Jack's nectar) before he proceeded to plunge down below to his mess quarters for the purpose of bringing up his tin pot, or pannikin, out of which it was his habit to quaff that delicious beverage.

A strong prize crew having been put on board her, the "Melpomene" sailed in company with her consorts for Bombay, whither they were bound. No time was lost in jury-rigging her, and before the week was out she was in good condition to take care of herself.

The Indiamen having a valuable cargo on board, divided the prisoners of war between them, and then setting a press of sail, made the best of their way to their destination, directing the "Melpomene" to follow.

All went well on board the frigate, though some of the officers were rather uneasy about her safety, for so battered was her hull that she certainly could not be called seaworthy; the prize captain said one day in my hearing that it was in spite of his earnest protest that she was left to find her way along the best way she could, and that he had repeatedly represented to the captains of the Indiamen that she ought to be scuttled, as were they to encounter bad weather, it was morally certain she would founder, and thus save them the trouble of sinking her. A terrible calamity was soon, indeed, to engulph the

gallant frigate, but it was not of the character appre-
hended by her officers.

One night, in the middle watch, I was listening
with amusement and pleasure to a conversation
between an old man-o'-war's-man, who was detailing
to a friend an account of the actions in which he
had participated in the East Indies while on board
Admiral Pocock's flagship, and spoke of the prominent part taken by the frigate on board which they
both then were, when a suspicion came over me that
I could distinguish a smell as of fire. Scarcely had
this thought presented itself to my mind, than the
officer of the watch came forward, and asking the
men whether they smelt anything like wool burning,
desired the first-mentioned sailor to go below, and
see if anything was the matter down there. This
man had just put foot on the ladder leading to the
lower deck, when the third officer came bounding up
the after-companion leading on to the quarter-deck,
and shouted out at the top of his voice, " Fire ! fire !
fire ! ring the fire-bell !" These words, replete with
such a fell import, rang over the silent decks with
the sound as of the archangel's trump at the last
day. For a moment it seemed to freeze the very
heart's blood of the three listeners, and to paralyze
their bodies, so that they could not move; but it was

only for this brief space of time, for hardly had the echoes of the dread announcement died away, than they made a simultaneous rush at the lanyard attached to my tongue—(would that all tongues of flesh had lanyards by which they could be effectually *held*)—and with might and main poured out on the midnight air such a volume of sound as would have roused the " seven sleepers," or any number of them (as it most certainly did on this occasion), had any such incentive to wakefulness been requisite after the stentorian tones of the aroused officer who gave the alarm.

Responsive to the summons, there streamed up from the lower deck a crowd of seamen, who repaired each man to his post with most commendable discipline, and with such promptitude that, before my alarum tones had ceased to ring, every soul was ready, and waiting for orders. Those told off as firemen repaired to search for the site of the fire, while " whips" were rove on the yardarms and canvas buckets prepared for bringing water from alongside, and the ordinary wooden buckets marshalled in rows to pass the water along. It was soon discovered that the fire was raging in the after part of the orlop deck, and in dangerous proximity to the powder-magazine. The captain first spoke of passing the powder up, and heaving it overboard; but fearful of the imminent danger there existed of a spark igniting the inflammable agent, he decided upon the safer course of flooding the magazine, which was accordingly carried out without a minute's loss of time. This completed, the officers and crew breathed with a feeling of comparative safety, and every nerve was bent to extinguish the fire, which was gaining ground with fearful rapidity. Very soon volumes of dense smoke were seen issuing from the after hatchways, and seen from the fore hatchways also, as the smoke rolled along the maindeck, and found vent anywhere.

The firemen were now obliged to come up on deck, being driven away by the heat and suffocating clouds of smoke. Orders were at once issued to prepare and victual the boats, and as these had all been kept by the late commander in a commendable condition for immediate service, little delay ensued before the respective officers reported every preparation made for abandoning the ship. Sorely against his will, the captain, after a hurried consultation with his two mates, decided upon adopting this course. The maintopsail was "laid to the mast," and the ship being hove to, the boats were lowered alongside, and quicky hauled forward, for the flames were now bursting through the maindeck ports, and it was impossible for the crew to lay into them from the after part of the ship.

The sick and wounded were first carefully distributed among the boats, and then with a discipline that would not have discredited a man-of-war, and in silence, the prize crew of the ill-fated " Melpomene" followed their comrades.   The boats pushed off, and none too soon, for the flames, spreading along the maindeck with surprising celerity, leapt up the tall masts and along the spars, setting fire to the sails, and thrust their forked tongues out of all the ports, licking the grim black muzzles of the guns, which, though deprived of all human companionship, yet defiantly frowned out upon the murkiness of night. So had they sullenly gaped when the tempest raged, when the storm-beaten waves lashed themselves into a hideous frenzy, and the winds raved and howled their loudest; so again when their iron throats belched forth a destructive hail of shot, and grape, and canister to the accompaniment of the lightning that lit up the night with quickly-recurring flashes, and of the thunder that shook every rib, and beam, and bolt in the sturdy frigate's oaken frame.   In like manner now, when the last act of the drama of the history of a gallant ship-of-war " from its cradle to its grave" was being enacted, the artillery stood their ground sullenly, and glared out into the night, and at the poor mortals, who, at length vanquished by an element more powerful than even the winds and the waves, abandoned their ship, and would no longer stand to their guns.

Was it with an expression of grim pity or of triumph that these mute iron sons of Mars, once the proud custodians of England's honour, regarded the men who had thus deserted them? I thought some such feelings must be theirs, for you must remember I also was left to my fate, and, though not gifted with powers of speech, could sympathize with my dumb fellows in misfortune, and understand their feelings.

CHAPTER XIII

THE fire raged through the deserted ship with intense fury, and lit up the horizon. It spread up the jury-mast which had been lately sent aloft and rigged with such trouble, and "laying" out along the yards with the celerity of a smart seaman, "picked up" the broad fields of canvas, and devoured everything, until the heel of the lower masts burning through, the masts and spars, together with all sails and cordage, came toppling from their giddy height, and crashed down on to the deck beneath, or over the side into the peaceful sea, which, after they had given vent to their fervid rage in a fierce hiss, finally extinguished them. The whole ship, from stem to stern, and from truck to keelson, was involved in the conflagration, as, unchecked by the resistance of man, it swept over everything, and like a plague of locusts in a fertile land, involved all alike in one common destruction. At length the fire, having done its work, died out, and left the once handsome frigate little more than a hollow and blackened shell. The guns having their carriages all burnt to pieces, fell, one by one, with a rattling noise like thunder into the hold of the ship ; and almost the only piece of wood-work the devouring element had spared was singularly enough that from which I was suspended. One end of this even had been destroyed, so that I fell over on one side, and every time the hull of the ship rolled on the long sullen swell that had now set in, I gave forth a half-subdued and monotonous sound.   All day and all night this mournful knell sounded over the solitary sea.   Not a sail came near us ; and the once proud frigate that had been ever noted for the swiftness with which she sped on the wings of the wind, now lay motionless, as far as any progress was concerned, and only rolled from side. to side, or pitched occasionally with a slow lifeless motion, as if conscious of the great calamity that had overtaken her.   So different all this was from the saucy curtsey she would make preparatory to starting on her way, when the sails first began to draw, or when, under a cloud of sail, with a smart topgallant breeze, she would dip her bows merrily and deep, sending the green seas flying over the forecastle to the intense admiration of the blue jackets, who spoke of the " old gal " as a jockey would of his mare after winning the Oaks.

I will not, however, descant on the painful theme, but will pass over the dreary days as they lengthened into weeks, until nearly a month passed away, when one night as I was pealing forth the same melancholy strains, forced from me by the necessities of my undignified position, I heard a loud voice shout in French, "Ship, ahoy!" No response came from the deserted vessel.

"Ship ahoy!" again rung out.

"I'll send a boat on board," was the welcome announcement the voice made when there was no reply to the second hail, and very soon a boat did come alongside, and an officer made his way up the side, and stared with astonishment at the hollow and blackened ruin of a fine ship. The French naval officer, which the stranger was, descended into his boat, and directing his crew to pull round to the bows, made his way by the head boards on to the remains of the forecastle, and calling to some of his men, removed me from my unpleasant position, and, returning to his ship, reported the condition of affairs, and informed the captain that with the exception of the bell which he had brought away, and the guns, which of course he could not remove, there was nothing worth fetching away in the abandoned ship.

My new home was a line-of-battle-ship, but it was only so temporarily, for on her arrival in France, whither she was bound, I was made over to the dockyard authorities, and placed in a storehouse at Toulon. Here I remained in obscurity for some years, until on a thorough overhaul being made by a new storekeeper—"New brooms," we know, "sweep clean"—I was brought to light, and as some ships were being fitted out for the purpose of prosecuting the war with Great Britain, I was placed in a ten-gun brig, and despatched to sea again, to my great delight.

I will pass over my adventures for the next ten years, and until I found myself, on my return to France, transferred to an old frigate whose bell had performed the suicidal act the poet conjures "Rude Boreas," that "blustering railer," to consummate— in short, it (for I suppose my readers will not allow that we bells have any sex) had "cracked its cheeks." I was accordingly taken out of the brig, and placed on board the "Artemise" frigate. It was during the height of the war of independence waged by the British Colonies in North America against the mother country.

The "Artemise" was the best ship I had yet seen in the French navy in respect of those qualities which are of the first necessity to a man-of-war. She was well commanded, well officered, well manned, and well found in every point of detail, while all on board her were thoroughly drilled and as smart a looking set of fellows as even an English admiral would wish to see. She carried forty-eight guns, distributed as follows: twenty-eight 18-pounders on her main-deck, fourteen 32-pounder carronades on her quarter-deck, and on her forecastle four 32's and two long 9's. Her crew, including officers, consisted in all of three hundred and forty-nine good men and true.

We sailed for the coast of America, and were employed in active service, our duties chiefly consisting in co-operating with the land forces, under Washington and Lafayette, or transporting troops and stores. It was a difficult and dangerous duty, as the English fleet was in great force on the coasts of America, and blockaded most of the ports. On one occasion we were blockaded under the guns of some strong fortifications in the York Town peninsula for some weeks by a squadron of the enemy, and though Captain Hamelin tried every ruse to draw off their attention so as to effect his escape, his every effort was frustrated by the vigilance of the British officers, and he was condemned to lie in inactivity.

This was most uncongenial to a man of his spirited temperament, and as he could not elude the British Navy, he determined to take advantage of the enforced repose to refit his ship. American officers often came on board from the fortress to smoke a cigar, or wile away the tedium by an inter-change of hospitalities. Many a yarn have I heard from their lips and from those of the officers of the "Artemise." There was one told by a Captain Milligan, of the American Cavalry, which impressed itself on my memory, and I will not apologize for laying it before my readers, whom I hope it may likewise interest.

"Six months ago," said Captain Milligan, " I was taken prisoner while reconnoitring with a detachment of cavalry in the neighbourhood of Baltimore, where a strong force of the British were encamped. I was sent with a number of the officers (rebels they call us) to a prison at Quebec, and as ill fortune would have it, I arrived a day or two after the British Commander-in-chief had come to a determination to retaliate in kind for the execution of two of his own officers, who had been shot by some one of our generals. It also happened that the rank of the two unfortunate officers was that of captain, and hence it was ordered that the victims were to be selected from those of the same standing. The officer who was in charge of us prisoners of war at this time, was a kind-hearted man, who strove all in his power to make our captivity as little irksome as possible, and was regarded by all the inmates of the prison with feelings of gratitude and affection.

" On the morning in question, this officer entered the room where the prisoners were confined, and desired all the officers to walk out into another room. I remarked that his face wore an expression of anxiety and sorrow, but as the prisoners who were daily expecting to be exchanged did not appear to regard the change with apprehension, I concluded that it must be habitual, although I had not remarked it before. His orders were obeyed with particular alacrity, for it was supposed the long-expected cartel had at length arrived, and that they were about to exchange their dreary prison quarters for home and freedom. After they had all gathered in the room, their countenances lit up with these agreeable anticipations, the officer came in among them, and with a face that looked graver and more sorrowful than ever, took a paper out of his pocket, and told them that he had a very unhappy duty to perform, the purport of which he had just received from the General Commanding-in-chief. He then, amidst the breathless attention of his auditors, proceeded to read an order for the immediate execution of two of the number in retaliation for the hanging of two English officers. It would be difficult to describe the blank expression of dismay in the faces of the astonished and horror-stricken group of officers, as the words of the fatal mandate dropped from the lips of the reader. When his voice had ceased to echo through the apartment, the men looked at each other with blanch faces, and a silence like death prevailed for some minutes in the chamber. The British officer seeing that his unfortunate prisoners were bewildered by the suddenness with which the terrible edict had come upon them, then suggested that perhaps the better way would be to place a number of slips of paper equal to the whole number of officers from whom the victims were to be drawn, in a box, with the word Death written on two of them, and the rest blank—the two who drew the fatal slips to be the doomed ones. This plan was unanimously agreed to, and a chaplain was appointed to prepare the slips.

"It was a study to watch the countenances of

of my comrades in misfortune, and the different methods by which they sought to kill time, ere the drawing began that was to decide their destiny in in this world. Some paced the room with rapid steps, and closely-knit brows and lips; some stood still, and gazed out of the window into the prison-yard, and gloomily regarded the objects before them, or the sentry with bayonet fixed, though these made no impression on their minds, which were occupied with far different thoughts of home, doubtless, and of the dear ones they would, perhaps, never more see; some few again talked and laughed loudly, but it was a forced gaiety, and almost more painful to behold than the mood of the others of whom I have spoken; some (only two they were in number) were on their knees, and were pouring out a passionate prayer for mercy, or, should it be ordered that they were to draw the fatal lot, then for fortitude from on high to endure the last final pang. All, without exception, bore the trying moments like brave men. These were soon past, though to some of us (myself among the number, I am not ashamed to say) they appeared like hours, for I was filled with frenzied anxiety to have it all over and know the worst, so that I might prepare myself for the last great change, or have the consciousness that I had returned to life once more.

"Presently the chaplain returned ; a great silence for the second time reigned in the apartment, and every eye was fixed on the clergyman and the bundle of slips in his hand, in which it may truly be said at that time that he ' held the issues of life and death.'

"The *modus operandi* of conducting the drawing was explained to us in a few words by the chaplain, and at a signal from him it at once commenced ; the officers advancing and taking out a slip, and, if it proved to be a blank, taking their places in another part of the room. How we whose turn had not yet come watched the countenances of the drawers as each man, according to his idiosyncrasy, tore open or slowly unfolded the slip of paper that was to be his death-warrant or his reprieve ; with what an intense and painful anxiety we marked, as one after another they defiled before the fatal box, and each one drew out a slip, that more than one-third had drawn blanks, and were restored to that dear life which we unhappy wretches, who stood awaiting our turn, under the dark shadow of the cloud of death, felt we had never until now sufficiently valued. Each man who drew a blank narrowed our chance—my chance—of ever setting eyes on my wife, or clasping to my breast again my little ones in my distant home in Carolina, and I alternately prayed to God, or

cursed my ill luck, while I stood there powerless to
avert the evil fate that was approaching me with such
rapid strides. One half of the captives—there were
eighteen of us in all—having drawn blanks, had exchanged gloomy looks of apprehension for a relieved
aspect they could ill disguise after escape from such
terrible peril, when an officer, Captain Thomas
Nattalie, drew a fatal death slip. Poor fellow! I
pitied him, and yet I could not restrain a feeling of
relief as I reflected with a sentiment of satisfaction
that my chance of being equally unfortunate was
considerably diminished thereby.

" My turn came next. I stepped forward, eagerly
seized a paper, when, oh horror! there appeared
before my eyes, as I hastily opened the slip, the
single word *Death!* I managed with difficulty to
retain sufficient command over myself to hide the
feelings of anguish that succeeded the first sensation
of blank dismay, and handing the slip to the chaplain he read the name out in full—Captain Joseph
Milligan, of the First Connecticut Mounted Rifles.

" I sat down by my friend and brother in misfortune without a word. We were removed from our
fellow-prisoners, and placed in a cell by ourselves, to
wait until the time fixed for our execution had
arrived. On finding myself comparatively free from

observation, I gave way to the full bitterness of my
heart, and so passed the first of the two hours
allowed us to settle our worldly affairs and our peace
with God. Within less than two hours then, and
before the sun went down, it would be all over for
us, and we should sleep in our lonely graves the
sleep that knows no waking. The thought was
maddening, but, after dwelling on it for some time,
it occurred to me that it was worth making an effort
to avert, or at least to postpone, our terrible doom ;
and straightway I fell to resolving all sorts of schemes
for delay, but dismissed them from my mind one
after another as impracticable or unpromising. At
length I thought of a plan, and hardly had I done
so than the officer in command made his appearance
with a guard, and ordered us out for immediate
execution. I at once demanded as a right conceded
by every civilized nation, that I might be permitted
to write to my wife and request her to come to me
at once, and bid me an eternal farewell. The commanding officer was at first taken aback, but undecided as to what course to pursue; and, being a
humane man, he, after some cogitation, consented to
grant a respite for a day or two, for the purpose of
enabling me to communicate with the English Commander-in-chief so as to obtain the necessary

sanction to see my wife, and he promised to forward the letter. This was done, and, to my great relief, permission was accorded as requested. My principal object, however, in petitioning for this respite was to enable my wife to take immediate steps to acquaint our Provisional Government with the perilous predicament in which Captain Nattalie and I were placed, and for them to secure hostages, and threaten retaliation should the orders of the English general be carried out. Everything was propitious, and events turned out as I had hoped and expected. My devoted wife did not let the grass grow under her feet, but immediately on receipt of my letter flew to the members of our Government, and so enlisted their sympathies by her prayers and tears, that they at once gave an English general high in command to understand that, unless our lives were spared, the capital penalty should be at once enforced on his son, a young aide-de-camp whom they had in their hands, having luckily captured him a short time previously when carrying despatches from his father.

"An order was at once forthcoming that our lives were to be spared, and thus to a clever ruse, and to the exertions of a true and loving wife, both my companion in misfortune and myself escaped from an imminent and terrible doom.   After a few more months' confinement we were all exchanged, but Captain Nattalie came out of the terrible ordeal with his hair white as snow.   He was a brave man, and had often faced death unflinchingly on the battle-field, but was not proof against the protracted strain on his mind caused by the uncertainty of his fate—a strain harder to endure than the prospect of immediate death."

To continue my biography: At length matters looked brighter as regarded our prospect of effecting our escape from the rigid blockade hitherto maintained.   Two of the blockading squadron made sail to Halifax, and the rest were driven out of sight of land by a storm, or stood off desiring to make a good offing.   The coast was clear, and Captain Hamelin, who had been fretting and fuming at his enforced idleness, was glad enough to take advantage of the opportunity, and put to sea as soon as 'the weather moderated.   He had not wasted his time, but had thoroughly overhauled and refitted his ship, so that the " Artemise " looked as if she had come out of dock, and was ready either to fight or fly, just as the mood might take her or the fates allowed.   It was not long before her capabilities in the former line were put to a severe test.

Early in the morning of the third day after putting to sea, we discovered a ship about eight miles off to the south-east, which it required little discernment to know was an English frigate, in all probability one of the blockading squadron. Captain Hamelin and his officers were desirous of engaging, but a calm that came on about eight bells, kept both frigates stationary. Every preparation was made for action, and the ship in her arrangements seemed to strike me as more like an English man-of-war than anything I had yet seen out of the service, while the bearing of all hands, from the captain to the cabin-boy, seemed to denote that they were inspired with confidence in themselves, and each other, a sure augury of victory, as I had come to learn. At noon a light breeze sprang up from the W.N.W., whereupon the English frigate stood towards the "Artemise" on the port tack under a crowd of canvas.

The "Artemise" kept on her course under all plain sail, the captain being desirous of drawing the enemy away a little, as he was afraid that some of her consorts were not far off. At three in the afternoon, finding the wind beginning to fall, and conceiving that he had drawn his enemy to a sufficient distance from interference on the part of her

21

consorts, if there were any, Captain Hamelin ordered his men to their quarters once more ; shortening sail he wore round, and running under his three topsails with the wind on his starboard quarter, steered to pass, and then cross, the stern of the English frigate, which, under the same sail, was now standing "close hauled" on the port tack. To avoid being thus raked, she tacked to the S.W. at a little after five, and hoisted her colours, which we had previously done.

It was at the close of a glorious day, with a light and balmy breeze, and the sea nearly as smooth as a mill-pond, that the ships drew near enough to commence an action remarkable for its obstinacy and the severe losses sustained by both combatants. The captain, taking out his watch, ordered three bells in the first dog-watch to be struck just as the "Artemise" had arrived within pistol-shot of the starboard or weather-bow of the British frigate ; and as one of the boys—poor little fellow, I pitied him, as I marked the pallor of his face, for indeed it was no place for a child twelve years of age—struck the bell with tremulous hand, the enemy replied by a broadside which convulsed the air with its terrible volume of sound, and sent a shower of shot crashing through the timbers and spars of the "Artemise,"

She, on her part, was not slow in accepting the challenge, and responded with a salvo from her artillery that shook and strained every joint of her fabric, and I doubt not did a vast deal more than shake and strain that of her adversary. After about three broadsides had been exchanged, the maintopsail of the " Artemise " fell aback in consequence of the braces having been shot away. Some hands quickly sprang up the rigging to reeve fresh braces or splice the old ones, according to what was necessary, but before the damage could be repaired, the " Artemise," instead of crossing the enemy, as she had intended, fell on board her; this collision caused the jibboom of the latter to carry away our jib and staysail, and either her boomkin or anchor fluke to knock away part of our larboard topside. The British frigate now opened a heavy fire of musketry from her tops, rigging, and every available spot aloft commanding our decks. Her seamen also threw hand-grenades upon our decks, which they hoped from the demoralizing effect these projectiles ordinarily have in warfare, would cause such confusion that they might be successful in an attempt to board, for which purpose a dense mass of sailors swarmed on her fore rigging ready to leap on board as soon as the opportunity offered. But the crew of the

"Artemise" did not so easily lose their heads, but replied by a hot and telling musketry fire that quickly cleared the enemy's rigging, and forced them to give up the. idea of boarding for the present. Finding this favourite British manœuvre out of the question, the enemy threw all aback and dropped clear of her opponent.

Setting his maintopgallant and maintopmast staysails, the jib being, as I have said, disabled, Captain Hamelin endeavoured to get his ship's head towards the bow of the British frigate. This he succeeded in doing, but in attempting a second time to cross the bows of his antagonist he failed, and once more fell on board her. The two ships after coming into violent collision, swung close alongside each other with the muzzles of their guns almost touching. Now ensued a scene of fearful mutual slaughter, to which indeed all that had gone before was as child's play. It was a quarter past seven, and getting dark, when the action assumed a complexion that was simply appalling. The men instead of being wearied or desirous on one side or the other of beating a retreat, appeared to have only warmed to their work, and enraged at the obstinacy of their opponents, fought their guns with almost a demoniac fury. The muzzles of the cannon, as I have said, were nearly locked, and the opposing seamen gunners snatched the sponges out of each other's hands, and struck at one another with them, or with the worms or rammers, or anything they could lay hands on ; and drawing their cutlasses they cut at the sponges or loaders, as they in carrying out their respective duties extended their arms beyond the port sills. At this time a party of our seamen, headed by the third lieutenant, attempted to lash the two frigates together, but failed, owing to the heavy fire of musketry, which the enemy in turn kept up from her tops and decks. So steady and well directed was this fusillade, that the third lieutenant and boatswain were killed, and the decks of the " Artemise " were soon nearly cleared of officers and men. Captain Hamelin, who was standing on the quarter deck, was now severely wounded from the same cause, and had to be carried below, the command devolving on the second lieutenant, the first having been killed at his post early in the action.

Thus progressed the sanguinary combat, which, however, it was plain, could not last long, if any survivors were to be left in either ship. Still neither side dreamt of yielding, but carried away by the mad frenzy of battle, blazed away with their great guns and small arms with unabated fury, struggled fiercely at the gun ports, thrusting and hacking at each other with boarding pikes and cutlasses, and sought to board through the same ports when the guns re-coiled.   At length the elements, or rather, certain physical forces came to the rescue; the concussion of the discharges from the cannon, acted as a repel-lent force, and the ships were mutually forced apart, and so in the almost calm state of the weather, they gradually receded from each other, their broadsides still bearing, and the respective crews continuing to work the guns, until at length they drifted out of gunshot, and all firing ceased.

It was a drawn battle.   All this fearful bloodshed and destruction had been absolutely destitute of any result, and as is usual in such cases, both the com-batants claimed the victory, though the warriors of neither nationality were entitled to it.   It was about a quarter past nine o'clock when the last gun was fired, and then, though fatigued and worn out by their great exertions, the crew of the " Artemise," without one word of complaint, proceeded to clear the decks and refit the ship aloft, as also the gun gear, so that they might be in a posi-tion to renew the action should the English frigate bear down upon them, with this object.   But it was clear that she also had had quite enough of it, and when morning broke was nowhere to be seen.

That was a terrible night succeeding the action. Luckily the fine weather continued, and only light airs, sufficient to give steerage way, moved the battered hull of the good frigate through the water. The decks were washed down, and all traces of the ghastly conflict sought to be removed, but it was not possible to control the moans of the wounded, or the frequent half-stifled cry of anguish as some poor mangled wretch tried vainly to check the sob or groan of agony that would find utterance from his lips, while the surgeon, or one of his assistants, amputated some limb torn by shot, or bound up with hasty hands, for there was abundance of work of this sort to be got through, some gaping gunshot or splinter wound.

Such are the inevitable horrors of every action, but they were greatly magnified in this instance, owing to the desperate character of the duel between two equally-matched ships. The dead were committed to the deep without any religious ceremony, for there was no chaplain, and every hand that could be spared was busied with the wants of the living; and when morning broke, it still found the gallant fellows, officers and men alike, busy at the work of repairing and refitting, or assisting the surgeon with the wounded—a duty that seemed as if it would never end.

The crew were regaled with spirits and biscuits, and then Captain Hamelin, anxious to arrive at some estimate of his losses, ordered all hands on the quarter-deck. Alas! the diminished length of the lines on either side of the deck, told its own tale of the havoc wrought by the desperate combat of the previous night. Of her three hundred and forty-nine officers and men, all told, that used to muster every morning, a hundred and ninety-two only answered the roll call! Of the absentees fifty-nine brave hearts were stilled for ever, and were now food for the fishes, and ninety-eight were numbered among those whose wounds were of a nature too severe to allow of their appearing on deck. Of the remaining one hundred and ninety-two, only about a hundred and sixty were absolutely free from all injury, and in a position to perform the duties of the ship. Though for a moment saddened by the thoughts called up by these losses, Captain Hamelin, who, though severely wounded in the shoulder, had caused himself to be brought up on deck, made an effort to conquer the weakness induced by his wound, and addressed his men in a short and spirit-stirring

address. In feeble tones he thanked them all for
the noble manner in which they had upheld the
ancient renown of their country, and though he said
they had reaped but a barren victory, he promised
them the opportunity of winning fresh laurels. The
brave fellows responded to the words of their chief
with vivas, and after being dismissed were allowed to
enjoy for the remainder of the day the rest they had
so well earned.

The damages the "Artemise" had sustained,
although they did not include a single fallen mast, a
result chiefly owing to the smooth state of the sea,
were very serious. Her masts and guns were all
badly wounded; her rigging, both standing and running, and her gear cut to pieces; and her hull all
riven and shattered with the storm of round shot
that had been poured into her at so short a range.
The English ship had lost her mizenmast, and was
equally riddled in her hull, and cut up as regards her
top hamper. She must also have suffered in an
equal measure in killed and wounded, as she did not
offer to renew the action, which a slight breeze that
sprang up during the night would have enabled her
to do had she been so inclined. Probably she, like
ourselves, had had enough of it, and though scorning
to yield or to fly, was not sorry that she drifted in a

direction opposite to that adopted equally involun-
tarily by the " Artemise." Captain Hamelin directed
his course to France, and the frigate arrived at
Toulon without any further adventure beyond an
unsuccessful chase of a British privateer. The
" Artemise" was put into dock on her arrival at
Toulon, and was found to be in so damaged a state
that it was decided by the naval authorities that she
should be broken up—a step also rendered necessary
by reason of her age. And so the old frigate,
having gallantly fought her last fight and acquitted
herself right nobly, was taken to the shipbreaker's
yard, and went the way of all flesh, and, indeed, for
that matter, of everything animate or inanimate.

At this time—early in 1781—France, assisted by
Spain, was making extraordinary efforts` to deprive
Britain of her boasted sovereignty of the seas. The
Spaniards were straining every nerve to capture
Gibraltar, and were pressing the siege of that stronghold by land, and its blockade by sea. To effect its
relief and supply its starving inhabitants with provisions, the British Government fitted out a fleet of
twenty-eight line-of-battle ships under the command
of Admiral Darby. The French boasted that they
would defeat the execution of this design, but the
British admiral, notwithstanding that a fleet of

twenty-six ships was lying in Brest harbour, and a still larger Spanish fleet was cruising in the Bay of Cadiz, set sail with a convoy of ninety-seven victuallers, as well as two fleets of merchantmen. The truth was, each of the allied nations was intent on effecting the objects most conducive to her own individual interests, and instead of acting in concert and crushing the British fleet, Spain only thought of recapturing Gibraltar, while France was occupied with her designs in America, as well as in the East and West Indies. The French Government accordingly bent every energy towards the fitting out of two fleets—one to be despatched to the East Indies, under De Suffrein, an officer who may certainly be placed in the front rank of French admirals, and the second to the West Indies, having for its commander the Count de Grasse.

Accordingly, I was taken out of the " Artemise," and, being considered a fine specimen of a man-o'-war's bell, as well as from the historical interest attaching to me, was forwarded to Brest, and, under the express orders of the Count de Grasse, was fitted on board his ship. I well remember the interest with which the gallant officer listened to the details of my career from the time I went to sea on board His Britannic Majesty's ship " Melpomene," to the day I was selected for the flag-ship of at that time the most popular admiral in the navy of the ancient foe of the said royal personage. This flag-ship was the famous "Ville de Paris," a first-rate line-of-battle ship, carrying 110 guns. She was, perhaps, the most powerful vessel afloat, and had been presented to Louis XV. by the city of Paris, and was said to have cost £176,000, a fabulous sum in those days to pay for a man-of-war, though in our time we have seen £360,000 expended on the construction of the "Warrior."

Admirals Count de Grasse and De Suffrein sailed from Brest on the 22nd of March, 1781, with the combined fleet of twenty-five sail of the line, and one ship of 50 guns, having on board six thousand soldiers, and convoying a fleet of nearly three hundred merchant-vessels. De Suffrein, soon after leaving port, parted company for the East Indies, taking with him five ships, and the remaining twenty-one vessels of war proceeded to Martinique, to effect a junction with the West Indian fleet already in those waters. The British Naval Commander-in-chief in the West Indies was Sir George Rodney, who, on learning the arrival of this large hostile expedition, detached Sir Samuel Hood, his second in command, with seventeen ships of the line to intercept them off

Fort Royal bay. A partial engagement ensued, but, although Count de Grasse had, with reinforcements, a majority of six ships, he did not care to close, being more anxious to secure the safety of his large and valuable convoy than to engage. He accordingly kept his fleet well together at a safe distance from his antagonists, while those of the latter that pressed into closer action received considerable damage. The Count de Grasse now formed a junction with nine ships of the line previously in the West Indies.

The French naval and military commanders undertook a combined expedition for the reduction of the island of St. Lucia, but, being foiled in this attempt, set sail for Tobago with the object of effecting its capture. Sir George Rodney, having completed the repairs of his ships, came in sight of our fleet with the whole of his squadron; but though the Count de Grasse, having changed his tactics, showed no disposition to avoid an engagement, the British admiral, notwithstanding that he had the advantage of the wind, did not think it prudent to run the risk. The French troops were landed under the command of the Marquis de Bouillé; but the inhabitants of Tobago, together with the small force of British troops, carried out a most protracted and gallant resistance. The French set fire to four plantations daily, and, by this savage mode of carrying on warfare, succeeded in forcing the governor to capitulate. Thus, somewhat disastrously for England, terminated the naval operations in the West Indies for the year 1781.

CHAPTER XIV.

THE Count de Grasse proceeded with the fleet, on board his flagship, to the Chesapeake, and, calling in at Hispaniola, received an augmentation of five sail of the line. His rival, Sir George Rodney, returned to England on account of his health, and the naval command devolved on Sir Samuel Hood, an officer scarcely less famous than his distinguished chief. In the meantime hostilities with varying success, but chiefly with results unfavourable to the mother country, had been progressing between Great Britain and her colonies.

It was to assist in a well-laid scheme for dealing a final blow at British power in the revolted provinces that the Count de Grasse sailed for the Chesapeake, for which station the Count de Barras, commanding a French squadron of eight line-of-battle ships, was also directed to steer. The French Commander-in-chief cast anchor in the Chesapeake on the 13th of August, and the Count de Barras sailed for the same

destination from Rhode Island five days before the
arrival of his superior, taking a circuit by Bermuda
to avoid the British fleet. Lord Cornwallis, the
British General in command of the troops in the
field, under Sir Harry Clinton, who remained at New
York, being desirous of possessing some strong post
as a place of security both for the army and navy,
had selected Yorktown and Gloucester Point, two
places separated by the York River, and nearly opposite each other; having fortified this point, he took
up a defensive position with his small force of seven
thousand men, and represented to Sir Harry Clinton
his urgent need of reinforcements.   At this time
the British army was parcelled out at various seaports; and in consequence it became manifest that
a naval superiority would secure success to either
party; it was with this object and to assist in carrying out the plans of Washington that the Count de
Grasse now brought so overwhelming a force to the
Yorktown Peninsula. Early in September, Admiral
Graves appeared off the Chesapeake, and made an
effort to relieve Cornwallis, but without success.
When he appeared off the Capes of Virginia, De
Grasse, apprehensive of the safety of the squadron
of the Count de Barras, which had not yet arrived,
put to sea, and an indecisive engagement took place

on the 7th of the month. There was little more than a distant cannonading, but small harm was done to either squadron, and no one was killed on board the " Ville de Paris." The British Admiral was willing to renew the engagement on the following day, but De Grasse, who had nothing to gain by fighting an action, wisely declined the perilous honour. He was soon after joined by the Count de Barras with his eight ships, when he possessed a very decided superiority. But Admiral Graves now felt the force of the axiom that " Discretion is the better part of valour," and sailed from the coast, when the French fleet re-entered the Chesapeake. During this time, according to a well-digested plan, the French and American forces, under the personal command of Washington, were on their march for Yorktown.

The combined army, amounting to twelve thousand men, assembled at Williamsburg on the 25th of September, and, five days after, moved down to invest Yorktown, while at the same time the Count de Grasse advanced to the mouth of York River with his whole fleet, so as to prevent Lord Cornwallis from retreating or obtaining succour by sea.

The British army was now completely hemmed in, and on the 6th of October the first parallel was

begun within six hundred yards of their lines; and
on the 9th and 10th the attacks of the besiegers
commenced with formidable energy, their shells
reaching the English ships in harbour, so that the
" Charon," frigate of forty-four guns, and a transport were burned. On the 11th of October the
second parallel was begun at the distance of two
hundred yards from the works, and then two redoubts
on the left of the British line were stormed by
columns of French and American soldiers, who vied
with each other in the reckless courage with which
they flung themselves on the enemy's fortifications.

It seemed to me as I heard the news of the daily
progress of the siege, to recall the old days before
Louisburg, and indeed had it not been for the
different language in which the intelligence was conveyed, I should have thought that I had been indulging in a long sleep, and that my past life was
all a dream. This idea would have been—to tell a
truth disagreeable to English ears—still farther en-
couraged when I pondered on the different spirit
with which the British conducted the siege then,
from that in which, their respective positions being
changed, they carried on the defence now. " Oh! "
thought I, burning with patriotic ardour, " for one
week, nay, for one day, of a Wolfe, a Townshend,

and a Boscawen." The men were lions, still, as was proved by the gallant manner in which, under the leadership of a brave officer, Colonel Abercrombie, they sallied out and spiked eleven canon, but they were commanded by a ——, but no, a man-o'-war's bell must not lower itself by being abusive.

No hopes of safety now remained for the British force, for no succour came from New York, where Sir Harry Clinton was dilly-dallying, and for the defence of which against an imaginary attack he was making elaborate preparations. Meantime one hundred guns were pounding away at Lord Cornwallis's works, which were now a mass of ruins, and so, after an attempt to escape in boats to Gloucester Point, which was frustrated by a violent storm, the British General proposed a cessation of hostilities for twenty-four hours, to settle terms of capitulation. To this, Washington, anxious "to save the effusion of blood," assented, and on the 19th of October a treaty was concluded, and the posts were given up; the troops and stores being surrendered to the Great American patriot, while the Count de Grasse received the submission of the ships and seamen. The honour of marching out with colours flying, which had been refused to General Lincoln, when he surrendered Charlestown in May of the previous year, was now by way of retaliation denied to Lord Cornwallis, who was with Sir Harry Clinton on the former occasion. Lincoln also was appointed to receive the submission of the Royal army, but beyond this humiliation, Washington behaved with great magnanimity to the vanquished. Five days after the surrender of Yorktown a British fleet, with seven thousand troops, arrived off the Chesapeake, but they were too late in warding off a blow that was fatal to the cause of their country, and returned to New York.

The Count de Grasse now sailed with thirty-two ships of the line for the island of Christopher, which he proposed to attack in company with the Marquis de Bouillé. The latter landed with eight thousand men, and threatened the islanders with a repetition of his excesses at Tobago, unless they forthwith surrendered. Sir Samuel Hood sought to interfere with his fleet of twenty-two sail, and succeeded in luring De Grasse from the coast by the offer of battle; but though by these means he succeeded in placing himself between the French army and fleet, and so cut off all communications, so great was the fear inspired among the people of St. Christopher's by the threats of the French general, that they surrendered without firing a shot. The British admiral preserved his fleet from attack by slipping his cables in the night, and getting silently under weigh. After this, the French were successful in reducing the islands of Nevis and Montserrat, until Barbadoes and Antigua alone remained to Britain of the Leeward group. After these conquests the French government projected an expedition against Jamaica, and a powerful reinforcement with large supplies was despatched under command of De Guichen, to enable the French and Spanish commanders to effect this object. Admiral Kempenfeldt succeeded in capturing twenty of these transports, but being in inferior force was unable to engage the powerful squadron that convoyed them.

Early in 1782, Sir George Rodney returned to the West Indies with a considerable fleet, and, meeting with Sir Samuel Hood, sailed for Martinique, whither he learned De Grasse had retired after the fall of St. Christopher's. The French fleet, at this time assembled in Fort Royal Bay, Martinique, consisted of thirty-three sail of the line, and two ships of 50 guns; and in this fleet were embarked 5,400 soldiers intended for the conquest of Jamaica. The design of the Count de Grasse was to proceed with all diligence to Hispaniola, and, after

joining the Spanish admiral, when their united
armaments would have numbered fifty ships, to bid
defiance to the British fleet, and wrest from them the
sovereignty of the West Indian waters. On the
morning of the 8th of April, the " Ville de Paris,"
with the rest of our fleet, proceeded to sea; and,
immediately after, Sir G. Rodney weighed and stood
towards us under all the sail he could carry. On
the following morning, off the island of Guadaloupe,
the British fleet gained so much upon us, that their
van and centre, including the flag-ship, were within
cannon-shot of our rear. A sharp cannonade now
ensued, which, however, proved partial and indecisive, owing to the wind being light; the greater
portion of their ships being becalmed under the high
lands of Dominica. However, there was some
heavy fighting, and two of our ships were disabled,
while those of the enemy were somewhat severely
handled.

During the course of the action, the " Formidable," the flag-ship of Sir G. Rodney, came abreast
of the " Ville de Paris," when the former ship threw
her maintopsail to the mast, as a challenge to the
French admiral ; but, though we were three miles to
windward, the Count de Grasse did not accept the
gauge of battle thus thrown down to him, but kept

his wind, and we did not fire a shot the whole day. There was good reason for this, as it was contrary to sound policy to engage the British fleet until we had an overwhelming preponderance; and had the Count been equally prudent on the 12th, his country would have been saved a disaster that was almost irremediable. Our Admiral was not particularly anxious to bring on a general engagement, and during the next two days, succeeded in keeping far to windward, and increasing the distance between the hostile fleets. The famous battle of the 12th of April, which gained a peerage for the immortal Rodney, would never have been fought but for an accident that put it out of the power of the Count de Grasse to defer the hour of trial. On the previous day (the 11th), as the fleet was sailing in close order, there being a strong breeze at the time, the " Zelé," a line-of-battle ship of 74 guns, fouled the " Ville de Paris," and, carrying away some of her spars through the violence of the collision, dropped to leeward in a crippled state. She would inevitably have fallen into the hands of the enemy, had not the Count de Grasse made a signal for the fleet to shorten sail, and allow her to overtake them. Rodney, seeing his opportunity, like a skilful sea-man was not long in availing himself of it, and, by dint of smart seamanship, succeeded in placing himself to windward of a large part of the opposing squadron, which consisted, at this juncture, of thirty ships fit for action—two having been disabled in the previous engagement.

By daybreak on the 12th April, the British line of battle was formed in an incredibly short time, and with a distance of one cable's length between the ships. Our fleet awaited the attack ; and, as the signal was given for close action by the British Admiral, his ships came up in splendid order, and ranged themselves against their opponents, passing along the line for that purpose. While doing so, they gave and received tremendous broadsides. After some time spent in close and deadly conflict, during which victory was long held in suspense, the British . Admiral executed a manœuvre which had never before been practised in naval tactics. In his own ship, the " Formidable," supported by the " Namur," the " Duke," and the " Canada," he bore down with all sail set on the enemy's line, within three ships of the centre, and succeeded in breaking through it in masterly style. The utmost consternation reigned on board the " Ville de Paris," and a portion of our ships, when they found themselves, by this manœuvre, cut off from the rest of the fleet.

" In the act of doing so," says Dr. (afterwards Sir Gilbert) Blane, the surgeon of the flag-ship, " we passed within pistol-shot of the ' Glorieux,' which was so terribly handled, that, being shorn of all her masts, bowsprit, and ensign-staff, but with the white flag nailed to a stump, and breathing defiance, as it were, in her last moments, she lay a motionless hulk, presenting a spectacle which struck our Admiral's fancy as not unlike the remains of a fallen hero."

As soon as Rodney had accomplished this manœuvre, the rest of his division followed him, wore round, and doubled on our ships—thus placing between two fires those of our ships, the " Ville de Paris" among the number, separated from the rest of the fleet.

Immediately after cutting the French line, Sir George Rodney made the signal for the van to tack and gain the wind of the enemy, which was accordingly done. The result of the action was now no longer doubtful, and, after a hopeless struggle, our ships struck their colours in succession. Though the victory was decided at the moment when the " Formidable" broke our line, the effect of it was not complete until the Count de Grasse, unable to continue the action, ordered the colours of the " Ville de

Paris" to be struck. "The thrill of ecstasy," writes an officer who was present, " that penetrated every British bosom, in the triumphant moment of the surrender, is not to be described."

The "Ville de Paris" had on board some 1300 men, including troops, and, being enveloped in a perfect hurricane of missiles, the slaughter on her crowded decks was terrible. By the best accounts that could be obtained, 300 men were killed and wounded on board her alone; her sides were riven with innumerable shot, and her rigging was so torn that she was reported as having " neither a sail left nor mast fit to carry a sail, so that, being unable to keep up with her friends during their flight, and falling now into the hands of our fleet, the Count de Grasse had done all that honour required, and was sufficiently justified in striking his flag." One of the prizes, the " Glorieux," presented a spectacle of horror when boarded, which impressed all beholders even amongst the scenes of carnage around. " The number killed was so great, that the survivors, either from want of leisure or through dismay, had not thrown the bodies of the killed overboard, so that the decks were covered with the blood and mangled limbs of the dead, as well as the wounded and dying, now forlorn and helpless in their sufferings."

After the surrender of the " Ville de Paris," Sir George Rodney sent Lord Cranstoun, one of the post-captains of the " Formidable," on board of us, to beg the Count de Grasse to remain in his late flag-ship if he chose. The French Admiral, however, voluntarily went on board the " Formidable" next morning, and remained there for two days. He bore his reverse with fortitude, and indulged in badinage with Sir Gilbert Blane, the surgeon of the " Formidable." He observed he had done his duty, and bitterly upbraided his government for not sending him a reinforcement of twelve ships, as he had requested, while he attributed his misfortune to those captains of his fleet who had deserted him, notwithstanding his repeated signals to them to return to his rescue.

The ships captured were, besides the flagship, the " Glorieux," " Cæsar," " Hector," 74's; the " Ardent," " Caton," and " Jason," 64's, and two frigates, besides a ship of the line sunk. The fate of one of these prizes, the " Cæsar," was most tragic. Soon after dark a cask of spirits caught fire, owing to the carelessness of an English marine, who was carrying a candle below to search for liquor. The flames spread so fast that they could not be extinguished, and, after burning for some time, the fire reached the powder-magazine, which, exploding, blew the ship to atoms. Upwards of 400 Frenchmen, including the captain, who had been severely wounded, together with the English officer who boarded her, with 58 seamen, perished miserably. Rodney, in his official despatch, placed the loss of the French at 9000 men killed and wounded, while 8000 prisoners remained in his hands.

The loss of men sustained by the British fleet in the actions of the 9th and 12th of April, amounted, on the other hand, to only 237 killed and 760 wounded. Although the British fleet carried 156 more guns, the total weight of their broadside was less by 4396 lbs. than that of their opponents; while the difference in the number of men were still more to their disadvantage. Those of the French vessels (I do not use the personal pronoun now, as I had once more changed hands to my great delight) that escaped, were reduced to wrecks.

Sir G. Rodney, in a letter to his wife, says "The battle begen at seven in the morning, and continued till sunset, nearly eleven hours; and by persons appointed to observe, there never was seven minutes' respite during the engagement, which, I believe, was the severest that ever was fought at sea, and the most glorious for England. Count de Grasse, who is at this moment sitting in my stern galley, tells me that he thought his fleet superior to mine, and does so still, though I had two more in number; and I am of his opinion, as his was composed all of large ships, and ten of mine were only 64's." In a letter to the same lady, dated the 4th of May, he says: "Count de Grasse, poor man, now begins to feel the very great misfortune that has befallen him. As to himself, he says he is easy, as he is conscious of having done his duty; but he fears that the disagreements that will certainly happen among the nobility of France will occasion much bloodshed. He owns France (as he himself says) is a century behind us in naval affairs. And," patriotically adds the British Admiral, "may they continue so!"

I must conclude this account of the celebrated battle of the 12th of April with a few words regarding the two commanders-in-chief. The "Ville de Paris" and the other captured ships of war proceeded to England, together with the Count de Grasse, who was the first commander-in-chief of a French fleet or army who had been a prisoner in England since the reign of Queen Anne, when Marshall Tallard was taken by the Duke of Marlborough, and confined at Nottingham. He landed at Portsmouth on the 1st of August, when he was received with every demonstration of respect and sympathy for his misfortune; but on his return to France he was disgraced by his government, and in the gardens of the Tuileries his life was nearly sacrificed to the fury of an exasperated mob.

Lord Rodney, having struck his flag, sailed from Martinique on the 22nd of July, and, after putting in at Kinsale, arrived in London at the end of September. He was received with enthusiasm by a grateful court and people, and was created a peer, with a pension of £2000 a year attaching to the title for ever. He lived principally in retirement after his return to his native land, and expired on the 23rd of May, 1792, after a few hours' illness, in the seventy-fourth year of his age, having been in the navy sixty-two years, upwards of fifty of which were passed in active service.

Much has been said and written about the credit due to Rodney for the invention and execution of this manœuvre of breaking the enemy's line, and doubts have arisen whether it was the effect of design on the present occasion. I suppose there never has been any great or original conception carried out with complete success, whether in war or the more peaceful domain of science, but that some one else was put forward as the originator.

Though this manœuvre may be described in the work on naval tactics by Clerk, it was expressly treated by a French writer, Père Hoste, as early as 1688, whose volume is considered the best extant on naval tactics. It is said, also, that it was frequently practised in the Dutch Wars. Whether, however, it was designed by Rodney, or suggested to him by another (his flag-captain, Sir Charles Douglas, and others, have been put forward), it is certain that his genius seized upon it at the critical moment, and that he was enabled, through the pains he had taken in training his fleet, to achieve by it a glorious result; as in armies so in fleets, that one is effectively the most numerous, that can bring the greatest number into action at a given point. "Breaking the line," does not necessarily form part of this tactical operation.

It is curious that on this same 12th of April, 1782, the French Admiral De Suffrein practised this manœuvre in an action with Sir Edward Hughes off Trincomalee, in Ceylon; that is, he threw the weight of his fleet on one division of the British, whilst a smaller part held the remainder in check. For obvious reasons it was omitted altogether by Nelson at the Nile, though the principle of the manœuvre was carried into execution, with what fatal effect is well known.

To return to the autobiography of so humble an individual (or article, perhaps, would be a more appropriate definition) as myself.

I said that a prize crew was put on board the " Ville de Paris." Guess my astonishment when I recognized some well-known faces among the British officers and seamen, whose jolly, weather-beaten countenances and pig-tails, I was as glad to see as if I had myself been blessed with a physiognomy and a pig-tail. The commanding officer was none other than William Duckworth; but so changed. He had been commander on board the Admiral's ship, and was sent to take charge of the prize with post rank. I was glad, indeed, to see his handsome face, which had not altered a bit, that is what I could see of it, for it was partially concealed by a pair of whiskers. The acting boatswain (Jury Bo'sun, he called himself) was Tim Johnson, another old friend of the reader's and of his humble servant the autobiographer, who had been advanced to this post on account of his gallantry as boatswain's mate of the flagship during the action of the 12th.

I longed to hear how all these happy results had

been brought about; how, indeed, the ship's company of the old "Melpomene" had managed to get outside the walls of a French prison, and I was at length enlightened by Tim Johnson himself, who, one evening over a pipe, confided his history to his messmate, the gunner, who had likewise been promoted from another ship in the British fleet for gallantry, From the former I learnt that the officers and crew of the "Melpomene" were exchanged for those of a French frigate of equal force, after they had been in prison only a few months; that on regaining his freedom he had accompanied his friend Morris to his estates in England, where the latter was received by his astonished friends and relatives as one risen from the dead, and the affair of the duel having long since blown over, he settled down into his old ways as a country gentleman. He was very kind to Johnson, whom he introduced to every one as a rough diamond of the best water, and his preserver, and did all in his power to make him happy.

Johnson at first liked the novelty and ease of his position, and, more than all, he liked the unlimited supply of grog—unlimited, that is, until his patron, fearful that he would drink himself into a premature grave, placed him on an allowance of a pint a day.

Johnson acquiesced in the arrangement; "it was more than he got at sea," was the thought with which he solaced himself, but the restraints of shore life became first irksome and then intolerable; at length his soul sickened for the excitement of a naval career in war time, and his health began to fail for the want of the invigorating breezes of the ocean, upon which it may almost be said with truth he had been cradled, and so at length, after a vain attempt on the part of his friend to induce him to remain, he took his departure, expressing his astonishment that any man could stand such a life, "and take to hunting hares, and such like, after chasing Frenchmen, which is something like sport." After serving in different ships, and various parts of the world, he was appointed to the "Formidable," Sir George Rodney's flag-ship, then fitting out for service, and was recognized by James Duckworth, whom the Admiral had appointed his flag commander. Thus they once more came together, and when the officer was appointed to the command of the stately prize, with the commission of a post-captain, he did not forget his old shipmate, but took him with him as his boatswain. I thought now of the last words I heard the latter exclaim as he went over the side of the "Melpomene," a prisoner, after her capture off

Brest, though I suppose the sturdy old sailor did not lay claim to a prophetic vision of the future when he uttered them.

On our arrival in England, I was taken out of the "Ville de Paris," I suppose as a trophy—though, unlike the treatment most trophies receive, I was put away out of sight in a lumber-room at Portsmouth; and, after lying there a great many years, unheeded by every one whose duty brought them into my company, on the breaking out of the Revolution, I was fitted on board one of the ships of the Royal Navy. Some other day, I may relate to you all the vicissitudes through which I passed during a naval war, the most memorable and glorious that our country has ever engaged in. Finally, in .1831, on the founding of the Royal United Service Institution (or the United Service Museum, as it was first called by his late Majesty, King William the Fourth, who, as a sailor king, took the greatest interest in its well-being), I, the old man-o'-war's bell, was placed with other naval curiosities in that interesting collection; and there I may be inspected by any visitor who, on presentation of his or her card, as the case may be—for the ladies like nautical relics—will be admitted to admire my proportions, and muse over the interesting historical associations with which, if I may be

permitted to say so without undue egotism, my
career is connected.

And now, here I am, safely moored at last! In
these peaceful days, when the talk I hear around me
is chiefly of Universal Expositions, deep-sea tele-
graphs, modern improvements in every department,
social, political, and military, and such dry-as-dust
topics, instead of glorious victories and frigate-
duels such as I have witnessed—in these degenerate
days (I speak solely, mind you, from the point of
view of an old-world salt, who has outlived not only
all his generation, but his era)—will it be believed,
they use me for the purpose of ringing all visitors
out when the hour for closing the museum has
struck. This undignified treatment daily excites my
ire, and induces in me longings that I could have
recourse to the Japanese custom of "happy dis-
patch," and either crack my sides, or have them
cracked by the modern porter—whether soldier or
sailor, in the Society's uniform of blue, without pipe-
clay, or pigtail, or any such thing—who causes my
tongue to wag in my cavernous jaws. Ah, well!
I suppose I ought to be contented; but old salts
are allowed the privilege of grumbling, and, as I
cannot have recourse to the mollifying influences of

a tot of grog and a plug of tobacco, why, I intend to avail myself of——

"Ring—a ring—a ring—a ring—a ring."

I started up, and found my old friend the naval porter regarding me with a broad grin on his face, and lugging away at the tongue of the bell beside which I had been enjoying a siesta on that hot summer afternoon.

A great poet, comparing the realities of dreamland with those of daily life, says:—

> "Sleep hath its world,
> A boundary between the things misnamed
> Death and existence."

This world, then, in which I had been living, was only a world of sleep; and as unrealistic was the dream which

> "In its development has breath,
> And tears, and tortures, and the touch of joy."

And yet, indeed, the dream seemed to me, as I stood for a moment rubbing my eyes, as much a reality as would a retrospect of my own life, had I indulged in it during that short summer hour. Thus, in the baseless fabric of a vision, melts away THE AUTO-BIOGRAPHY OF A MAN-O'-WAR'S BELL.

Simmons & Botten, Printers, Shoe Lane, E.C.

GEORGE ROUTLEDGE & SONS'
JUVENILE BOOKS.

7 6 Dante's Divine Comedy. Translated by H. W. LONGFELLOW. 1 vol., crown 8vo, cloth.

The Poetical Works of Lord Lytton. With Frontispiece and Vignette. Fcap. 8vo, cloth.

Hogg on the Microscope. With 500 Illustrations and 8 Coloured Plates.

Andersen's Stories for the Household. 8vo, cloth, gilt edges, with 240 Illustrations.

Robinson Crusoe. With 110 Plates by J. D. WATSON.

In cloth, gilt edges, **6s.** each.

6 0 Routledge's Every Boy's Annual. Edited by EDMUND ROUTLEDGE. With many Illustrations, and beautiful Coloured Plates.

Shipwrecks ; or, Disasters at Sea. By W. H. G. KINGSTON. With more than 100 Illustrations.

The Adventures of Robinson Playfellow, a Young French Marine. With 24 Plates, and many Woodcuts.

More Bab Ballads. By W. S. GILBERT. With Illustrations by the Author.

Travelling About. By Lady BARKER. With 6 Plates and 5 Maps.

Ridiculous Rhymes. Drawn by H. S. MARKS. Printed in Colours by VINCENT BROOKS. 4to, fancy cover.

Pepper's Boy's Play-book of Science. 400 Plates.

D Aulnoy's Fairy Tales. Translated by PLANCHE.

Planche's Fairy Tales. By PERRAULT, &c.

Pepper's Play-book of Mines, Minerals, and Metals. With 300 Illustrations. Post 8vo, gilt.

Motley's Rise of the Dutch Republic. Crown 8vo, cloth, gilt.

An Illustrated Natural History. By the Rev. J. G. WOOD, M.A. With 500 Illustrations by WILLIAM HARVEY, and 8 full-page Plates by WOLF and HARRISON WEIR. Post 8vo, cloth, gilt edges.

Lord Lytton's Dramatic Works. Crown 8vo, cloth, gilt edges.

Routledge's Five-Shilling Books.

s. d.

Grimm's Household Stories. With 240 Illustrations by WEHNERT. Crown 8vo, gilt. — 5 0

Hans Andersen's Stories and Tales. 80 Illustrations, and Coloured Plates.

Walter Crane's Picture Book. With 64 pages of Coloured Plates. Cloth, gilt edges.

Country Life. Illustrated by Poetry, and 40 Pictures by BIRKET FOSTER.

Sage Stuffing for Green Goslings ; or, Saws for the Goose and Saws for the Gander. By the Hon. HUGH ROWLEY. With Illustrations by the Author.

What the Moon Saw, and other Tales. By HANS C. ANDERSEN. With 80 Illustrations, and Coloured Plates.

Chimes and Rhymes for Youthful Times. With Coloured Plates. (Uniform with " Schnick-Schnack.")

Buds and Flowers. A New Coloured Book for Children. (Uniform with " Schnick-Schnack.") Small 4to, cloth.

Schnick-Schnack. Trifles for the Little Ones. With Coloured Plates. Small 4to, cloth.

Watts' Divine and Moral Songs. With 108 Woodcuts, engraved by COOPER.

Original Poems for Infant Minds. By JANE and A. TAYLOR. With Original Illustrations by the Best Artists, engraved by J. D. COOPER.

Little Lays for Little Folk. Selected by J. G. WATTS. With Original Illustrations by the best living Artists, engraved by J. D. COOPER. 4to, cloth, gilt edges.

Sing-Song. A Nursery Rhyme-Book. By CHRISTINA G. ROSSETTI. With 120 Illustrations by ARTHUR HUGHES, engraved by the Brothers DALZIEL.

The Picture Book of Reptiles, Fishes, and Insects. By the Rev. J. G. WOOD, M.A. With 250 Illustrations. 4to, cloth.

—————————— **Birds.** By the Rev. J. G. WOOD, M.A. With 242 Illustrations. 4to, cloth.

—————————— **Mammalia.** By the Rev. J. G. WOOD, M.A. With 250 Illustrations. 4to, cloth.

Routledge's British Poets.

EDITED BY THE REV. R. A. WILLMOTT.

Illustrated by FOSTER, GILBERT, CORBOULD, FRANKLIN, and
HARVEY, elegantly printed on good paper, fcap. 8vo,
gilt edges, bevelled boards.

s. d.

5 0 1. **Spenser's Faerie Queen.** Illustrated by COR-BOULD.

2. **Chaucer's Canterbury Tales.** Illustrated by CORBOULD.

3. **Kirke White.** By SOUTHEY. Illustrated by BIRKET FOSTER.

4. **Southey's Joan of Arc, and Minor Poems.**

6. **Pope's Poetical Works.** Edited by CARY.

7. **Milton's Poetical Works.** Illustrated by HARVEY.

8. **Thomson, Beattie, and West.** Illustrated by BIRKET FOSTER.

10. **Herbert.** With Life and Notes by the Rev. R. A. WILLMOTT.

12. **Cowper.** Illustrated by BIRKET FOSTER. Edited by WILLMOTT.

13. **Longfellow's Complete Poetical Works.** With Illustrations. Fcap. 8vo.

14. **Longfellow's Prose Works.** Fcap. 8vo.

16. **Burns' Poetical Works.** Illustrated by JOHN GILBERT.

17. **Fairfax's Tasso's Jerusalem Delivered.** Illustrated by CORBOULD.

18. **Percy's Reliques of Ancient English Poetry.**

19. **Scott's Poetical Works.** Illustrated by COR-BOULD.

21. **Wordsworth.** Illustrated by BIRKET FOSTER.

22. **Crabbe.** Illustrated by BIRKET FOSTER.

25. **Moore's Poems.** Illustrated by CORBOULD, &c.

26. **Byron's Poems.** Illustrated by GILBERT, WOLF, FOSTER, &c.

29. **Bennett's Poetical Works.** Portrait and Illustrations.

s. d.

31. **Campbell's Poetical Works.** Illustrated by W. HARVEY. 5 0

32. **Lover's Poetical Works.** With a Portrait.

33. **Rogers' Poetical Works.** With a Portrait.

36. **Dryden's Poetical Works.** With a Portrait, &c.

37. **Mrs. Hemans' Poems.**

Routledge's Five-Shilling Juvenile Books.

In fcap. 8vo and post 8vo, Illustrated by GILBERT, HARVEY, FOSTER, and ZWECKER, gilt.

Marryat's Children of the New Forest.

Marryat's Little Savage.

Lilian's Golden Hours. By Silverpen.

Boy's Treasury of Sports and Pastimes.

The Queens of Society.

The Wits and Beaux of Society.

Entertaining Knowledge.

Pleasant Tales.

Extraordinary Men and Women.

Dora and her Papa. By the Author of "Lilian's Golden Hours."

Great Battles of the British Army.

The Prince of the House of David.

The Pillar of Fire.

The Throne of David.

The Story of the Reformation. By D'Aubigne.

Popular Astronomy and Orbs of Heaven.

Once upon a Time. By Charles Knight.

White's History of England.

The Spectator. Gilt edges.

The Winborough Boys. By the Rev. H. C. Adams. 5 0

The Prairie Bird. By the Hon. C. Murray.

The Great Sieges of History. With Coloured Plates.

Cooper's Leatherstocking Tales.

Great Battles of the British Navy. With Coloured Plates.

Memoirs of Great Commanders. With Coloured Plates.

The Playfellow. By Harriet Martineau. With Coloured Plates.

The Family Arabian Nights. With Coloured Plates.

The Adventures of Robin Hood. With Coloured Plates.

Holiday Stories. By Lady Barker.

Half Hours with the Best Letter Writers. By Charles Knight.

Characteristics of Women. By Mrs. Jameson.

Royal Princesses of England.

What Men have Said about Women.

Routledge's Four-and-Sixpenny Juveniles.

A NEW SERIES OF JUVENILE WORKS.

All well Illustrated, and bound in an entirely New Binding,
expressly designed for them.

s. d.   **List of the Series.**

4 6 *The Orville College Boys.* | *Tales upon Texts.* By the
By Mrs. Henry Wood. | Rev. H. C. Adams.
Wonderful Inventions. By | *Pictures from Nature.* By
John Timbs. | Mary Howitt.
Æsop's Fables. With Plates | *Stephen Scudamore the*
by H. Weir. | *Younger.* By A. Locker.
The Illustrated Girl's Own | *Hunting Grounds of the*
Treasury. | *Old World.*
The Boy's Own Country | *Watch the End.* By
Book. By Miller. | Thomas Miller.
The Forest Ranger. By | *Last Hours of Great Men.*
Major Campbell | *Robinson Crusoe.* With
Pleasures of Old Age. | 300 Plates.

In fcap. 8vo, cloth, gilt edges, price 4s. each.

4 0 **Every Girl's Book.** By Miss LAWFORD. With many
Illustrations.

Every Little Boy's Book. By EDMUND ROUTLEDGE.
With many Illustrations.

Routledge's Album Series.

In cloth gilt, price 3s. 6d., beautifully printed on toned paper.

3 6 **Otto Speckter's Fables.** With 100 Coloured Plates.
A New Edition. 4to, cloth, gilt edges.

Routledge's Sunday Album for Children. With
80 Plates by J. D. WATSON, Sir JOHN GILBERT, and others.

The Boys' and Girls' Illustrated Gift-Book. With
many Illustrations by McCONNELL, WEIR, and others.

The Child's Picture Fable Book. With 60 Plates
by HARRISON WEIR.

The Coloured Album for Children. With 72 pages
of Coloured Plates.

The Picture Book of the Sagacity of Animals.
With 60 Plates by HARRISON WEIR.

The Boys' Own Story Book. Many Illustrations.

s. d.

Album for Children. With 180 page Plates by 3 6
MILLAIS, Sir JOHN GILBERT, and others. Imp. 16mo, cloth.

Popular Nursery Tales. With 180 Illustrations by
J. D. WATSON and others. Imp. 16mo, cloth.

Child's Picture Story Book. With 180 Plates.
Imp. 16mo, cloth.

A Picture Story Book. Containing "King Nutcracker," and other Tales. 300 Illustrations. Imp. 16mo, cloth.

Mixing in Society. A Complete Manual of Manners.

The Children's Bible Book. With 100 Illustrations,
engraved by DALZIEL.

A Handy History of England for the Young.
With 120 Illustrations, engraved by DALZIEL.

Child Life. With Plates by OSCAR PLETSCH. Gilt
edges.

Petsetilla's Posy. By TOM HOOD. Plates by F.
BARNARD. Gilt edges.

One by One. A Child's Book of Tales and Fables.
With 50 Illustrations by OSCAR PLETSCH, and others.

Rhyme and Reason. A Picture Book of Verses for
Little Folks. With Illustrations by WOLF, and others.

The Golden Harp. Hymns, Rhymes, and Songs
for the Young. With 50 Illustrations.

Griset's Grotesques. With Rhymes by TOM HOOD.
Fancy boards.

The Children's Poetry Book. With 16 Coloured
Plates. Square, cloth.

Out of the Heart: Spoken to the Little Ones. By
HANS ANDERSEN. With 16 Coloured Plates. Cloth.

The Nursery Picture Book. With 630 Illustrations.
Folio, boards.

Bowman's Juvenile Books.

With Plates, fcap. 8vo, cloth gilt.

The Boy Voyagers.	*The Young Exiles.*	3 6
The Castaways.	*The Bear Hunters.*	
The Young Nile Voyagers.	*The Kangaroo Hunters.*	
The Boy Pilgrims.	*Young Yachtsman.*	
The Boy Foresters.	*Among the Tartar Tents.*	
Tom and the Crocodiles.	*Clarissa.*	
Esperanza.	*How to make the Best of It.*	

ROUTLEDGE'S

Three-and-Sixpenny Reward Books.

With 8 Illustrations, fcap. 8vo, bevelled boards, gilt sides.

3 6 *Ancient Cities of the World.*
Great Cities of the Middle Ages.
Robinson Crusoe. Coloured Plates.
Sandford and Merton. Coloured Plates.
Evenings at Home. Coloured Plates.
Swiss Family Robinson. Coloured Plates.
Edgeworth's Popular Tales. Coloured Plates.
———— *Moral Tales.* Coloured Plates.
———— *Parents' Assistant.* Coloured Plates.
———— *Early Lessons.* Coloured Plates.
The Old Helmet. By the Author of "The Wide, Wide World."

The Wide, Wide World.
The Travels of Rolando. 1st Series.
Celebrated Children.
Edgar Clifton.
The Lamplighter.
Melbourne House.
Seven Wonders of the World.
Queechy.
Ellen Montgomery's Bookshelf.
The Two Schoolgirls.
The Pilgrim's Progress. With Coloured Plates.
The Girl's Birthday Book. With many Illustrations.
The Word; or, Walks from Eden.
Glen Luna Family.
Mabel Vaughan.

ROUTLEDGE'S

Three-and-Sixpenny Juvenile Books.

Foolscap 8vo, with Engravings, gilt.

3 6 *Hans Andersen's Tales.*
Heroines of History.
Sketches and Anecdotes of Animal Life. By Rev. J. G. Wood.
Grimm's Home Stories.
Animal Traits and Characteristics. By Rev. J. G. Wood.
Wood's My Feathered Friends.
White's Selborne. 200 cuts.

The Four Sisters.
The Golden Rule.
Boyhood of Great Men.
Footprints of Famous Men. By J. G. Edgar.
Rev. J. G. Wood's Boy's Own Natural History Book.
Lillieslea. By Mary Howitt.
Heroines of Domestic Life.
Tales of Charlton School. By the Rev. H. C. Adams.

THREE-AND-SIXPENNY JUVENILES—continued.

s. d.
3 6

Schoolboy Honour. By Rev. H. C. Adams.

Red Eric. By R. M. Ballantyne.

Louis' School Days.

Wild Man of the West. By Ballantyne.

Dashwood Priory. By E. J. May.

Freaks on the Fells. By R. M. Ballantyne.

Lamb's Tales from Shakspeare.

Balderscourt; or, Holiday Tales. By Rev. H. C. Adams.

Rob Roy. By James Grant.

The Girl of the Family. By the Author of "A Trap to Catch a Sunbeam."

Paul Gerrard, the Cabin Boy. By Kingston.

Johnny Jordan. By Mrs. Eiloart.

Ernie Elton, at Home and at School.

The Village Idol. By the Author of "A Trap to Catch a Sunbeam."

Children of Blessing. By Author of "The Four Sisters."

Lost among the Wild Men.

Percy's Tales of the Kings of England.

Boys of Beechwood. By Mrs. Eiloart.

Papa's Wise Dogs.

Digby Heathcote. By Kingston.

Hawthorne's Wonder Book.

The Doctor's Ward. By the Author of "The Four Sisters."

Will Adams. By Dalton.

Little Ladders to Learning. 1st series.

Ditto. 2nd series.

The Child's Country Book. By T. Miller. Coloured Plates.

The Child's Story Book. By T. Miller. Coloured Plates.

Uncle Tom's Cabin.

Tom Dunstone's Troubles. By Mrs. Eiloart.

The Young Marooners.

Influence. By the Author of "A Trap to Catch a Sunbeam."

Jack of the Mill. By W. Howitt.

Patience Strong. By the Author of "The Gayworthys."

Dick Rodney. By J. Grant.

Jack Manly. By J. Grant.

Don Quixote. (Family Edition.)

Our Domestic Pets. By Rev. J. G. Wood.

History for Boys. By J. G. Edgar.

Through Life and for Life.

Saxelford. By E. J. May.

Old Tales for the Young.

Harry Hope's Holiday.

Boy Life among the Indians.

Old Saws new Set. By the Author of "A Trap to Catch a Sunbeam."

Hollowdell Grange.

Mayhew's Wonders of Science.

——— *Peasant - Boy Philosopher.*

Barford Bridge. By the Rev. H. C. Adams.

The White Brunswickers. By Rev. H. C. Adams.

A Boy's Adventures in the Wilds of Australia. By W. Howitt.

Tales of Walter's School Days. By Rev. H. C. Adams.

The Path She Chose. By F. M. S.

Little Women. By L. Alcott.

Routledge's British Poets.

(3s. 6d. Editions.)

Elegantly printed on tinted paper, fcap. 8vo, gilt edges,
with Illustrations.

s. d.

3 6 *Longfellow.* * Complete.
Cowper. *
Milton. *
Wordsworth. *
Southey.
Goldsmith.
Kirke White.
Burns. *
Moore. *
Byron. *
Pope.
James Montgomery.
Scott. *
Herbert.
Campbell. *
Bloomfield. *
Shakspeare. *
Chaucer. *
Willis.

Golden Gleanings.
Choice Poems.
Shakspeare Gems.
Wit and Humour.
Wise Sayings.
*Longfellow's Dante—Para-
diso.*
——— *Purgatorio.*
——— *Inferno.*
Lover's Poems. *
*Book of Familiar Quota-
tions.*
Bret Harte.
Leigh Hunt. *
Dryden. *
Ainsworth. *
Spenser. *
Rogers. *
Mrs. Hemans. *

Volumes marked * are kept in Morocco and Ivory Bindings,
price 7s. 6d.

Mayne Reid's Juveniles.

In fcap. 8vo, cloth gilt, with Illustrations.

3 6 *Bruin.*
The Boy Tar.
The Desert Home.
Odd People.
Ran away to Sea.
The Forest Exiles.
The Young Yagers

The Young Voyagers.
The Plant Hunters.
The Quadroon.
The War Trail.
The Bush Boys.
The Boy Hunters.

Routledge's Standard Library.

In post 8vo, toned paper, green cloth, **3s. 6d.** each.

s. d

The Arabian Nights.
Don Quixote.
Gil Blas.
Curiosities of Literature. By Isaac D'Israeli.
1,001 Gems of British Poetry.
The Blackfriars Shakspeare.
Cruden's Concordance.
Boswell's Life of Johnson.
The Works of Oliver Goldsmith.
Routledge's Pronouncing Dictionary.
The Family Doctor.

Ten Thousand Wonderful Things.
Sterne's Works.
Extraordinary Popular Delusions.
Bartlett's Familiar Quotations.
The Spectator.
Routledge's Modern Speaker.
1,001 Gems of Prose.
Pope's Homer's Iliad and Odyssey.
Book of Modern Anecdotes.
Josephus.

3 6

Routledge's Three-Shilling Juveniles.

Under the above title Messrs. G. ROUTLEDGE & SONS are about to issue a New Series of Juvenile Books, all well Illustrated and well bound in a New and Elegant Binding.

List of the Series.

Boys at Home. By C. Adams.
Cecil Raye.
Dogs and their Ways.
Our Holiday Camp. By St. John Corbet.
Helen Mordaunt. By the Author of "Naomi."
Romance of Adventure.
The Island Home.

Play Hours and Half Holidays.
Walks and Talks of Two Schoolboys.
Hildred the Daughter.
Hardy and Hunter.
Fred and the Gorillas.
Guizot's Moral Tales.
Frank Wildman.

3 6

Routledge's One-Syllable Series.

By MARY GODOLPHIN.

In 16mo, cloth gilt, with Coloured Plates, price **2s. 6d.** each.

Bunyan's Pilgrim's Progress.
Evenings at Home.

Swiss Family Robinson.
Robinson Crusoe.
Child's First Lesson Book.

2 6

Routledge's Half-Crown Juveniles.

Fcap. 8vo, Illustrated by the Best Artists, gilt, **2s. 6d.** each.

s. d.

2 6 *Arbell.*

Eda Morton and her Cousins. By M. M. Bell.

Gilbert the Adventurer.

The Lucky Penny, and other Tales. By Mrs. S. C. Hall.

Minna Raymond. Illustrated by B. Foster.

Helena Bertram. By the Author of "The Four Sisters."

Heroes of the Workshop, &c. By E. L. Brightwell.

Sunshine and Cloud. By Miss Bowman.

The Maze of Life. By the Author of "The Four Sisters."

The Twins; or, Sisterly Love.

The Wide, Wide World.

The Lamplighter. By Cummins.

The Rector's Daughter. By Miss Bowman.

The Old Helmet. By Miss Wetherell.

Deeds, Not Words.

The Secret of a Life.

Queechy. By Miss Wetherell.

Sir Roland Ashton. By Lady C. Long.

Sir Wilfred's Seven Flights. By Madame de Chatelaine.

Ellen Montgomery's Book-Shelf. With Coloured Illustrations.

The Two School Girls. With Coloured Illustrations.

The First Lieutenant's Story.

Melbourne House. By Miss Wetherell.

The Word; or, Walks from Eden.

Rough Diamonds. By J. Hollingshead.

The Medwins of Wykeham. By the Author of "Marian."

The Young Artists.

The Boy Cavalier. By the Rev. H. C. Adams.

Gilderoy, the Hero of Scotland.

Lamb's Tales.

Stories of Old Daniel.

Extraordinary Men.

Extraordinary Women.

Life of Napoleon.

Popular Astronomy.

Orbs of Heaven.

Pilgrim's Progress. By Offor.

Friend or Foe: A Tale of Sedgmoor. By the Rev. H. C. Adams.

Tales of Naval Adventure.

Matilda Lonsdale.

The Life of Wellington.

The Glen Luna Family.

Uncle Tom's Cabin.

Mabel Vaughan.

Christian Melville.

The Letter of Marque.

Routledge's Books for Young Readers.

Illustrated by ABSOLON, GILBERT, HARRISON WEIR, &c.,
square royal, gilt, **2s.** each.

s. d.

Amusing Tales for Young People. By Mrs. Myrtle.

The Donkey's Shadow, and other Stories.

The Broken Pitcher, and other Stories.

The Little Lychetts. By the Author of "Olive," &c.

The Great Wonders of the World.

My First Picture Book. 36 Pages of Coloured Plates. 16mo, cloth.

A Visit to the Zoological 2 0 *Gardens.*

The Richmonds' Tour in Europe.

Aunt Bessie's Picture Book. With 96 Pages of Plates.

Little Lily's Picture Book. With 96 Pages of Plates.

The Story of a Nutcracker. With 234 Pictures.

Old Mother Hubbard's Picture Book. 36 Pages of Coloured Plates.

Two-Shilling Gift-Books.

With Illustrations, strongly bound in cloth.

Ten Moral Tales. By Guizot.

Juvenile Tales for all Seasons

Conquest and Self-Conquest.

Evenings at Donaldson Manor.

Praise and Principle.

Grace & Isabel (M'Intosh).

Charms and Counter-Charms.

Gertrude and Eulalie.

Robert and Harold.

Robinson the Younger.

Amy Carlton.

Robinson Crusoe.

Laura Temple.

Harry and his Homes.

Our Native Land.

Bundle of Sticks.

Family Pictures from the Bible.

Hester and I; or, Beware 2 0 of Worldliness. By Mrs. Manners.

The Cherry Stones. By Rev. H. C. Adams.

The First of June. By Rev. H. C. Adams.

Rosa: A Story for Girls.

May Dundas; or, The Force of Example. By Mrs. Geldart.

Glimpses of Our Island Home. By Mrs. Geldart.

The Indian Boy. By Rev. H. C. Adams.

Ernie Elton at Home.

The Standard Poetry Book for Schools.

Try and Trust. By Author of "Arthur Morland."

Swiss Family Robinson.

Evenings at Home.

---

s. d. TWO-SHILLING GIFT-BOOKS—continued.

2 0 *Sandford and Merton.*
Ernie Elton at School.
John Hartley.
Jack of all Trades. **By T.** Miller.
The Wonder Book.
Tanglewood Tales.
Archie Blake.
Inez and Emmeline.
The Orphan of Waterloo.
Maum Guinea.
Adventures of Joseph Hawse-pipe.
Todd's Lectures to Children.
Marooner's Island.
The Mayflower. **By Mrs.** Stowe.
Anecdotes of Dogs.
Mr. Rutherford's Children.
The Play-Day Book. **By** Fanny Fern. With Coloured Plates.
Emma. By Jane Austen.
Mansfield Park. By Austen.

Northanger Abbey. By Jane Austen.
Pride and Prejudice. By Jane Austen.
Sense and Sensibility. By Jane Austen.
Village Sketches. By the Rev. C. T. Whitehead.
The Boy's Reader.
The Girl's Reader.
Spider Spinnings.
Stories for Sundays. By the Rev. H. C. Adams. 1st series.
Stories for Sundays. By Rev. H. C. Adams. 2nd series.
Adventures among the Indians.
Cousin Aleck.
The Doctor's Birthday. By the Rev. H. C. Adams.
Walter's Friend. By the Rev. H. C. Adams.
Little Women. 1st series.
Little Women. 2nd series.

The Hans Andersen Library.

In 13 Books, fcap. 8vo, gilt, 1s. 6d. each.

---

1 6 *The Red Shoes.*
The Silver Shilling.
The Little Match-Girl.
The Darning Needle.
The Tinder Box.
The Goloshes of Fortune.
The Marsh King's Daughter.
The Wild Swans.

Everything in its Right Place.
Under the Willow Tree.
The Old Church Bell.
The Ice Maiden.
The Will o' the Wisp.
Poultry Meg's Family.
Put Off is Not Done with.

Each Volume contains a variety of Tales, a Frontispiece in colours, and an average of 16 other Pictures, engraved by the Brothers DALZIEL.

Routledge's Eighteenpenny Juveniles.

In square 16mo, cloth, with Illustrations by GILBERT, ABSOLON, &c.

s. d.
1 6

Peasant and Prince. By Harriet Martineau.

Crofton Boys. By ditto.

Feats on the Fiord. By do.

Settlers at Home. By ditto.

Holiday Rambles; or, The School Vacation.

Little Drummer: A Tale of the Russian War.

Frank. By Maria Edgeworth.

Rosamond. By Maria Edgeworth.

Harry and Lucy, Little Dog Trusty, The Cherry Orchard, &c.

A Hero; or, Philip's Book. By the Author of "John Halifax."

Story of an Apple. By Lady Campbell.

The Cabin by the Wayside.

Memoirs of a Doll. By Mrs. Bisset.

Black Princess.

Laura and Ellen; or, Time Works Wonders.

Emigrant's Lost Son. By G. H. Hall.

Runaways (The) and the Gipsies.

Daddy Dacre's School. By Mrs. Hall.

British Wolf Hunters. By Thomas Miller.

Bow of Faith (The); or, Old Testament Lessons. By Maria Wright.

Anchor of Hope; or, New Testament Lessons. By Maria Wright.

Mrs. Loudon's Young Naturalist.

Accidents of Childhood; or, Stories for Heedless Children.

Annie Maitland; or, The Lesson of Life. By D. Richmond.

Lucy Elton; or, Home and School. By the Author of "The Twins."

Daily Thoughts for Children. By Mrs. Geldart.

Emilie the Peacemaker. By Mrs. Geldart.

Truth is Everything. By Mrs. Geldart.

Christmas Holidays. By Miss Jane Strickland.

Rose and Kate; or, The Little Howards.

Aunt Emma. By the Author of "Rose and Kate."

The Island of the Rainbow. By Mrs. Newton Crossland.

Max Frere; or, Return Good for Evil.

Rainbows in Springtide.

The Child's First Book of Natural History. By A. L. Bond.

Florence the Orphan.

The Castle and Cottage. By Perring.

Fabulous Histories. By Mrs. Trimmer.

School Days at Harrow.

Mrs. Barbauld's Lessons.

Holidays at Limewood.

Traditions of Palestine. By Martineau.

On the Sea. By Miss Campbell.

Games and Sports.

The Young Angler.

Athletic Sports.

EIGHTEENPENNY JUVENILES—continued.

s. d.

1. 6 Games of Skill.
Scientific Amusements.
Miriam and Rosette.
Ruth Hall. By Fanny Fern.

The Picture Book of Animals and Birds.
Boy Life on the Water.
Original Poems. Complete. By A. and J. Taylor.

Routledge's Shilling Song-Books.

EDITED AND COMPILED BY J. E. CARPENTER.
Fcap. 24mo, boards, with fancy covers.

1 0

Modern.
Popular.
Universal.
Comic.
National.
Humorous.
New British.

New Standard.
The Entertainer's.
The Comic Vocalist.
New Scotch.
New Irish.
The Moral.
The Religious.

The Master Jack Series.

In small 4to, fancy cover, each with 48 pages of Plates.

1 0

Master Jack.
Mamma's Return.
Nellie and Bertha.
The Cousins.
Tales of the Genii.
Sindbad the Voyager.
Robin Hood.
Prince Hempseed.

The Enchanted Horse.
Dame Mitchell and her Cat
Nursery Rhymes.
The Tiger Lily.
The Lent Jewels.
Bible Stories.
My Best Frock.

Routledge's One-Shilling Juveniles.

In post 8vo, price 1s., well printed, with Illustrations.

s. d.

Grace Greenwood's Stories for her Nephews and Nieces.

Helen's Fault. By the Author of "Adelaide Lindsay."

The Cousins. By Miss M'Intosh.

Ben Howard; or, Truth and Honesty. By C. Adams.

Bessie and Tom; A Book for Boys and Girls.

Beechnut: A Franconian Story. By Jacob Abbott.

Wallace: A Franconian Story. By Jacob Abbott.

Madeline. By Jacob Abbott.

Mary Erskine. By Jacob Abbott.

Mary Bell. By Jacob Abbott.

Visit to my Birth-place. By Miss Bunbury.

Carl Krinken; or, The Christmas Stocking. By Miss Wetherell.

Mr. Rutherford's Children. By Miss Wetherell.

Mr. Rutherford's Children. 2nd series. By Miss Wetherell.

Emily Herbert. By Miss M'Intosh.

Rose and Lillie Stanhope. By Miss M'Intosh.

Casper. By Miss Wetherell.

The Brave Boy; or, Christian Heroism.

Magdalene and Raphael.

The Story of a Mouse. By Mrs. Perring.

Our Charlie. By Mrs. Stowe.

Village School-feast. By Mrs. Perring.

Nelly, the Gipsy Girl.

The Birthday Visit. By 1 0 Miss Wetherell.

Stories for Week Days and Sundays.

Maggie and Emma. By Miss M'Intosh.

Charley and Georgie; or, The Children at Gibraltar.

Story of a Penny. By Mrs. Perring.

Aunt Maddy's Diamonds. By Harriet Myrtle.

Two School Girls. By Miss Wetherell.

The Widow and her Daughter. By Miss Wetherell.

Gertrude and her Bible. By Miss Wetherell.

The Rose in the Desert. By Miss Wetherell.

The Little Black Hen. By Miss Wetherell.

Martha and Rachel. By Miss Wetherell.

The Carpenter's Daughter. By Miss Wetherell.

The Prince in Disguise. By Miss Wetherell.

The Story of a Cat. By Mrs. Perring.

Easy Poetry for Children. With a Coloured Frontispiece and Vignette.

The Basket of Flowers. With a Coloured Frontispiece and Vignette.

Ashgrove Farm. By Mrs. Myrtle.

The Story of a Dog. By Mrs. Perring.

Rills from the Fountain: A Lesson for the Young. By Rev. Richard Newton.

s. d.

ONE-SHILLING JUVENILES—continued.

1 0 *The Angel of the Iceberg.*
By the Rev. John Todd.
Todd's Lectures for Children. 1st series.
———————— 2nd series.
Little Poems for Little Readers.
Minnie's Legacy.
Neighbourly Love.
Kitty's Victory.
Elise and her Rabbits.
Happy Charlie.
Annie Price.
The Little Oxleys. By Mrs. W. Denzey Burton.
Book of One Syllable. With Coloured Plates.
Little Helps. With Coloured Plates.
Uncle Tom's Cabin, for Children.
Aunt Margaret's Visit.
Keeper's Travels in Search of his Master.
Richmond's Annals of the Poor.

Child's Illustrated Poetry Book.
The New Book of One Syllable.
Blanche and Agnes.
The Lost Chamois Hunter.
The Gates Ajar.
The Sunday Book of One Syllable.
Mrs. Sedgwick's Pleasant Tales.
Uncle Frank's Home Stories.
Village Sketches. 1st series.
———————— 2nd series.
Our Poor Neighbours.
Tales in Short Words.
Watts's Songs.
Æsop's Fables.
Language and Poetry of Flowers.
Stuyvesant.
Susan Gray.
Original Poems. 1st series.
———————— 2nd series.
Nursery Rhymes.

Price 1s. each.

1 0 *Dance Album.* With Rules and Music. Cloth, gilt edges.
The Nursery Library. 12 Books in a Packet. 1st and 2nd series.
Stories for Sundays. By Rev. H. C. Adams. Two series. 12 Books in Packet.
Routledge's British Reading-Book. Plate on every page, demy 8vo, cloth.
Routledge's British Spelling-Book. Demy 8vo, cloth.
A Coloured Picture-Book for the Little Ones. Small 4to, fancy cover.
Routledge's Comic Reciter. Fcap. 8vo, boards.
——————— *Popular Reciter.* Fcap. 8vo, boards.
Ready-Made Speeches. Fcap. 8vo, boards.
The Nursery Library. 12 Books in a Packet.

Christmas Books.

Fcap. 8vo, boards, 1s. each, with fancy covers.

s. d.

New Charades for the Drawing Room. By Author of "A Trap to Catch a Sunbeam."
Riddles and Jokes.
The Dream Book and Fortune Teller.

Acting Proverbs for the Drawing Room.
Fly Notes on Conjuring.
Original Double Acrostics. 2nd series.
A Shilling's Worth of Fun.

1 0

Routledge's Ninepenny Juveniles.

With Coloured Plates, 18mo, cloth, gilt.

Ally and her Schoolfellow.
Loyal Charlie Bentham.
Simple Stories for Children.
A Child's First Book.
Story of Henrietta.
Stories from English History.
Life of Robinson Crusoe.
Little Paul and the Moss Wreaths.
Watts' Divine Moral Songs.

Cobwebs to Catch Flies.
Barbauld's Hymns in Prose.
Prince Arthur.
A Winter's Wreath.
Twelve Links.
Easy Talks.
Susan and the Doll.
Juvenile Tales.
Six Short Stories.
The Captive Skylark.

0 9

Routledge's Sixpenny Story Books.

Royal 32mo, with Illustrations.
These are also kept in Paper Covers, price 4d. each.

History of My Pets.
Hubert Lee.
Ellen Leslie.
Jessie Graham.
Florence Arnott.
Blind Alice.
Grace and Clara.
Recollections of My Childhood.

Egerton Roscoe.
Flora Mortimer.
Charles Hamilton.
Story of a Drop of Water.
The False Key.
The Bracelets.
Waste Not, Want Not.
Tarlton; or, Forgive and Forget.

0 6

SIXPENNY STORY BOOKS—continued.

s. d

0 6 *Lazy Lawrence, and the White Pigeon.*
The Barring Out.
The Orphans and Old Poz.
The Mimic.
The Purple Jar, and other Tales.
The Birthday Present, and the Basket Woman.
Simple Susan.
The Little Merchants.
Tale of the Universe.
Robert Dawson.
Kate Campbell.
Basket of Flowers.
Babes in the Basket.
The Jewish Twins.
Children on the Plains.
Little Henry and his Bearer.
Learning better than Houses and Lands.
Maud's First Visit to her Aunt.
Easy Poems. Plain edges.
The Boy Captive. By Peter Parley.
Stories of Child Life.
The Dairyman's Daughter.
Arthur's Tales for the Young.
Hawthorne's Gentle Boy.
Pleasant and Profitable.
Parley's Poetry and Prose.
Arthur's Stories for Little Girls.
Arthur's Last Penny.
The Young Cottager.

Parley's Thomas Titmouse.
Arthur's Christmas Story.
The Lost Lamb.
Arthur's Stories for Little Boys.
Arthur's Book about Boys.
Arthur's Organ Boy.
Margaret Jones.
The Two School Girls.
Widow and her Daughter.
The Rose in the Desert.
The Little Black Hen.
Martha and Rachel.
The Carpenter's Daughter
The Prince in Disguise.
Gertrude and her Bible.
Bright-eyed Bessie.
The Contrast. By Miss Edgeworth.
The Grateful Negro. By Miss Edgeworth.
Jane Hudson.
A Kiss for a Blow.
Young Negro Servant.
Lina and her Cousins.
The Gates Ajar. Plain edges.
Sunday School Reader.
Hearty Staves.
Contentment better than Wealth.
Robinson Crusoe.
Patient Working no Loss.
No such Word as Fail.
Tales of Truth & Kindness.
Edward Howard.

Routledge's Miniature Library.

In 64mo, 6d. each, cloth gilt, with Coloured Frontispiece.

s. d.
0 6

Language of Flowers.	*Ball Room Manual.*
Etiquette for Gentlemen.	*Handbook of Carving.*
Etiquette of Courtship and Matrimony.	*Toasts and Sentiments.*
Etiquette for Ladies.	*How to Dress well.*

Routledge's Sixpenny Songs.

EDITED BY J. E. CARPENTER. Fcap. 48mo, fancy covers.

0 6

Fireside Songster.	*Family Song Book.*
Home Songster.	*Amusing Songster.*
British Song Book.	*The Social Songster.*
The Select Songster.	*Songs for all Seasons.*
The Convivial Songster.	*The Droll Ditty Song Book.*
Merry Songs for Merry Meetings.	*The Whimsical Songster.*
The Funny Man's Song Book.	*Highland Songster.*
The Fashionable Song Book.	*Blue Bell Songster.*
Drawing-Room Song Book.	*Shamrock Songster.*
The Laughable Song Book.	*Mavourneen Songster.*
The Sensation Songster.	*The Sacred Song Book.*
Everybody's Song Book.	*The Devout Songster.*
The Social Songster.	*Songs for the Righteous.*
	Songs of Grace.

Routledge's Sixpenny Handbooks.

In royal 32mo, 6d. each, with Illustrations, boards.

o 6 *Swimming and Skating.* By the Rev. J. G. Wood.
Gymnastics.
Chess. With Diagrams. By G. F. Pardon.
Whist.
Billiards and Bagatelle. By G. F. Pardon.
Draughts and Backgammon. By G. F. Pardon.
Cricket.
The Cardplayer. By G. F. Pardon.
Rowing and Sailing.
Riding and Driving.
Archery.

Brother Sam's Conundrums.
Manly Exercises: Boxing, Running, Walking, Training, &c. By Stonehenge, &c.
Croquet. By Edmund Routledge.
Fishing.
Ball Games.
Football.
Conjuring.
Quoits and Bowls.
Shooting.
Fireworks.
Skating.
Swimming.

Routledge's Fourpenny Juveniles.

For List see Sixpenny Juveniles, on page 21.

Little Ladders to Learning.

Each Illustrated with 125 Woodcuts by JOHN GILBERT, HARRISON WEIR, and others. Crown 8vo, sewed, in fancy covers, 6d. each.

o 6 *Things In-doors.*
What we Eat and Drink.
Animals and their Uses.
Birds and Birds' Nests.
Fishes, Butterflies, & Frogs.
Trees, Shrubs, and Flowers.
City Scenes.

Rural Scenes.
Country Enjoyments.
How Things are Made.
Soldiers and Sailors.
Science and Art.
Geography and Costume.